THE SOUTHERN KILLER

PETER O'MAHONEY

D1707562

The Southern Killer: An Epic Legal Thriller
Joe Hennessy Legal Thrillers Book 3

Peter O'Mahoney

Copyright © 2023
Published by Roam Free Publishing.
peteromahoney.com

1st edition.

ALSO BY PETER O'MAHONEY

In the Joe Hennessy Legal Thriller series:

THE SOUTHERN LAWYER
THE SOUTHERN CRIMINAL

*****

In the Tex Hunter Legal Thriller series:

POWER AND JUSTICE
FAITH AND JUSTICE
CORRUPT JUSTICE
DEADLY JUSTICE
SAVING JUSTICE
NATURAL JUSTICE
FREEDOM AND JUSTICE
LOSING JUSTICE
FAILING JUSTICE
FINAL JUSTICE

THE SOUTHERN KILLER

JOE HENNESSY LEGAL THRILLER BOOK 3

PETER O'MAHONEY

CHAPTER 1

THE APRIL heat rose through the Lee Correctional Institution in Bishopville, South Carolina.

Criminal defense attorney Joe Hennessy hated the place. He hated the smells of urine that wafted along the humid air, he hated the smells of male body odor that seemed to dominate every corner, and he hated the overwhelming cries of anguish that echoed down the halls.

He stood against the back wall in the narrow room, arms folded, waiting for the prisoner to arrive. The concrete walls were lined with condensation. A dirty puddle in the front corner of the room added to the dampness. The thick humidity circled him, wrapping around his body and drenching him in a disgusting wetness. There was no ventilation.

The door to the prison meeting room opened. The first guard stepped in and checked the room. Another guard escorted the prisoner, John Cleveland, inside. The prisoner was led to the metal table in the middle of the room and then cuffed on the hook at the edge of it. The guard checked the cuffs were tight.

The first guard looked at Hennessy, and Hennessy nodded his response. The guard grunted and turned, locking his stare on Cleveland for a long moment, then exited the room, slamming the heavy door behind him.

Hennessy didn't move. His face was emotionless as he stared at the prisoner who had no hope of ever being released. Hennessy leaned his towering frame against the far wall. He had removed his tie, leaving the top collar of his white shirt undone, and rolled his sleeves up to his elbows.

John Cleveland raised his eyes to look at the lawyer. He was a tall African American man, and the orange prison uniform was tight over his muscular frame. His glare was unflinching.

"Didn't think you'd come."

"I didn't want to," Hennessy said. "But curiosity got the better of me."

Cleveland sniffed and looked around the room, scanning his eyes over the cracks in the walls. "This place ain't much, but it's home."

"I'm not here to chat." Hennessy's jaw clenched. "You said you've got information for me."

"Now, now, now." Cleveland chuckled and smiled. He was missing more than a few teeth. The ones that remained were stained yellow. "That's not the Southern hospitality I'm used to from an older gentleman like yourself. Where's ya manners? How about you tell me a few things before we get down to business? How's the outside world? Has much changed in Charleston since I was locked up fifteen years ago? How are the beautiful women out there? Tell me they're still looking good."

"You've got five minutes before I walk out that door. Start talking."

Cleveland grunted and pulled at the chains holding his wrists close to the table. His hands couldn't move far. "I need your help, lawyer boy."

"And why would I help you?"

"Because I can help you." Cleveland sniffed again. He leaned forward, bringing his face close to his hands, and rubbed his nose. He looked up at Hennessy, waiting for him to respond. Hennessy didn't. The lawyer kept his arms folded, not moving from the back wall. Cleveland looked around the room again and then back to Hennessy. "I need you to get my daughter out of prison."

Again, Hennessy didn't respond.

"She was arrested, and I need someone to help her. She's my flesh and blood, but I've only seen her twice in my life. Once just after she was born and then once when her mother brought her here. I check on her when I can, you know, using the internet we get back here, but for most of her life, I've been locked up. Her mother died when she was about twelve, and I couldn't look after her 'cause of these bars. I let her down in so many ways."

Hennessy stared at the man who was the number one suspect in his son's unsolved murder over twenty years earlier. The defense lawyer had spent much of the last two decades in the darkness of grief, unable to forgive himself for not solving the crime that tore him apart.

A year after losing his son, Hennessy had left the city of Charleston, moved Upstate, and bought a vineyard to name in Luca's honor. He remained there for twenty years, happy to have escaped his past. But after the inconsistent weather caused several poor crops, he was forced to return to law in the Low Country to earn enough money to keep the banks out of Luca's Vineyard. He wasn't going to let the banks take Luca's legacy.

"My baby girl doesn't deserve to be locked up." Cleveland offered a half smile. "I can't let my flesh and blood have this life. I can't let her stay behind bars. She needs to be better than me."

"Tell me what she's in for."

"The murder of her stepfather, Dennis Fenton. He was a pig of a man. I should've taken care of him many years ago. He was a cop but got charged by the Feds for drug trafficking in a sting with the motorcycle gang, the Rebel Sons. He spent five weeks behind bars, up in Lieber Correctional. The screws tell me she was acting in self-defense, but the State lawyers want her locked up because she killed an ex-cop. I heard that Fenton tried to rape her, and she was defending herself. She's got a lawyer, one of the court ones, but he's useless. She needs a good lawyer. She needs you."

Hennessy held his glare on John Cleveland. "In return for what?"

"If you get my daughter out of prison, I'll tell you everything I know."

"About?"

"What happened to your son."

Hennessy stormed forward, slapping his hand on the metal table. He leaned over the flat surface, staring at Cleveland. Cleveland didn't flinch.

"What do you know?" Hennessy snarled, all signs of courtesy vanishing in the blink of an eye. "And how do I know you're telling the truth?"

"The van they found. It had blood on the walls, didn't it? You would've seen it. A red smear down the corner near the rear doors. They never released that to the public, did they?"

Hennessy reacted, grabbing Cleveland by the throat and lifting his chin. Cleveland struggled back, but his cuffs were tight. He couldn't move far.

"What do you know?" Hennessy snarled.

"Everything."

"Tell me what you know."

Hennessy pressed his fingers into the prisoner's throat. Cleveland clenched his jaw and flexed the muscles in his neck. He turned his eyes to meet Hennessy's.

"You get 'er out of prison first, then I'll tell you everything. That's the deal, and I ain't saying another word until you do."

Hennessy shoved Cleveland backward against the chair and then released his grip. He walked to the other side of the room, pacing the floor. He turned and stared back at Cleveland. "How can I trust you?"

"You can't, but I'm the only hope you've got." Cleveland stretched his neck and then returned his glare to Hennessy. "Get my baby girl free, and I'll tell you the truth about what happened to your son."

CHAPTER 2

NO WORDS, strength, or drive can cure the deep agony of unresolved grief.

The unanswered questions can sit heavy, deep in a person's soul, weighing them down until they learn to accept its dark embrace. For some, they learn to tolerate that pain, to sit with it, and then move forward. Step after step. Moment after moment. Task after task. They progress to new experiences, holding on to the memories as a part of them. For others, the burning questions are unshakable. So they run. They run from the aching, the damage, and the anguish. They run from the darkness, the wallowing pit of nightmares, and the heavy weight of the past. Some run to the church, some run to the bottom of a bottle, but for Joe Hennessy, he ran from his life in Charleston.

After moving back to his home city, he found the recollections were unavoidable. On some days, triggered by a fleeting memory, the unresolved grief would come flooding back, filling his body with anguish and his eyes with tears.

As he sat in the cab of his pickup truck, rain tapping on the window, he remembered one of the last days he spent with his forever ten-year-old son— on Folly Beach, cooled by gentle summer rain, they ran and they laughed, and they played and they wrestled. A warm breeze was blowing off the Atlantic ocean. Storm clouds sat heavy on the distant horizon. The smells of summer filled the air. Luca threw the football as a perfect spiral from twenty yards away, and Joe couldn't have been prouder. He ran to his son, exchanged a high-five, and lifted him up in celebration. In that hug, full of pride and joy, love and tenderness, Luca had gripped him tight. As Hennessy sat in his truck, he could feel that grip around his shoulders again.

He wiped his eyes with the back of his shirt sleeve. He had wrestled with the deal all night, not managing a wink of sleep, his mind a mess of possibilities. Could he trust a lifer like John Cleveland? No chance, he concluded, but Cleveland knew details about the van that were never released to the public. The promise of information from the unsolved case was too great to resist. If there was a chance to find the truth about what happened to Luca, he had to take it. He had to take the risk.

He grabbed the paperwork his assistant had put together that morning. He opened the file and read the first page. Alicia Fenton, born Alicia Cleveland, had lived a hard life. Her mother passed when she was just twelve, five years after her father, John Cleveland, was sentenced to life in prison for the murder of a banker and his wife in a robbery gone wrong. With no other close family, Alicia was left in the care of her recently acquired stepfather, a detective named Dennis Fenton.

Dennis Fenton had his problems with the law, convicted as a part of a federal drug bust on an outlaw motorcycle gang in Charleston. The drug bust hit the Rebel Sons hard, and Fenton was caught up in the middle of it. He was sentenced to fifteen months but only spent five weeks behind bars. A few hours after his release, he was dead, courtesy of Alicia and a baseball bat to the back of the head.

Hennessy returned the paperwork to his briefcase, snapped the locks shut, and climbed out of the truck, looking up to the sprawling Sheriff Al Cannon Detention Center in North Charleston. The brutalist architecture was confronting. It was a large concrete block structure that housed over a thousand inmates awaiting trial in Charleston County.

After twenty-five minutes of security checks, he was waiting in the prison interview room. The meeting room in the Detention Center was cleaner than the one at Lee Correctional, but there was still no life in it. White was the predominant color. The walls were white, the table and chairs were white, and the floor tiles were white. The prison-supplied pen was white. The ceiling was white. The only spot of color was the orange door. The lack of color alone was enough to drive most people insane.

After fifteen minutes, Alicia Fenton was escorted into the room. She was a slight eighteen-year-old with the skin tone of a person born to a white mother and black father. Her easy features looked innocent, but her steely eyes told a different story. Her shoulders were turned forward, and she kept her head bowed slightly, her black hair dangling over her face. The blue-and-white-striped prison uniform was too large for her slight frame.

"Hello, Miss Fenton. My name is Joe Hennessy, and I'm here to help you."

"Call me Alicia. I hate the name Fenton. It's not my birth name. My stepfather forced me to change my name when I was young, but I want to change it back to my mother's name." Her annunciation was clear, and her tone was well-educated. "And I'm sorry to disappoint you, but you've been sent to the wrong place. I can't afford a private lawyer. They've given me a public defender."

"I've offered to do this case pro bono." Hennessy opened his briefcase and removed a file. "That means I'm doing it for free."

"Why?"

"John Cleveland has something I need."

"That guy? I'm surprised he even remembers who I am."

"He remembers you."

"Whatever." She shrugged and looked away.

"I've looked at your file, and I can see that you lost the bail hearing due to the violent nature of the crime." Hennessy opened the file and looked at the first page. "You've been charged with one count of murder under section 16-3-10 of the South Carolina Code of Laws. This state does not define levels of murder, for example, first or second-degree murder, and all forms of killing with malice aforethought come under this charge. That means they believe you had the intent to kill your stepfather. What can you remember about that day?"

"I don't even know where to begin," Alicia replied. "He beat me a lot, and he raped me once."

"John Cleveland?"

"No. I'd only met John twice. I remember my mother took me to see him once in prison, which was enough. I don't even know what he's like as a person. All I know is that my birth father is a killer." She shook her head. "I'm talking about Dennis Fenton, my stepfather and guardian. And I bet my court case against him isn't in those files, is it?"

Hennessy flicked through the pages of his file. "And what court case would that be?"

"The one where Fenton was found not guilty of raping me as a minor." She shook her head, blinking back tears. "Dennis had those records sealed after he was found not guilty. It was so stupid of me to think that the courts could help me. I was fifteen years old, and I was taken out of his care while the court case happened. Then he was found not guilty, and they just sent me right back to him. They said I was lying for attention. And I can tell you the beatings got a lot worse after that court case."

"I don't have a record of your previous court cases, but we'll get one." Hennessy checked the file. "Why don't you tell me what happened that night?"

"When Dennis was sent to prison for fifteen months, I thought I was safe. I thought I had fifteen months to sort my life out and get out of there. I was already planning how to save enough money to get away. I never wanted to see that ugly prick again. But then he showed up five weeks later. I had no idea he was coming back. Got out for good behavior, he said."

"And his name was on the lease of the house you were staying at?"

"He owned the apartment, but he transferred the ownership to my name before the court case. He declared bankruptcy so that the court would look on his behavior leniently. That was his lawyer's advice, and I think it worked. They originally talked about putting him away for five years. I signed all the paperwork, and then he said I had to sign the deed back over to him once he was released from prison. He was so manipulative."

"So that night, on April 15th, you weren't expecting him to come home?"

"No. I didn't think he'd be back for months, and I thought he'd at least tell me a week or two before he came back." A tear escaped down her cheek. "That night, he came in stinking of hard liquor. He had a bottle of whiskey in his hand and said he was celebrating his release. He'd already drunk half the bottle and told me he had a few more bottles in the car. He told me it was expensive whiskey, and I should have some."

"Did you?"

"No. I thought he would've spiked it. He was so drunk already, and he continuously tried to reach under my skirt, and when I slapped him away, he punched me in the face and then tried to push me to the floor. He told me he was going to have me and that I should just stay quiet. It'd be easier if I was drunk, he said. That's when I screamed. Dennis got up to check the door was locked."

"Is that when you hit him?"

"There was a baseball bat nearby, and I picked it up and just swung it. It was self-defense. He attacked me, and I defended myself. I thought it was obvious that it was self-defense." She shook her head again. "I can't believe they locked me up. It's because I'm a black girl, and he's a white cop, isn't it?"

"No. You're locked up because you hit a man with a baseball bat, and he died," Hennessy stated. "Usually, you'd be covered by the Protection of Persons and Property Act, but as this was your stepfather's residence, it changes things. We'll still apply for protection under the Act. If I were your lawyer, we would first lodge a motion for the case to be dismissed."

"How would you do that?"

"The first step for us is to lodge a motion to have an evidentiary hearing under the protection of the Act. That hearing will be our chance to have this case thrown out before it even gets to trial. The Stand Your Ground laws and the Castle Doctrine were codified under the Act, which allows you to be free from prosecution if you were acting in self-defense."

"I told the Public Defender I wanted to get off on self-defense, but he doesn't think I can win it because I hit him in the back of the head. He told me to take the deal and didn't even suggest a hearing."

"If we can show that the threat to you still existed when you hit your stepfather, we've got a chance at self-defense. You have a legal right to defend yourself, but there are rules for how and when you're permitted to act. In South Carolina, there are four elements of self-defense. One—you didn't instigate or attack another person and then claim self-defense. Two—you were, or you believed you were, in imminent danger of losing your life or sustaining serious bodily injury. Three—a reasonable person would also believe they were in imminent danger if they were in your place. And four—there was no other probable means of avoiding the danger. However, because the attack occurred in your home, you had no duty to retreat."

"I think all those points apply to my situation."

"Good. Because if this makes it to trial and we raise the issue of self-defense, and the prosecution can't disprove one or more of these elements beyond a reasonable doubt, the jurors must acquit you. Once we have raised self-defense, the State has the burden of disproving, beyond a reasonable doubt, at least one of the elements." Hennessy opened another file and read more lines of information. "However, I hope the case doesn't have to go that far. If you were acting in self-defense, the Protection of Persons and Property Act affords you the right to be free from prosecution. If we succeed, you'll be free to go after the hearing. If the judge rules against us, we go to trial and present self-defense."

"Does that mean you can get me out of here?"

"Our best chance is the evidentiary hearing. If the judge allows the hearing, we'll present a case to state you were acting in self-defense and should be free from prosecution." Hennessy flicked open another page. "And if that doesn't work, we have the option to negotiate a deal for manslaughter. In South Carolina, manslaughter is defined as the killing of another person but without the malice necessary for murder. Manslaughter is punishable by a minimum sentence of two years, while the minimum for murder is thirty."

"But why didn't the other lawyer do all this?"

"Because he has many cases on his books, and yours looks like the State will offer a good deal for manslaughter further down the track. I'm sorry to say it, but if the case makes it to trial, given what we know already, it's highly possible the jury will find you guilty of murder."

"I don't want a deal. I want to get out. I was acting in self-defense. My stepfather was going to rape me."

"If you want me to take on this case, I need to convince the public defender to pass it to me, although that won't take much effort. It's your decision, but I would like to help you." Hennessy took five pages out of his briefcase and slid them across the table. "You'll need to sign these papers for me to represent you."

She looked at the papers and nodded.

Hennessy nodded in return, but doubt plagued him. From what he'd seen so far, he didn't like his chances—not of winning, nor of getting the information from John Cleveland.

CHAPTER 3

MOTHER NATURE wasn't modest when she made South Carolina.

From wooded river valleys to whisper-thin barrier islands, from stunning beaches to picturesque fields, from the salt marshes to the gorgeous weeping willows, the beauty of South Carolina was unmistakable. And the jewel of the Palmetto State was the elegant city of Charleston. It was an easy city to love. The cobblestone streets, the breathtaking architecture, and the Low Country lifestyle made the city a tourist hotspot, but it was the genuine Southern hospitality that made the place so special.

Hennessy sat on a wooden bench in Washington Square Park, across from the Charleston Judicial Center. The bugs were loud, and the air was thick with humidity, but the shade of the sprawling oak trees provided some relief. Located behind City Hall at the corner of historic Meeting and Broad Streets, Washington Square Park was the first public park in Charleston, opened in 1818. A large statue of George Washington, once a visitor to the streets nearby, stood proudly near the entrance.

After fifteen minutes of gathering his thoughts, Hennessy drew a deep breath, stood, and walked toward the Judicial Center, briefcase in hand. He hadn't told Wendy, his wife of thirty years, about the case, but he knew he couldn't hide it for long. He could never lie to her. He was in Charleston to earn money to keep the bank out of their vineyard, and she would question why he was doing pro-bono cases. How could he explain the case to her without telling the whole truth? He knew he couldn't. She would see straight through him. She always did.

He passed through security and greeted his assistant Jacinta in the hall outside the courtrooms. She pointed toward courtroom five, and he thanked her. As he stepped into the courtroom, the murmurs ceased. Five cops were sitting in the back row of the public gallery. Older men. Lifelong cops who were willing to do anything to protect their brotherhood. Their glare told Hennessy all he needed to know.

After the first glance, he ignored them, taking up his seat at the front of the room. Assistant Solicitor Aaron Garrett nodded to Hennessy as he sat down. Hennessy nodded his response. Garrett was a young black man still in the early stages of his career, but his path seemed certain—work his way up through the ranks of the Circuit Solicitor's Office, making many connections along the way, before stepping into the fiery pit of politics. His smile was charming, his tone charismatic, and he was in the shape of a driven man who had the time and energy to spend two hours in the gym every morning.

Moments after Hennessy had sat down, Alicia Fenton was escorted in next to him, and the murmur of voices began again.

The bailiff called the room to order, and Judge Nancy West entered through a door near the front of the room. She walked to her bench as if she was riding a set of wheels, almost gliding over to her chair with just a brief grin to the audience. Judge West was a thin woman in her late fifties, although she could've passed for someone a decade younger. Thanks to her yellow glasses and dyed brown hair, she looked vibrant, and her skin glowed as if she'd only eaten organic food her entire life.

She took her seat, wished the courtroom a good morning, and accepted her paperwork from the bailiff. She opened her laptop, clicked several buttons, and then opened the files on her desk. She ran her eyes across each page, barely pausing as she flicked through the folder.

"Mr. Hennessy, I see that the defense has lodged a motion to apply for an evidentiary hearing under the Protection of Persons and Property Act."

"Your Honor," Aaron Garrett stood and began his argument before Hennessy could respond, "the State would like to oppose any such hearing. This is not a typical stand-your-ground scenario. The victim, Dennis Fenton, wasn't a random intruder. He was the defendant's stepfather. His address is listed as the apartment where the attack took place, and as such, the defendant has no protection under this Act."

"Your Honor, if I may respond without being interrupted." Hennessy stared at Garrett for a long moment. The venom from Garrett's words surprised Hennessy, but he looked behind him and saw the police officers nodding at each other. Hennessy drew a breath and looked back at the judge. "The motion is for an evidentiary hearing, not for a decision. We're not making arguments for the decision today."

"There are precedents for denying a hearing," Garrett continued. "In the State v. Fanning, 2016, the South Carolina Supreme Court held that there's no right to a full evidentiary hearing to determine if a defendant is entitled to immunity under the Protection of Persons and Property Act."

"Your Honor," Hennessy's voice raised, "the right to immunity from prosecution afforded under the Act is meaningless if the defendant is barred from presenting evidence to the court to support their claim."

"In Fanning, 2016," Garrett continued, "the Supreme Court held that the trial court is required only to make a determination whether the Act applies but is not required to conduct a hearing before making the decision. Based on this precedent, I argue that the defendant has no legal claim under this Act. The Act clearly states that it doesn't apply if the victim has a right to be in the home, such as a resident, an owner, a tenant, or a titleholder to the property. The victim was a resident of the home in which he was attacked, making any further arguments null and void. The defense can still argue for protection under self-defense law, but the immunity under this Act does not apply."

"The Act states that the defendant is immune from prosecution, and it's a true immunity. Therefore, it's a complete block to court action, and we have a chance to prove this before trial." Hennessy's voice was firm. "This is not simply an affirmative defense. Black's Law Dictionary defines 'immune' as to be 'exempt from a duty or liability' and 'prosecution' as 'a criminal proceeding in which an accused person is tried.' The victim was attempting to rape the defendant. She has a right to self-defense."

"And the defendant will have the chance to present their case for self-defense at trial." Garrett knocked his hand on the table. "This is a legal issue, and the Act does not cover the defendant's situation."

"The intent of the Act is clear, and it was defined by the General Assembly. I refer to the South Carolina Code of Laws, section 16-11-420. They explicitly state that the Act finds that persons residing in this State have a right to expect to remain unmolested and safe within their homes. And that its proper for law-abiding citizens to protect themselves, their families, and others from intruders and attackers without fear of prosecution or civil action for acting in defense of themselves and others. We have to afford this defendant that right."

"Your Honor," Garrett argued, "the victim resided at this residence, meaning the Act doesn't apply here!"

"I argue that he wasn't a resident." Hennessy slapped a file shut. "The victim was not on the ownership deed, he was not paying rent, and only hours before the incident, he was a resident of the Lieber Correctional Center. The homeowner was not aware that he was returning from prison. He wasn't due to be released for another fourteen months."

"And his address on his release papers was listed as the apartment where the incident occurred!"

"Just because he writes it on a piece of paper doesn't mean the property owner approves his residence there!"

"Enough, Gentlemen," Judge West interrupted them.

Hennessy turned to glare at Garrett. The prosecutor struggled to stand still, the anger bubbling inside him.

"Thank you for your arguments. I can see this is a

contentious issue," Judge West continued. "Under the State Carolina Code of Laws, the Protection of Persons and Property Act, Section 16-11-410, affords a person the right to act in self-defense and be immune from prosecution. I've considered what was presented in the memorandums and the motion documents, and given what I've heard here today, I agree that the court should consider if the defendant has protection under the Act. We will conduct an evidentiary hearing to determine whether the Act applies. Anything further on this date?"

"Nothing from the defense, Your Honor."

"Mr. Garrett?" Judge West asked when the prosecutor didn't respond.

Garrett drew a long breath, holding back his disappointment in the decision. "Nothing from the State."

"Then, we stand adjourned."

Hennessy turned to his client and gave her a nod of approval. She mouthed the words 'Thank you,' before being escorted out of the courtroom again.

As Hennessy stood to leave, Garrett stepped over to him. Garrett looked at the police officers still seated at the rear of the courtroom. "The victim was a cop, Hennessy. You should know that this isn't going to be easy."

Garrett turned and left, not allowing Hennessy the opportunity to respond.

When Hennessy stepped out of the courtroom ten minutes later, the five older police officers were waiting for him in the hall. They formed a line blocking his path. Towering over them, Hennessy pushed past, brushing into their shoulders.

They didn't say a word, but their presence told him

one thing—if he wanted the information from John Cleveland, he needed to fight against the whole system.

CHAPTER 4

ALICIA FENTON sat on the hard bed with her back pressed against the wall.

She looked up to the only window she could access, a tiny eighteen-inch by twelve-inch gap sporting three bars set into the thick concrete. She saw a speck of blue, cloudless sky beyond the bars, just enough to remind her that the outside world continued on without her. As the sun headed toward its highest point of the day, the sky turned white and hazy. Soon, it felt like she was swimming against the humidity. There was little to no ventilation in the cells and certainly no air-conditioning. Prisoners were locked up to be punished for past sins, and little was more punishing than the Southern humidity.

The cell was the only place where Alicia felt safe enough to let her guard down, although even then, she didn't drop it completely. It was a prison, and she knew enough to understand that danger could come for her at any moment, taking on many different forms to try and get close to her.

While the danger of prison was enough to dominate her mind, it was during the quiet times in her cell that the reality of the situation truly hit home. She shared the cell with another inmate, but Ruth spent most of her time three doors down with a few of her 'homies,' as she liked to call them.

Continuing to stare out the window, Alicia tried to imagine where she would have been at that moment were it not for her sudden detour to prison, thanks to a man she loathed. Dennis Fenton may have been her stepfather and had given her a place to live when her mother died, but the man always had ulterior motives when it came to helping others. He wasn't one to go out of his way to offer up the kindness in his heart. If there was something in it for him, he would find a way to get it.

The memories played through her mind like a 4th of July parade, each horrific moment of abuse on a slow-motion reel she felt powerless to stop. A tear escaped and slowly cascaded down her face as the memory of the first time he had put his hands on her played out. What she remembered most vividly was the beating in her chest as he lay beside her, the distinct smell of cheap whiskey on his breath.

It had started as beatings. When the rage got too much for Dennis, he rained down a heavy parade of punches on her helpless soul. He always apologized the next day, explaining that he didn't know how to control his anger. He blamed it on his PTSD, but it was all the same for her. The day he raped her when she was fifteen was the worst. She tried to shut that day out, but the nightmare always had a way of finding its way back into her consciousness.

Alicia closed her eyes, squeezing them shut to force every hint of sadness out of them. She wiped the remaining tears away and focused on school and the friends she had made since joining community college. Nursing wasn't a career choice she made on a whim. For Alicia, it was everything. The thought of helping so many others was something she had known she wanted since an early age. She pictured her patients already, the elderly, the vulnerable, the young, and those with nowhere else to turn. She wanted to make each of their lives better.

Another tear threatened to break free as the image of herself in a nurse's uniform blinked out, replaced by the vision of her sitting behind bars for years to come. With his final act in the living world, the man who should have protected her had influenced her immediate future. He had ensured that whatever dreams she had for her destiny would take a drastic detour.

She wanted to scream as she closed her eyes again. She wanted to let out all the rage that continued tormenting her. It felt like a heat, boiling away inside her, an anger she felt powerless to release. If she managed to scream, the others would hear and come to investigate. That would bring unwanted attention to her, and she already had a sign that not everybody accepted her into the unit.

She had always felt like an outsider. Being the daughter of a black father and a white mother meant that she never quite fit in. Her skin was black but not dark, and she felt she had no connection to her African American heritage after her father was locked up. But even before he was put away for murder, she never saw the man. Her mother, of English descent, told her to be proud of her black heritage, but she knew nothing of her past. When Dennis Fenton married her mother, he told her never to speak of her black heritage. She knew he secretly hated having a black stepdaughter.

From the moment she arrived in the detention center, Alicia had seen how some other inmates looked at her, as if sizing her up in a way fighters sometimes did just before a bout. Bad feelings rose when she saw those eyes watching her. She tried her best to avoid it by remaining in her cell.

"Alicia?" She snapped her eyes open, her heart missing a beat as the voice caught her off guard. Despite the lack of malice in the tone, it still surprised her enough to jump, and the girl in the doorway giggled. "Sorry, didn't mean to scare you."

"I'm not scared," Alicia said as she tried to see who the voice belonged to. The tears made it hard for her to focus, and she didn't want to bring attention to them by wiping her eyes.

"You been crying?"

As the girl stepped forward, Alicia linked the voice to a face she knew well. Jada Wallis may not have been the closest of her friends at high school, but she was a familiar face, and given the distinct lack of coldness in her tone, it gave Alicia hope that she had found an ally.

Jada sat down beside Alicia and hugged her. Alicia felt a rush of relief and didn't want to let go at first. The hug gave her a sense of security, something she hadn't felt since arriving in the unit.

"What happened to you?" Alicia asked.

"Got into a fight with my neighbor," she said as she pulled back. "Cops took her side and threw me in here. But the real question is what are you doing in here? You were smart in school. Girls like you aren't supposed to end up back here."

Alicia couldn't answer at first. She tried to shake her head to show a lack of strength to talk about it. But despite trying to fight back the tears, the feelings were too powerful.

Jada saw Alicia's lips quiver with emotion and immediately held her arms back out. "Aw, come here, babe."

Before Alicia had a chance to fight it, her emotions bubbled to the top and began pouring out in a wave of uncontrolled sobs. She couldn't help it; all she could do was let it go as her newfound friend held her tight.

It took Alicia five minutes to get herself back under control, the pair sitting in near silence once the tears slowed again. Alicia didn't speak for a long time, content to lean into the arms of someone else. Once she was all cried out, Alicia pulled back and smiled at Jada for the first time.

"I'm sorry," she whispered. "Things haven't been easy."

"I can see that," Jada said as she held Alicia's hand. "Just be sure not to do that out there." She looked to the door, then leaned in a little as she lowered her voice. "Some girls out there don't mind preying on the weak. If you cry out there, you'll be torn apart."

"Is it really that bad?"

"Girl, you're inside with some pretty twisted people right now," Jada said, not mincing her words. "And we're just the detention center. It gets worse. They transfer you to Graham Correctional in Columbia if you get convicted. That's where the real terror starts. Still, most of 'em here are out for themselves, despite what they might tell you. You'd be wise to grow a set of eyes in the back of your head."

It was advice Alicia didn't find surprising, although hearing it firsthand finally confirmed her darkest fears.

She knew she was in trouble, she knew prison would be dangerous, and she was beginning to realize how bad it would be.

CHAPTER 5

JOE HENNESSY stepped out of his car and walked toward Salty Mike's, a legendary local dive bar near the Safe Harbor marina. It was five in the afternoon, but the humidity was so thick it felt like the cabin pressure of an airplane, and the skies were so hazy it was hard to make out the shape of the clouds.

The beauty of Charleston ran deeper than the picture-perfect streets and well-maintained history. The real beauty of the Southern city lay in the small cafes and bars, in the hidden restaurants. It was off-the-beaten-track, down the alleyways, behind the façade with the buildings untouched by time, standing strong since the 1700s. It was in the genuine hospitality that made a person feel like family instantly. It was in the outdoor lifestyle, where people of all social classes spent their days on the water—boating, swimming, or fishing. It was the beat of the year-round summer lifestyle that made the place so special. And Salty Mike's was the essence of that lifestyle.

Hennessy flapped his shirt as he entered the bar, trying to cool down. It took a moment for his eyes to adjust to the darkness. He greeted Major, the bar's dog who loved all the attention he received, and then he ordered a Palmetto State IPA. The bartender chatted about the heat for a moment and then pointed outside where Hennessy's investigator, Barry Lockett, was sitting.

Lockett was leaning back on a chair directly under the outdoor fan with his phone in front of him. He had an enormous smile across his face.

"What's so funny?" Hennessy approached his investigator.

"I love reading about history, but this one's got me." Lockett looked up from his phone, shaking his head. "I was reading about the Great Whiskey Fire of Dublin in 1875. More than ten people died."

"That doesn't sound very funny. Dying in a fire would be horrific."

"Oh no, they didn't die in the fire."

"No?"

"Oh no, these Irishmen died because the whiskey factory was on fire, and they didn't want to waste the drink. All the deaths from the Great Whiskey Fire were from alcohol poisoning." Lockett laughed. "The barrels of whiskey were burning, and whiskey was pouring down the street, so these Irish locals drank it as quickly as possible."

"How very Irish." Hennessy chuckled. "My favorite Irish saying is they don't call it a hangover, they call it the 'Irish Flu.'"

Lockett laughed and turned to the laminated menu on the bar. "You hungry? If you are, don't look at anything but the popcorn shrimp. It's legendary."

Lockett's massive hand reached out and hugged the sweaty glass of beer. He took another sip and let out a moan of satisfaction. Australian-born, beer had been a constant part of his life since he was fifteen. He was a large man with two sleeve tattoos and ripping muscles. His broad frame intimidated most, but his cheeky grin and Australian accent were disarming.

The view from the back deck of Salty Mike's was worthy of a postcard. Looking out to the marshes and beyond, the marina and the Ashley River were framed by storm clouds on the horizon.

Hennessy loved the bar. It was a dive bar where the drinks were strong, the conversations long, and the atmosphere relaxed. Behind them, the bar's patrons continued about their business, a hum of voices rising and falling like waves. Occasionally, someone would get a little too excited by a story they shared, their voice rising above the others before their audience erupted into laughter.

The bar catered to many but always hung on to the old salty sea dogs who didn't mind a great tale with a cold beer. They sat in small groups, scattered across the many tables, and always had one person in the middle of some tall story about the one that got away or the worst storm of the season. Two young men walked past, wearing wet shorts and sweaty button-ups, followed by a small Corgi, laughing loudly about their day on the water. One of them patted Lockett on the shoulder and then sat down nearby.

Hennessy and Lockett ordered food and it arrived quickly. The waitress set down two small platters before wishing them an enjoyable meal and moving on to her other tables. Hennessy tried the first piece of popcorn shrimp and felt his mouth fill with spices. It was good, and he began to feed each piece into his mouth rhythmically, pausing briefly for a sip of beer to wash the food down. The men ate in silence, the way people did when food was too good to pass up.

Within minutes of taking his first bite, Hennessy emptied his plate with a final head shake of satisfaction.

He sat and watched a small boat float past in the distance, a father and son sitting at opposite ends. The kid held a fishing rod out beside him. He was about to turn and say something to Lockett when the kid did something which grabbed his attention. Just as they were close enough for their voices to travel across the water, the boy called for his dad to speed up. What grabbed Hennessy's attention were the specific words the boy used and the memory of Luca speaking the same words during one of their fishing trips. "Ready to fill the buckets, Dad?"

As the father called back to his son, Hennessy felt his chest tighten ever so slightly by the words, the memory brief but intense. He looked away from the boat, desperate to forget the pain, and focused on a distraction.

"I've got a new case," Hennessy began. Work always had a way of pushing the emotions down. "Alicia Fenton, a young black girl, has been charged with murdering her white stepfather, who was an ex-cop. She says it was self-defense, but the prosecution sees it differently. It looks like the police department has pressured them to press charges against the girl. I need your help to investigate."

"How can she afford your fees?"

"She can't."

Lockett raised his eyebrows, questioning his answer.

"Her birth father has information I need."

"Must be important information."

"It is."

"Alright." Lockett sipped at his ale. "Then tell me what you need."

"I need you to start with a complete background check on her stepfather, Dennis Fenton. He's a former cop who got caught up in a Federal drug sting of an outlaw motorcycle gang and spent five weeks of a fifteen-month sentence in prison. He pleaded not guilty and protested his innocence, and the police force stuck by him. But he was dead not even five hours after his release." Hennessy took a sip of beer and set his glass down. "Fenton was trying to rape his stepdaughter, and she defended herself. It sounds simple, but we have two problems—one, she hit him in the back of the head when he was walking away, and two, apart from a small mark on her eye, there was no evidence of his assault on her."

"Sounds like you're up against it." Lockett whistled. "Cops making it hard?"

"They're not going to make it easy. They're a brotherhood, a family, and so they should be. They see some of the worst things life has to give, and they do it to protect the community. They need to protect each other." Hennessy stared out at the water as another boat floated past. "And in this current environment, they need to know that the Solicitor's Office has their back. They've had several cops charged over the last few years, and the gap between the Solicitor's Office and the police force is turning into a chasm. The prosecution needs an easy win to show the police department they're still on the same side."

"Even at the expense of the truth?"

"Life isn't black and white." Hennessy shrugged. "A lot of the world exists in the gray, and cops are no exception. These people risk their lives to protect the community. We have to respect that."

"Trust in authority is important." Lockett nodded and sipped his beer. "But you break that trust, and you'll have a hard time trying to regain it."

"True," Hennessy nodded. He flapped his shirt. The fan in the top corner of the deck was working overtime. It was having little effect against the humidity. "But what would the streets look like without the cops?"

"Safer for some people, I imagine," Lockett said. "So, what are you going to do?"

"I need to prepare for a Protection of Persons and Property Act hearing. We'll try to get her off on self-defense. The hearing is a week and a half away, so I need you to look into Dennis Fenton and see if there is any sign that he could've tried to rape his stepdaughter on his return from prison. Did he write anything on social media? Did he tell anyone he knew, or do we have a witness that could help us?" Hennessy looked out at the water again. He knew the case would be challenging, but they were also fighting the police department, making it almost impossible to win. "And I've also got another case I need to focus on."

"You're a busy man."

"My books are full," Hennessy sipped his drink. "But that's the life of a defense lawyer—there's always more than one case to focus on, and there's always more than one client to defend."

CHAPTER 6

HENNESSY LOVED walking the streets of Charleston just after dawn.

The early mornings were gentle, a time before the city was bathed in a sultry heat. Walking with a takeaway coffee in his hand, he wandered through the alleyways, taking in the sights, before he stopped to read one of the signs that marked the spot where the majority of the international slave trade took place.

The city of Charleston was still coming to terms with its history, good and bad. Its place in the revolution and the civil war was celebrated, but its role in the international slave trade was taking longer to accept. For all the city's appeal, for all its stunning beauty and colorful history, Charleston was also home to a brutal chapter of the past. It was a city shaped by slave labor, and beneath the facade of the wealthy city was the cruel narrative of Jim Crow and Ku Klux Klan violence. Those wounds of the past were deep, causing generational pain, but the healing work had begun. The city's past was far from perfect, but it was embracing its beautiful Gullah culture.

Hennessy read the details on the sign, shook his head, and then wandered back to his office on Church Street in Downtown Charleston. On the second floor of a plain red brick building, Hennessy's law office was a stone's throw away from the beating heart of law and justice in the Low Country. He walked up the stairs and into the reception area, greeted Jacinta, who had come in early, and then sat in his separate office. He had rented the space for cheap from an old associate, who mentioned it had been empty for years.

Hennessy sat behind his desk for the first hour of the morning, which was a wasteland of legal pads, law books, witness statements, and police reports. He made notes, checked precedents, reviewed papers, and studied potential witness profiles. He continued to review the files for the upcoming evidentiary hearing, trying to focus on the Alicia Fenton case.

He was so consumed by the work that he didn't hear Jacinta at his door. Jacinta Templeton was an organized woman with a love for hard work. In her mid-thirties, she had a sweet smile that charmed every person she met. With a five-year-old son at home and a husband in banking, her life was busy, frantic at times, but she preferred it that way.

"Your ten o'clock is here." Jacinta said as she entered and tidied up the loose files. "This one is a paying client, so I suggest you give him your full attention."

Jacinta winked at Hennessy, and then left the room to greet the client. She returned a moment later, leading the client into the room.

"Mr. McDermott, good morning."

Brandon McDermott was a steady man in his fifties, solid, broad-shouldered, and with large hands that looked like they'd worked every day since he was fifteen. He was clean-shaven with short-cropped hair. He wore blue jeans with a brown belt and brown boots, and his flannel shirt was tucked in.

"Sorry, I'm early," he said. "Just a little keen to get going."

"No problem. Can Jacinta get you anything? A coffee? Glass of water?"

"No, I'm fine, thank you."

"If you need anything, just ask," Jacinta said. She sat on the chair next to him with her notepad ready.

"I'm not used to these kinds of situations," McDermott continued. "Never been arrested before, in fact. Never had any trouble with the law, not even for speeding."

Hennessy could sense the man's nerves and waved a hand for him to calm down and relax. He knew the best way to get the information he needed was to slow people down, or more precisely, their brains down.

"Take your time, Mr. McDermott. I've reviewed the charges and the evidence that the prosecution has sent us during discovery. They've charged you with Grand Larceny, claiming you stole more than $2000 worth of whiskey. That's a lot of whiskey, so why don't you start at the beginning and tell me what happened that night."

"Well, I guess you could say that it began about a month ago. My father passed away suddenly. I guess it was because of the grief that I was drunk."

"I'm sorry for your loss."

"Thank you. Not an easy thing to get used to."

"Were you close?"

"We used to be. He retired to Savannah with his second wife. After that, he struggled to find the time to spend with us, and I didn't get down there enough. It left me with a lot of regrets." McDermott swallowed hard and continued. "I must've been on a decent downer when I decided to go looking for more booze."

"So, you admit you were drunk?"

"Yeah, well, a bit hard to deny that. I mean, I ended up in a park passed out for most of the night."

"I'm sorry, go on."

"So, there I was at about 8pm, hoping for more booze from the Whiskey and Vine Liquor store, off Market Street, but the guy behind the counter refused to serve me. Said I had enough, and he wouldn't let me buy anything."

"How did you react to that?"

"Not well."

"Were you violent toward him?"

"A little. I was trying to drown out my grief and needed more alcohol. When he knocked me back, I got pretty wound up. I pushed him out of the way and took one of the expensive bottles from behind the counter. I then threw two fifty-dollar bills on the table. I paid for it. I didn't even steal it."

Jacinta took notes, her hand whizzing across the page in a near blur.

"What happened next?"

McDermott lowered his tone and looked down at his hands in embarrassment. "What happened next was me being a complete idiot."

"We've all been there," Hennessy offered.

"Not like this," McDermott said. "After another lengthy verbal tirade, I ended up outside and…" He paused to shake his head as he scratched his chin. "I felt my anger taking over and ended up breaking the nearest thing I could find. The security camera wasn't as severe as throwing a brick through the huge shop front window, so I focused my rage on it. I threw the brick at the security camera four or five times and smashed it to bits. A few guys got up in my face, and I ended up leaving. As I walked away, I remember drinking the whiskey like it was a bottle of water. Next thing I know, I was lying on some park bench in the early hours of the morning, a bottle of half-empty expensive whiskey next to me. I completely blacked out after going to the liquor store."

"That's not what the police say happened," Hennessy said. "According to them, you returned shortly after closing time, broke into the store, and helped yourself to five more bottles of expensive whiskey. The whiskey was a prized collection, the most expensive in the store, held behind a glass case and worth around $500 a bottle. Two bottles of Pappy Van Winkle and three bottles of Orphan Barrel, they claim. They claim you stuffed them in a backpack and then fled back to the park and that you dropped them off before you fell asleep on the bench."

"Only, that's not what happened, Mr. Hennessy. You have to believe me."

"The internal security camera wasn't working at the time, which means you effectively destroyed your only chance at a clear alibi."

McDermott rubbed his eyes and groaned. "The irony, right?"

"The irony is right," Hennessy said. "And now the police have charged you with grand larceny for stealing five bottles of very expensive whiskey, and nobody can verify your story. The one issue they have is that they haven't been able to locate the missing bottles yet."

"And here's the thing, Mr. Hennessy. This charge

could ruin me. I mean quite literally. I run a small construction company, and the Catholic school where I'm currently managing a project for a new science building has zero tolerance for these sorts of things. A charge like this will effectively end my business."

"I take it they view their public image seriously?"

"Serious enough to include a clause in the initial building contract. Anyone who brings the school into disrepute will have their contract terminated, effective immediately. And I've heard that they've done it before. That's why I have to beat these charges. If I don't, twenty people will lose their jobs."

"Do you have a copy of the contract?"

"Not here, but I can get it for you."

"Good. That'll be our starting point," Hennessy said. "Now, I'd like to take you through the legal process and what I expect will happen."

McDermott nodded, and for the next hour, they discussed the case and the potential avenues they had to proceed. There was already a deal on the table from the prosecution for a suspended sentence, but McDermott said that any sentence would see the construction contract torn up. He said he couldn't do that to his staff. He would fight it the whole way, even if he was guilty. Hennessy agreed.

After an hour, they shook hands solidly, and Hennessy told him they would be in contact again in the next month.

"How do you think we'll fare?" McDermott asked as he walked toward the door.

"I can't promise you a clean getaway from this mess, Mr. McDermott," Hennessy began, "but we'll use all our best tactics to fight this in court."

CHAPTER 7

JOE ARRIVED at the vineyard, a two-hour-and-forty-five minute drive inland from Charleston, late on Friday afternoon.

He ate dinner with Wendy and his sixteen-year-old daughter Casey, who discussed plans for her upcoming seventeenth birthday. Joe smiled as she talked about inviting some of her oldest friends, people she'd known for her entire life. After dinner, he walked along the edge of the property with Casey, listening to her stories about the final years of high school.

"And are you studying hard?"

"Of course. I'm learning all sorts of things." Casey smiled. "This week, I learned that nothing starts with 'n' and ends with 'g.'"

"What?" Joe squinted. "Netting, nag, negating. Lots of words start with 'n' and end with 'g.' What are they teaching you down there?"

"Seriously?" Casey laughed. "Nothing starts with 'n' and ends with 'g.' Get it? The word 'nothing' starts with 'n' and ends with 'g.'"

"Ah." Joe laughed. "That's good. But Casey, I've also learned something this week."

"At your age? I'm impressed."

"I learned why boxers don't make love the night before a fight."

"What?" Casey giggled. "Why is it that?"

"It's because they don't like each other very much."

Casey burst out laughing, and her innocent laughter brought a broad smile to Joe's face. They wandered for a while longer, swapping more jokes, stories, and tales of their weeks. As time ticked past 9.05pm, they arrived back at the house, and he wished her goodnight. He couldn't think of a more perfect Friday night.

Life was simple in the vineyard, and Joe loved it that way.

He woke Saturday morning next to his wife, with the sun shining in the open curtains and the vineyard stretched out before them. The view from their bedroom had always been breathtaking, but as he stood in front of the floor-to-ceiling window looking out over the landscape after a long week, he felt a calmness wash over him.

Wendy watched him as he stood silently, his frame haloed by the sunshine. When he turned to find her staring, he smiled. "Didn't wake you, did I?"

"Not at all," she said, patting the bed for him to return. He did, climbing in and lying close enough for them to cuddle while still looking out into the day. They lay in each other's arms for a while, enjoying a moment of serenity before the inevitable jobs set in. When they heard Casey in the kitchen, they rose and ate breakfast together. After Casey hurried out the door to a yoga session with her volleyball team, Joe smiled again.

"She's growing up fast, isn't she?" Joe said as he blew the steam off his second coffee.

"She's growing up to be an amazing woman, but

she's definitely a teenager." Wendy smiled. "She's lovely as long as I don't ask her to do anything, give her any kind of advice, say the wrong thing, do the wrong thing, or breathe in any kind of way."

"We had the same with Ellie and look at her now. Studying to become a lawyer at NYU."

"We did." Wendy drew a breath and turned the conversation to work. "Do you want to tell me why you've taken on a pro-bono case?"

"It's a simple enough case," he answered. "We have a hearing next week to get her off before the trial. Hopefully, it goes in our favor."

Wendy didn't press the issue. "I have an early morning meeting with one of the wedding planners for another ceremony next weekend. I think one of the staff wants a hand to run the irrigation lines down the south end. And the fence along the west side needs tightening, and I think there may be a hole in some of the netting near the driveway."

There was a moment when Wendy looked over at him and smiled, but the genuine emotion lay hidden beneath. Joe spotted it for the barest of seconds, a little moment where the real emotion revealed itself.

"I'm on it," Joe said and made another cup of coffee.

The weekend was much busier than he'd anticipated, but Joe didn't complain. He loved working the lands, getting his hands dirty, and being surrounded by some of the most beautiful nature in the State. He helped the staff lay new irrigation lines, fixed the fences, and replaced some of the torn netting. Wendy spent the weekend busy at the small store and café on the other side of the vineyard, helping to organize the area for another wedding the following weekend.

It wasn't until late Sunday afternoon that Wendy and Joe finally sat down for more than a few minutes without someone needing either of them. With a beer in one hand for himself and a glass of wine in the other for Wendy, Joe took the drinks out onto the porch, where his wife sat in one of the chairs with her eyes closed. The sun lounge was raised slightly higher than usual to keep her sitting upright. Joe paused long enough to watch her for a few seconds and smiled. After all the years together, his love for her felt as strong as ever.

She sensed his presence and looked up. "Still perving on me?"

"You're still the hottest woman I've ever met," he said as he walked over to her and set it down on the table beside her before taking his seat. "Got you a drink."

"Thank you, my love," Wendy said, picked up the glass, and took a sip. He heard her sigh as she held the glass and rested it on her lap.

"Feels good to get through another weekend," she whispered.

"I'll drink to that."

Silence fell over them for several minutes. The beautiful South Carolina landscape lay before them, with the low-hanging sun giving just enough warmth. The view from the porch usually made up for any shortfalls in conversation, and they could've sat like that for hours. But the sensation hung a lot heavier on him when he knew there was more to the silence than just a simple lack of words. As he took another sip and held the drink in his mouth for a few seconds, he knew the timing would never be more perfect for explaining why he took the pro-bono case.

"I have to tell you something," Joe began. Wendy turned and looked at him, but instead of a look of curiosity on her face, he saw anticipation. "This may not be easy to take, and I apologize in advance for the anguish it might cause, but there's a reason I've taken on the Alicia Fenton case. Alicia Fenton's father was the one who initially contacted me. The details about his relationship with his daughter aren't that important, but what is, is the fact he's been in prison for most of her life. John Cleveland is in for murder, serving a life sentence, and will likely die behind bars."

"John Cleveland?" she whispered. "Why would you help him?"

He took a deep breath, feeling the pulse of his heartbeat thumping at the walls of his chest. He looked at her and tried to smile, but it didn't work this time.

"Because he's offered something."

"What is it?"

"He told me he knows what happened to Luca." Her fingers spasmed slightly as her other hand rose to touch his. He could feel her begin to shake. "He knows who murdered our boy, and when I get his daughter out of prison, he's going to share everything he knows. That's how he's paying for her defense."

A tear slipped down Wendy's face as she grabbed him with her free hand. He leaned forward, and they held each other.

"I wanted to tell you sooner, but I just couldn't. I didn't want to put you through unnecessary stress in case I failed."

"When will you know if you get her out?" she

whispered, her voice thick with emotion.

"On Friday, we go to an evidentiary hearing to prove she should be immune from prosecution." Joe drew a breath. "If we win, we'll know the truth about Luca's death by next weekend."

CHAPTER 8

HENNESSY'S WEEK hadn't gone well.

He'd talked to all the witnesses in Alicia's case, he reviewed every file and checked every legal precedent in South Carolina, but he couldn't find a breakthrough. Exhausted at the end of the week, Hennessy stepped into courtroom five of the Charleston Judicial Center.

He was early and the courtroom was empty. Over the next thirty-five minutes, several other people entered the courtroom behind him. The same five police officers present at the last hearing walked in and sat in the back row. They all glared at Hennessy but didn't say a word. The burly officers sat with grumpy frowns that seemed to be permanently etched on their faces. Despite his drug charges, Dennis Fenton was still part of their brotherhood. He was still a murdered cop to them.

At 9.55am, Aaron Garrett entered the room, followed by a junior assistant. After they sat down, Alicia Fenton was led from a side door to the defense table. She was still in her prison uniform, scruffy looking, and still cuffed at the hands and feet. She said nothing as she sat next to Hennessy.

Five minutes later, the clerk at the front of the room read the case number and then asked the room to rise for Judge Nancy West. The judge walked in, followed by her assistant, and sat down. She adjusted her bright yellow thin-rimmed glasses, cleared her throat, and opened the file on her desk. Once she was settled, Judge West looked out to the waiting lawyers.

"Welcome to the court today. This is an evidentiary hearing to present evidence about whether the Protection of Persons and Property Act should be considered in the case of the State versus Alicia Jane Fenton. The intention of the Act is for those acting in self-defense to be immune from prosecution. Mr. Hennessy, you may begin your argument."

"Thank you, Your Honor." Hennessy stood. "We've lodged a motion to have an evidentiary hearing, pursuant to South Carolina Code of Laws, Section 16-11-450, supported by an affidavit and a memorandum. The Act clearly states that a person who uses deadly force pursuant to the stand-your-ground law is to be immune from criminal prosecution or civil actions. This is a legal requirement in South Carolina."

"Your Honor," Garrett stood and argued before Hennessy could continue, "this is not a case to consider the Protection of Persons and Property Act. First, the victim was struck in the back of the head, which indicates that he was clearly walking away. Self-defense is only viable so long as the person is being attacked. The law clearly states that once the threat has stopped, you cannot continue to defend yourself by attacking the other person. And we have precedents for this." Garrett opened a file on his desk as he talked. "In the State v. Oatley, the defendant argued he was immune from prosecution under the Protection of Persons and Property Act, however, it was found not to be the case because the use of deadly force was not warranted to prevent the defendant's own death or bodily injury. In that case, the trial court found there was no force to be used because the victim had turned their back and was walking away. The threat was over, and so the Act didn't apply."

"Your Honor, if I may finish my arguments without being interrupted." Hennessy glared at Garrett, paused, and then turned back to the Judge. "The Act clearly states in Section 16-11-450, that 'A person who uses deadly force as permitted by the provisions of this article or another applicable provision of law is justified in using deadly force and is immune from criminal prosecution for the use of deadly force.'"

"But Your Honor—"

"And the intent of this section of the law has been defined by the General Assembly." Hennessy raised his voice to continue over Garrett's attempt to interrupt him. "The General Assembly stated that 'persons residing in this State have a right to expect to remain unmolested and safe within their homes,' and that 'no person or victim of crime should be required to surrender his personal safety to a criminal, nor should a person or victim be required to needlessly retreat in the face of intrusion or attack.' The defendant was being attacked. In this case, she was physically injured, and the victim was attempting to rape her."

"Your Honor, this hearing is about the law, not some wild storytelling by the defense," Garrett argued. "Even if we ignore the fact the victim was walking away and the threat to the defendant had ended, the presumption provided under this section of the law does not apply if the victim has the right to be in the residence. The victim was once the owner of the apartment and was still a resident at the time of his death. Because the victim was a resident of the property, the Act cannot be applied."

"The victim was no longer the owner of the property. He transferred the ownership of the apartment to the defendant five months earlier. He had also previously been in prison until that night, and his sentence still had another fourteen months to run. He should've been in prison, however, he surprised the owner of the apartment on his return. His residence was in the Lieber Correctional Center, not this address on Logan Street. His name was not on the title, he was not renting a room from the owner, and he was not a resident in the five weeks prior to that night."

"This is about the law! The victim's address is listed on his prison release papers. He was a resident of the apartment before he went to prison, which means he had the right to be there. He had his belongings in the apartment. He lived in this apartment. And he intended to come home to this apartment. Under the law, the Protection of Persons and Property Act does not apply! And this is about the law, not some fanciful argument that the man didn't reside there. The defendant has no protection under this Act because the victim resided there."

"In her own home, where she lived alone, the defendant was protecting herself against an attempted rape—"

"There's no evidence of that!"

"The defendant had previously lodged complaints with the police department about her rapist—"

"And the man was found not guilty!" Garrett slapped his hand on the table. "The victim was struck in the back of the head in his residence! The Act does not apply!"

"Because the attacker was struck in the back of the head is not evidence that the threat had ended. We don't know if the attacker was picking up a knife, gun, or another weapon to continue the attack."

"Ok, Gentlemen." Judge West raised her hands to settle the courtroom. "Let's calm this down again. Apart from the issues raised, is there any other evidence that needs to be considered in my decision?"

"No, Your Honor," Garrett said. "We have lodged our complete arguments in the affidavit, and our main point is that because the victim resided at this residence, protection under this Act cannot be applied. We've attached the letters addressed to the apartment and the bills that show he was still paying the power bill. The defense can argue for self-defense at trial, if they so wish."

"Mr. Hennessy?"

"Nothing further from the defense, Your Honor," Hennessy said. "Our complete arguments are lodged in the affidavit, however, our main point is that she was acting in self-defense against a person who did not reside at the residence for the previous five weeks, and the victim was not supposed to be a resident again until his prison sentence finished, which was fourteen months later."

"This is an interesting issue, and you both have strong arguments. On the one hand, he's clearly a resident of the apartment, as he still pays the power bill, and his belongings are still there. And on the other hand, he was residing at a different location for the previous five weeks, albeit forcefully, and he wasn't due back for another fourteen months. What legally defines residence? That's the question I will have to consider. So having reviewed the arguments earlier and listening to what has been said today, we will adjourn until I make a decision."

Judge West hadn't rejected the motion outright.

It was a small win for the defense, and it signaled the case would be a fight to the end.

CHAPTER 9

JUDGE WEST delivered her decision five days later—the defense's application for protection under the Protection of Persons and Property Act was refused.

Judge West agreed that the victim legally resided at the residence, despite his prison sentence, and because of this, the defendant did not fall under the protection of the Act. She noted that while the victim had removed his name from the apartment title, he was still a resident, as evidenced by his address on his prison release papers. She scheduled the case for trial.

Five days after Judge West delivered her decision, prosecutor Aaron Garrett called and asked for a meeting with Hennessy. Hennessy agreed as quickly as he could, knowing the prosecution was rattled by the argument for self-defense. He knew a better deal was coming. As he prepared for the meeting, he told Jacinta that he expected a deal for voluntary manslaughter between two to five years.

Hennessy stepped inside the building at 101 Meeting Street. Inside the entrance, the title of the Ninth Circuit Solicitor was displayed proudly on the wall beneath the Seal of South Carolina. The American Flag stood on one side of the name, and the South Carolina State Flag on the other.

While other states referred to the position of

Circuit Solicitor as the District Attorney, the 1868 South Carolina Constitution, South Carolina's fifth constitution, established one elected Solicitor for each judicial circuit, totaling sixteen judicial circuits in the state.

Assistant Solicitor Aaron Garrett was waiting near the entrance of the office. Garrett shook hands with Hennessy solidly, made a few comments about the heat and humidity, and then led Hennessy through the halls to his office. Garrett's private office was spacious and modern. There was a clean, white desk with only a computer monitor, a Scandinavian-styled couch, and a plain white bookshelf filled with red-colored law books. A piece of art on one wall and an indoor plant in the corner. The air-conditioner was working overtime, and the room felt cool, a great relief from the outdoors.

"Can I get you anything?" Garrett asked as he sat down behind his desk and indicated for Hennessy to take the seat on the other side. "Hot drink? Cold drink?"

"No, thank you," Hennessy said as he sat down. "I'm fine."

"How's the vineyard?"

"It's fine, but I'm not here to chat."

"Really? Joe, that's not the Southern way. We have to make small talk for a few moments before we get down to business. I had a delicious Merlot from North Carolina the other week, but I can't think of the name of it. Do you have much competition across the border?"

"Sorry, Aaron, but I'm here for business."

"I know another defense lawyer just like you. He's all work and no play. The guy works fifty-five-hour weeks and still doesn't have time for a little chat, which is a pity because he seems like a decent guy. As I said, he seems just like you."

"You really are a talker, aren't you?"

"I love to talk. My mother says that's why I'm a lawyer."

"What's the offer?"

"Alright, alright." Garrett brought a file across his desk and opened it. "But I'll tell you, I was impressed with your work on the evidentiary hearing. It was a mighty fine effort you put in court. You almost convinced the judge that there was no reason to even have a trial."

Hennessy nodded but offered no verbal response.

"Down to business then," Garrett said. "Alicia Fenton murdered an ex-cop, plain and simple. You managed to get a PPPA hearing, but you won't win it at trial. It's clear that she hit him in the back of the head with a baseball bat, and apart from a minor cut on her forehead, you have no other evidence of an assault."

"Fighting off a rapist is a valid defense."

"Not if you hit them in the back of the head as they walk away."

"Tell that to the media."

"I won't have to. I'll tell it to the courts." Garrett shook his head. "There's no evidence of attempted rape. You've read the reports yourself. Your client showed no signs of physical injury apart from a small mark above her eye. She submitted to a rape kit at the request of the arresting officers, and there was no evidence of rape or even attempted rape."

"A woman defending herself against a man trying to rape her has to show signs of violence, or else she isn't believed?"

"Not necessarily, but in this case, there's a distinct lack of evidence, which would show how things happened according to your client. This is nothing more than an angry teenager who lashed out at her stepfather and killed him."

"Their history is another story."

"And you won't get a chance to bring that up in court. He was found not guilty." He paused and locked eyes with Hennessy. "Due to the sensitivity of the case, the records were sealed, and a media gag was placed over them. You won't get to talk to the media about that trial."

"He raped his stepdaughter when she was fifteen. Doesn't your moral compass at least go off a little bit?"

"He was found not guilty in a court of law. We have to respect the process. And again, there's zero chance you'll be able to present that in court. No judge in this state will allow those records to be presented at trial."

"It's her truth."

"It's not the truth in a court of law."

Hennessy leaned forward, studying the man opposite him. "Dennis Fenton was a disgraced cop with a history of sexual assault allegations, drug abuse, and deep connections to outlaw motorcycle gangs. He was sentenced to fifteen months in prison for his involvement with drug deals. Why are you protecting him?"

"He was still part of the police brotherhood." Garrett leaned back in his seat. "Ever since this office decided to weed out corruption in the city, the relationship between the Circuit Solicitor's Office and the police department has been strained. There's no denying that. And we need them to cooperate with us for the justice system to flow smoothly. This is our chance to build our connection again. To prove that we've got their back."

"She was defending herself."

"So she says," Garrett sighed and looked up to the air-conditioner vent as a cool gust of air blew through. "Many people knock the cops, but their job is one of the hardest in any community. We need to respect them. We need to respect the effort they put in, and we need to respect their dedication to their service. And right now, they feel like they're being attacked from every angle. The media are after them, the bleeding heart youngsters are after them, and the general public doesn't trust them. It used to be a respected profession, a place that attracted the noblest of people, but it's all changed. I even had one case come across my desk where a retail worker spat on a cop for just walking into the store. Where's the respect for what they do? Where's the respect for all the risks they take?"

"They don't have an easy job."

"Did you know that the number of applications the State has received for permanent disability pensions has increased five-fold in the last two years? Ninety percent of those applications have come as a result of PTSD. We're pushing our cops past the limit and not supporting them when they fall over. PTSD is a real condition, and it has dire consequences."

"And this is what you'll tell the court to make them feel sorry for Fenton?"

"Of course, I will. PTSD is a documented condition that Fenton suffered from. And any chance you have of making him out to be the bad guy will be wiped away from their sympathy for him. Years earlier, he arrived at a single-vehicle car crash to find the driver was decapitated, and then he had to try and save the mutilated body of a baby. Both he and his partner at the time, Detective Sean Carver, were deeply affected by that. Who wouldn't be? They both suffered PTSD because of the work they had to do in service to the community," Garrett said. "For every cop that dies in the line of duty, two die from suicide. Think about that, Hennessy. These people risk their lives day in and day out, and when they need us, we don't help them."

"So that's his excuse for falling into bed with the one-percenters?"

"That's what he said during his trial for the drug charges. The morphine helped him relax and forget about what he saw on the day of the car accident, and the motorcycle gangs could get it for him. And given his position, they were happy to supply him as long as they got something in return. The Rebel Sons ran drugs through Charleston. And we know Fenton gave them a free passage through so he could calm his PTSD."

"My research tells me that Internal Affairs were looking at both Dennis Fenton and Sean Carver in connection to the Rebel Sons, but only Fenton got busted. Sean Carver is somehow still a detective, and perhaps not coincidently, he was also the one who picked up Fenton from Lieber Correctional upon his release."

"I don't know what you're suggesting, but Detective Carver has not been charged with anything. If you got your hands on the report, you'd know that

Detective Carver was warned by Internal Affairs not to have any contact with the Rebel Sons, or he would lose his job. He knows he can't go near the gangs anymore."

"Sean Carver picked up Fenton from the prison and drove back to Fenton's apartment. Carver's history is an important piece of this puzzle, and his past will be exposed as part of this case."

"Are you suggesting you'll expose his past to the media?"

"I'll do what I need to." Hennessy leaned forward. "What's the new offer?"

"We're willing to admit that perhaps this case isn't cut and dry. We'll put an offer on the table for manslaughter under section 16-3-50, and she will note that this crime was under intense passion. She does ten years and then gets on with her life."

"Ten years?"

"It's about as good as it's going to get. You won't receive an offer less than that. We need the police department to know we still have their backs."

Hennessy held his stare on Garrett for a long moment, and when Garrett didn't flinch, he stood and offered his hand. "I'll take it to my client."

Garrett shook with Hennessy. "You don't want to take this to court. There will be a lot of upset police officers if this one makes it into the courtroom."

Hennessy didn't respond. He picked up his briefcase, turned, and left the office. He walked through the halls, said goodbye to the secretary, and stepped out into the bright sunlight covering the street. It took a moment for his eyes to adjust.

"Joe Hennessy."

Hennessy turned and saw South Carolina Senator

Richard Longhouse standing just outside the wooden doors of 101 Meeting Street, a cigarette pinched between two fingers. Longhouse drew a drag and then puffed out a cloud of smoke.

Neither man attempted to shake hands, a sign of the animosity between them.

"Tell me, Counsellor," Longhouse said, pausing long enough to take another drag from his smoke. "Since when does a man working to save his vineyard take on pro-bono cases?"

"That's none of your business."

"Ah, but it is." Longhouse smiled as he stepped closer to Hennessy. His grin was filled with fakeness. In his fifties, Longhouse was a Charleston man through and through. Tall and slim, he was well-groomed, taking great pride in his appearance. His olive skin was tanned, and his hair was dyed brown. He had a thick mustache that looked like it was combed. Dressed in black trousers and a white shirt, he presented as a respectable member of society, but those who knew him knew that was far from the truth. "Dennis Fenton was a cop, and the Charleston police department and I are good friends."

"You're a corrupt man. I have no time for you."

"Come on, Joe, we used to work together. You and me in the Solicitor's Office. Do you remember those days twenty years ago? We used to fight the same fight." Longhouse shrugged and then flicked his cigarette to the gutter. "I've got a word of advice for you because maybe you've forgotten how things work in Charleston. Everyone is connected here. We're all in each other's business, and we all scratch each other's backs. It's the Southern way." Longhouse stepped closer. "The police department has helped me in the past, and I've helped them. And nobody wants Fenton's past brought out in the open. Think long and hard before you take this case to trial."

Hennessy's jaw clenched, holding back the urge to hit the man.

Longhouse sensed Hennessy's rage and then nodded over his shoulder. Sitting by the street, next to a Charleston PD patrol car, were two of the older police officers that were previously present in court.

Hennessy turned back to Longhouse and stepped close, towering over him. "I'll warn you once, Longhouse. Stay away from me, and stay away from my case."

CHAPTER 10

THE HUMIDITY was thick in the Sherriff Al Cannon Detention Center.

When the temperature rose, the heat became trapped in the halls and windowless rooms, creating a stale stench that lingered for months. The foyer and the guards' rooms were air-conditioned, but everywhere else was subject to fluctuations in weather and humidity.

Hennessy waited in the interview room, reviewing the case files, dabbing his forehead with a cloth to prevent sweat dripping onto the papers. He waited twenty-five minutes in the stuffy air before the door to the room opened.

Alicia came into the room uncuffed and sat opposite him. Her head was downcast. She was skinnier now, and her face looked gaunt. Her skin had lost its vibrancy, and her eyes looked tired. He greeted her, and she responded with a brief nod.

"It's ok that the hearing didn't go our way. It's the first step in a long process. What we've done is signaled to the prosecution that we're going to fight this one every step of the way," Hennessy said. "And as expected, the prosecution didn't like that. They thought they had an easy win, but now they know this is going to be a battle. As expected, they called to offer a new deal. I met with the Circuit Solicitor's

Office this morning, and we spent some time discussing your case and, in particular, we talked about what a plea deal would look like."

Alicia looked up at him, a brief sense of hope lighting up in her eyes. "You were great in court. Thank you for doing that."

"Don't thank me yet." Hennessy exhaled loudly. "As you know, the judge didn't rule in our favor, but it's forced the prosecution to rethink their position. They know if they take it to trial, they'll be in for a fight, so they don't want to do that. They've offered to reduce the charges from murder to voluntary manslaughter."

"How long in prison?"

"Ten years."

"Ten years?" Alicia didn't move. Her eyes looked at his, then slowly dropped to her hands, where she was twisting her fingers together. He could only watch on as she grappled with whatever realization was now ravaging her mental state. "Or I take it to trial and risk getting life for murder?"

"That's correct."

She shook her head. "This is political, isn't it? It's because he's a former cop, isn't it?"

Hennessy's jaw clenched and relaxed.

"You don't have to say it," she continued. "I know it's true. If he wasn't an ex-cop, I would've walked out of here. I know they have power and authority, and I just have to accept it. He was respected in the police department before his downfall and, even after his conviction, he still had a lot of friends there."

Alicia stood and walked to the far corner of the room, hiding her expression from him. From where he sat, he couldn't see her face. She stood frozen, a statue gazing beyond the wall, and all Hennessy could do was wait.

"He first beat me when I was twelve. My mother had died a few months earlier, and then he saw that car crash with the baby and the decapitated mother. He was different after that. It was like his whole personality had changed. He became angry, drunk, and violent. I was so scared of him, but I didn't have anywhere else to go. I didn't have any other family. He beat me so badly one time that I couldn't go to school for a week. I had to wait until the bruising on my face went down. I never did anything wrong, but he'd always find a reason to beat me." She paused for a long moment, shaking a little. "And then, when I was fifteen, he came home really, really, drunk. That's when he raped me. I was so broken after that. I went and saw the nurse at the school, and she took me to the hospital and then to the police station. We went to court, went through this whole process, but it was no use. I couldn't beat the system then, and I probably won't beat the system now. After I lost the court case, they just sent me back to his care, like I was his to own. How stupid. After that, he stopped drinking as much but started turning to drugs. Morphine, I think. Instead of being violent and out of control, he was just useless."

She turned to face Hennessy again. Her face appeared calm and controlled. The fear he had seen previously remained but with much less intensity. It looked as if she had accepted the news he had brought her, and rather than fight it, she would accept her fate.

"It is what it is, I guess," she whispered as she looked across at him, and Hennessy felt a dagger strike his heart. "You can't beat a system designed to keep you down, can you?"

"I'm preparing our defense for trial. We'll argue that you acted in self-defense, and if we get a good jury, we have a strong chance to win. This isn't over."

"Can I testify? Can I get up there and tell them what he did to me?"

"It's your choice, but I don't think it's a very good idea."

"Why not?"

"While it's completely your decision, you have to remember that the burden of proof is on the prosecution, so that forces the jury to decide whether there's enough proof to convict you. If you don't testify, the jury has to look at the evidence, and only the evidence presented in the trial."

"And if I do?"

"If you testify, the question for the jury doesn't become about the facts or the lack of them. The question becomes about your credibility and whether you're telling the truth. That places you at an extreme disadvantage because the prosecution will do everything in its power to confuse you on the stand and make you look untrustworthy. One slip of the tongue on the stand and the jury will forget about everything else. Instead of focusing on the facts, they will make their decision based on you. The rest of the court case won't even matter."

"If it will get me out of here, I can handle it."

"Criminal trials are extremely emotional and stressful, which makes us all vulnerable to making mistakes. You'll face skillful, experienced attorneys whose job it is to make you look like a liar. They'll confuse you so that you'll change the answer to a basic question, and they'll pounce upon any tiny little mistake. And unfortunately, even though jurors are expected to be impartial, it's only normal that people maintain their natural biases in a courtroom. You're a young girl with a motive to lie about self-defense. You don't deny that you hit him, so the prosecution will make it look like you acted out of rage and then made up the self-defense story later to stay out of prison. The case will only be about whether the jurors believe you."

"But how else do I tell my side of the story? All I want to do is tell the truth."

"We tell your side of the story through the witnesses we present in the trial." Hennessy leaned forward and crossed his arms on the table. "My investigator is gathering background information about anyone connected to this case, and that'll form the basis of our strategy. Can you tell me anyone I should talk to? Anyone who would've seen how Dennis treated you. I need to know if you can think of anyone who would talk about his behavior and testify for us in court."

"Edith Chapman," she answered quickly. "That's Dennis' sister. She lives in Wilmington, North Carolina, about two hours north. She's a lovely woman who tried to get me taken out of Dennis' care after the rape. She knows what her brother did to me."

"That's good. Anyone else?"

"There was a woman who lived across the street who would look after me if the beatings became too bad. Maria Don. She knew what was happening, but I don't think she'll testify. She's terrified of authority and the courts. Her husband is currently in prison for murder, but she's certain that he's innocent. She'll talk to you, but I don't think she'll testify."

"I'll talk to them," Hennessy said. "We've taken one roll of the dice, and now it's time to build for the next step in the process. But I have to warn you, there's still a long way to go, and it's only going to get tougher."

CHAPTER 11

HENNESSY HADN'T been sleeping well.

It was too hot, and the bugs were too loud. Night after night, he tossed and turned, constantly waking to check the air-conditioner was working, but it was making little difference. The thoughts about Alicia that rumbled through his head prevented any sense of calm.

The drive to the Logan Street address was mostly in silence, his thoughts drifting back to the deep agony of grief. The streets of Charleston did that to him. It awoke memories he'd long pushed down. He knew his life was good—he had an amazing wife who understood him, he had two amazing daughters that tested him, and he owned a picturesque vineyard that challenged him, but there was always a small thought in the back of his mind, one thought that tested his limits. For the last twenty years, the same thought kept coming back. Back then, he was a lawyer in the Circuit Solicitor's Office, a prosecutor working for justice in Charleston, but even with every resource at his fingertips, he never found his son's killer. Over the years, he had tried to push the thoughts about his son's murder away, tried to bury them deep inside, but Alicia's case had pushed them back to the foreground. The thoughts that rumbled through his head prevented any sense of calm.

He parked in front of Alicia's apartment. The sidewalk was deserted, and the only sound came from a dog barking somewhere down the street, no doubt sitting on a balcony for a bit of fresh air. The single-level red brick apartments were squashed next to each other, with a small step and yard at the front of each.

He walked across to house number five and paused long enough to note the crime scene tape still dangling from one edge of the door. As if to give the case some extra sense of reality, Hennessy slowly reached out and touched the door, holding his palm against the cold timber for a few seconds.

"She's not home," a voice called out from behind, startling Hennessy enough to pull his hand back. He looked over and saw an older woman standing in the doorway of the apartment across the road.

"I know," Hennessy said as he crossed the street. The woman eyed him suspiciously. "I'm actually here to see you. Mrs. Don, isn't it?"

"Who are you? I ain't interested in no door-to-door salesmen."

"I'm not selling anything. My name is Joe Hennessy. We spoke on the phone earlier."

The face of Maria Don was emotionless, neither happy nor sad, though in her wrinkles were written the memories of both joys and sorrows. Her hair was dark as the shadows of the night, and her eyes were gray as the clouds. An African American woman in her seventies, she looked like she had lived a hard life. She studied Hennessy without giving any indication of what she was thinking. When he was close enough, she nodded her approval and waved for him to enter.

Her lower-floor duplex apartment was directly across the road from the Fenton home. Hennessy first noticed that she had no air-conditioner, and the ceiling fans did little to cool the room down. The apartment was nothing like Hennessy had imagined when he first spotted the woman. He imagined a place filled with memories, walls covered in photos of children and grandchildren, perhaps interlaced with a few pets along the way. Instead, there was nothing even remotely close. Not a single family photo could be seen, with the walls bare, except for a single framed picture of a London double-decker bus. The single wall unit, which sat almost next to the couch, had just a single shelf of books, and even then, only barely enough to fill it. He spotted just one name he recognized, Stephen King, but couldn't determine which book it was. The rest of the shelves held half a dozen knick-knacks between them.

"Lovely home you have," Hennessy said as he accepted her gesture to take a seat on the well-worn couch.

"Thank you," the woman said, picked up a pile of knitting, and sat it on the table beside her seat.

"Have you lived here long?"

"Long enough to know that the world is a better place without the likes of Dennis Fenton in it."

Blunt and to the point, Hennessy thought to himself. He liked that.

"I ain't testifying if that's what you're gonna ask me next," she snapped before he responded to her comment. "I'm just a lonely old woman living here, and I don't need people trying to shut me up for talking. It ain't worth the risk."

"Which people?"

"The cops."

"Any in particular?"

"You heard of Sean Carver?" She studied his expression. "Yeah, you've heard of him. He's been snooping around here since Dennis died. Making comments that the police control this area, and if someone wants to mess with the law, they have to answer to him. I don't trust him one bit."

"He said that to you directly?"

"Not those words, but men like him don't have to say it."

Hennessy nodded. "How well do you know Alicia?"

"I know her well enough."

Figuring it best to get to the point, Hennessy dropped the charade and bit the bullet. "I understand it can be frightening to deal with—"

"I ain't testifying in no court," the woman snapped, cutting him off mid-sentence. "I don't know how many times I have to say it, but I ain't going up against those cops. I saw what they did to my innocent husband, and we're still paying the price. When Dennis died, I told the cops that I saw nothing and heard nothing that night, and that's what I'll tell you as well. If you put me in front of a judge, that's what I'll tell them too."

"But that's not true, is it?"

She looked away.

"Alicia is facing life in prison," he said, hoping his tone held enough empathy. "She'll spend the rest of her life behind bars if nobody comes forward to offer her some support." He leaned forward in his seat. "Especially from people like yourself, people who knew her stepfather." For a moment, Hennessy thought she would change her mind. Her face relaxed a little, losing the stern edge as the corners of her mouth pulled slightly outward. He was sure she was about to smile, apologize, and then agree. "Can you please tell me what you know about that night?"

"Are you recording this?"

Hennessy shook his head.

"Alright. I'll tell you what I saw, but it doesn't go further than us. I ain't telling the police this." She drew a breath, hesitated, and then continued. "I was sitting on the front step, having a smoke at around 9pm, and I saw the car pull up. It was a nice car. A new Mercedes. Dennis Fenton got out of the passenger seat. I remember it was Fenton because I was sure he was supposed to be in prison."

"Did you see who was driving?"

"No, but it was a new car. Real nice. As soon as I saw Fenton get out, I knew it would be trouble. He was drunk and yelling stuff over and over. I sat on the step for a while, and I watched him storm into his apartment. I felt sorry for Alicia, but what could I do? I can't go up against the cops. Look at what they did to my husband. If I tried to stop Dennis, I would've ended up behind bars as well."

"What happened after you saw Dennis enter the apartment?"

"I saw a big biker-looking guy talk to the driver of the car and then wait by the door of Dennis' apartment. I thought it was really weird, so I waited to see what would happen. I heard a scream. Then Alicia ran out, calling for help. The guy in the Mercedes stepped out and helped her, and the biker went into Dennis' apartment. That was it. I went back inside my apartment then. I didn't want no trouble."

"If you could testify about what you saw that night, it would help Alicia."

"You done?" The tone sounded as cold as ice. "I'm not in the habit of repeating myself, Mr. Lawyer. I said I'm not testifying, and I mean it."

Hennessy and Maria Don sat staring at each other for a few more seconds. The steely look in her eyes told Hennessy the woman stood firm, and no amount of pleading would change her mind.

"Thank you for your time."

She didn't respond, but she followed Hennessy to the door. She shut the front door the second he stepped outside. As he walked back onto the street, he saw a new Mercedes parked out front. The shiny exterior caught his eye, but it was the man next to it that gathered his full attention.

Hennessy approached the man leaning against the front of the vehicle. He recognized the man from the photos in the police files. "Sean Carver?"

The man didn't respond, but it was clear to Hennessy that he'd gotten the name right.

Sean Carver looked like trouble, like a man who crossed everyone to get what he wanted. His arrogance was apparent as he stood on the street, arms folded across his chest. His light brown hair was graying at the sides, and his weathered skin made him look ten years older than his age of forty-five.

As Hennessy approached, Carver turned and entered his black Mercedes. Carver started the whisper-quiet engine and rolled away. Hennessy stood on the street, watching the car disappear into the distance. He turned back to Maria Don's house and saw her looking through the blinds at the car. When she saw Hennessy looking at her, she moved away from the blinds.

One thing had become clear to Hennessy—the

further he dug into the case, the more dangerous it was becoming.

CHAPTER 12

HENNESSY DROVE the scenic route to Wilmington, North Carolina, starting the three-hour drive along Highway 17 just after sunrise. He needed to know if Edith Chapman would testify about her brother's behavior with Alicia, and he preferred to ask that question face-to-face, allowing him the chance to assess the strength of her potential testimony.

Hennessy arrived in the pleasant city just after 10am, already three coffees into his day. He drove to the neighborhood of Carolina Place, an affluent community where mature and majestic oak trees stood in front of stately homes.

Edith Chapman was tending to the roses in front of her home, a zest for life radiating off her. She wore a colorful dress, a bright red hat, pink shoes, and yellow garden gloves. In her sixties, she appeared a picture of good health, and as she reached over one bush to trim the other, she looked as nimble as a teenager.

"May I help you?"

"Hello, Ma'am. My name is Joe Hennessy. My assistant phoned you yesterday."

"Ah, yes. This is about Dennis and Alicia, isn't it?"

"It is."

"Then you'd better come in." She removed her gloves and led Hennessy into the house, turning left once they stepped inside the open door. The dining room was spacious and elegant, with orange dahlias in a vase in the center of the wooden table. "Coffee, tea, or a coke?"

"Sweet tea, please," Hennessy replied.

Edith turned into the kitchen, retrieved a pitcher of sweet tea from the refrigerator, along with a tray of ice from the freezer drawer. She collected two glasses on her way back and set them down on the table. She poured a generous amount into the tall glasses, dropped two ice cubes into each, and looked on hopefully as Hennessy took the first sip.

"You know the way to a man's heart." Hennessy smiled. "This is delicious."

"Oh, good." She took her glass and sat at the other end of the table. She drew a long breath and then sighed. "It's so sad about what happened to Dennis."

"It can be hard to process these types of situations."

"Oh no. Not that." She waved his comment away. "I was almost relieved when I heard the news about his death."

"Why is that?"

She took another long breath and exhaled. "Dennis was spiraling out of control, and it was getting worse and worse. I thought prison might sort him out, but when I went to see him back there, it was clear he was high on something. He said he could get whatever he wanted behind bars and spent most of his days as high as a kite." She took another long, slow breath and then looked out the window to the leafy surroundings. "No, when I said it was sad what happened to him, I was talking about the incident. He was a good man before that. Honorable. Tough. Reliable. His wife died of a heart attack, which was hard enough, and only a month later, he saw something that changed him. He never told me what it was. He refused to talk about it to me, but it changed him. He started to run away. First, it was alcohol, and then it was drugs. My husband's a doctor, and we tried to help Dennis so many times, but the addictions always drew him back. Whether it was the drink, gambling, or in the end, morphine, he was always looking to get the next hit."

"That must've been tough to watch," Hennessy said, then turned the conversation in another direction. "I take it you knew he wasn't doing right by Alicia?"

"Not doing right by her," she scoffed. "That's one way to say it. I tried my hardest to get her out of there once her mother passed, but nobody would listen. I knew it wasn't my brother doing these horrible things to her. It was the PTSD. When I heard he raped Alicia, I insisted she stay with me during the trial. She was such a lovely girl, always cleaning up and helping around the house. After the jurors made the wrong decision in the trial, Dennis demanded that she return to his house. I guess it was a sense of control for him. We couldn't do much about it. After the court decided about her custody, the police showed up to take her back. I cried for a week after that. That poor girl."

Edith played with the edge of the tablecloth, attempting to disperse some of her nervous energy.

"Did you ever see Dennis hit Alicia?"

"I did. The first time I saw Dennis give her a backhand across the mouth, I ran out and slapped him so hard that his ears must've rung for a week."

"Did you ever see him do anything sexual?"

"No, but when I went to visit him in prison, he said that he couldn't wait to get his hands on her. It was disgusting, and I told him as much, but he was so high he didn't even think twice about it. He wasn't really making much sense."

"He said that directly to you?"

"He did."

"Do you remember his exact words?"

She sighed and tipped her glass of sweet tea to the side. The ice clinked against the edge of the glass. "He said, 'I can't wait to get my hands on that sweet piece of tail.' And then he said that he 'owns her.' It was disgusting." She fought back a tear and then sighed again. "And Alicia used to talk about how Dennis watched her in the shower. She was only fourteen at the time, and she had this creepy stepfather watching her shower every night."

"Did you report it to anyone?"

"I reported it to everyone. We tried everything. Child services, the courts, the police, nobody did anything. The problem was that Dennis knew everyone in power. It's like that in small cities. A few well-connected men get to do whatever they want."

"Did you see any other abuse?"

"Not directly, but she talked about how he would often rub his hands all over her." She paused and sighed. "She cried a lot when she was here. I asked her to tell people at the school, but she said that would only make it worse. If Dennis found out, he would only beat her harder."

"I'm really sorry you had to hear that from her."

"So am I, Mr. Hennessy."

Hennessy sat back in his chair and spotted a photo in the corner of the room. It was Edith and Dennis, twenty years earlier, with broad smiles on their faces.

"Like I said," Edith turned to the photo when she noticed Hennessy's attention, "he was a different man before the incident. He worked so hard to serve his community and was a good family man. But…" Her head dropped as she fought back the tears. "None of us could help him."

"If the case went to trial, would you testify about Dennis' behavior?"

"Yes. Absolutely. I loved my brother, but I can't defend that behavior. If you call me to the stand, I'll tell the court everything I know."

"Thank you," Hennessy responded. "Your testimony will be a very important part of Alicia's defense. My assistant will be in touch at a later time, but we'll need you to draft a statement of the facts as you know them, and it's likely we'll head to trial in around five to eight weeks."

She bit her lower lip. "Mr. Hennessy, Dennis never shared with us what the incident was. His wife died, and he had to deal with this incident, but I never knew what it was. My little brother was suffering, and I never found out what caused it. Do you know what happened?"

Hennessy nodded.

"Can you please tell me?"

"Are you sure you would like to know?"

"Yes." She looked into her sweet tea. "Yes, I do."

"There was a single-vehicle car accident." Hennessy watched the woman fight back tears as she stared into her sweet tea. "Dennis and his partner were the first to arrive at the scene. The mother…"

Hennessy sighed. "Are you sure you want to know?"

"Please," she whispered.

"The mother was decapitated, and the baby in the back was badly mutilated. Dennis worked hard to save the baby, but she died in the hospital."

Edith worked hard to fight back the tears, and when she couldn't hold them in any longer, she stood, the tears flowing down her cheeks. "I'm sorry, Mr. Hennessy. I need some time."

"That's ok," Hennessy stood and rested a caring hand on her shoulder. "Take all the time you need."

CHAPTER 13

THE PRISON walls looked like they were covered in a lining of sweat. Alicia did her best to avoid touching them, keeping far away from the walls.

During her time in prison, she couldn't bring herself to let out the real feelings which seemed to torment her day and night. Others did, where the endless screams from those who didn't care seemed to go on for hours at a time.

As she was escorted back to her unit by Maria Gonzales, one of the nicer guards she had come to know during her time inside, Alicia wondered what life would be like if she wasn't that kind of person, someone too afraid to speak up. She had been struggling with it her entire life, always considered too weak by those around her. Prisoners took advantage of such a thing, but despite her friend Jada telling her she needed to change to survive this place, she still couldn't bring herself to let go.

As Gonzales led her past one of the adjoining units, Alicia could hear the voices from behind the wall, the faint rumble occasionally punctuated by someone yelling over the top of everyone else. She wondered what it would be like to be that person, the alpha in the wolf pack, the one to speak whatever was on their minds without considering the consequences.

As if I could ever do that, she thought to herself as

they reached their destination. Gonzales unlocked the door and gestured for Alicia to step inside. As she passed the guard, Gonzales whispered something to her that came as a surprise.

"Watch your back in here," she said, and Alicia briefly stopped to look at the guard. At first, she thought the warning came from a place of spite, a warning of an intended attack as if the guard was mocking her. But the look had been the exact opposite. The pause lasted barely a second, but it was enough for Alicia to see a different side of the guard. Behind the tough exterior, the uniform, and the intimidating tool belt the guard wore around her middle, there was a caring woman.

"Thank you," she whispered back and continued into the rowdy inside of a prison unit notorious for assaults and drugs.

Screaming and laughing greeted Alicia as she entered, with several girls chasing each other around the common area like a couple of schoolchildren. Someone had taken the other's shoe and was running around waving it in the air. From initial appearances, it looked as if it was just a game, a fun distraction from the endless monotony of prison life. Unfortunately, the fun was only one-sided.

To begin with, both women were opposites of one another. The first looked fit and strong, running with the agility of a pursued rabbit. The one running after her couldn't have spent more than a fleeting thought about physical activity during the previous decade. Her face almost lit up with exhaustion, her cheeks beaming red with heat. The person doing the chasing was anything but happy about the ensuing run. The look on the woman's face resembled a cartoon, her anger ready to explode into a raging storm. The one holding the shoe would occasionally pause and hold the item out to her pursuer but then snatch it back and take off again.

"Give it back to her," someone near the back called, sounding more annoyed than supportive.

Alicia looked toward the upstairs balcony where her cell sat. Jada would still be at work in the laundry and, since she didn't trust anybody else, she knew her best bet was to return to the cell and wait for her friend to return. The more she could avoid being out with the rest of the unit's population, the less chance she had of getting involved in a conflict.

She'd barely made it to the stairs before she heard someone call out to her in a voice that sounded anything but inviting.

"Hey, new girl, why don't ya come and sit 'ere?"

The woman calling her was named Deb. She wasn't quite the top dog of the unit but yearned for the position. Alicia looked as she sat with one arm around her girlfriend while another inmate sat on her other side, all three staring at Alicia with wry grins. With her thick arms covered in tattoos, Deb looked scarier than any man Alicia had met and felt her cheeks heat up as she considered her options.

"I said come here," Deb repeated, and a few of the girls turned their attention from the chase to the new situation appearing before them.

Alicia had two choices, and neither felt appealing. She could go to the woman and see where that path led her, or she could ignore the inmate completely and take her chances back in her cell. While her cell gave her a sense of separation from the rest of the unit, it didn't offer any protection. The doors remained unlocked during the day, which meant anybody could simply follow her inside. Alicia forgot about it as she foolishly chose the second option.

"Hey, I'm talking to you," Deb called as Alicia turned back to the stairs and continued. She heard shuffling behind her as she walked up the stairs before footfalls followed her up.

Thinking she could at least get to the top of the stairs first and reconsider her position, Alicia looked up and saw someone already blocking her way, another inmate standing at the top of the stairs with her arms folded across her ample chest. It was another one of Deb's accomplices, although Alicia didn't know her name.

"Better do as you're told, sweet cheeks," the woman said, and Alicia paused her climb to look behind her.

The previous look of bemusement on Deb's face had vanished as she climbed the stairs toward her. The rest of the unit fell silent in anticipation of the confrontation which was about to unfold.

Alicia held her breath.

The beating in her chest hit the next level.

She knew a confrontation would eventually find her, but she didn't imagine it happening in such a public setting.

All eyes were on them as Deb reached the step just beneath Alicia's, and the woman didn't stop until the tip of her nose touched the much smaller woman.

Her breath reeked of stale cigarettes, bad enough for Alicia to gag.

Deb grabbed her victim around the throat.

Visions of her stepfather grabbing her flashed through Alicia's mind as Deb's slap caught her on the side of the head.

Stars flashed before her eyes as the hand returned for a vicious backhander that filled her mouth with the stale taste of blood.

"Mackenzie!" someone screamed, and before Alicia could react, the attacker let go of her, turned, and tried to lash out at the two officers who had already closed the distance between them. Through her watery eyes, Alicia could see Gonzalez standing at the door.

Deborah Mackenzie was removed from the unit in handcuffs after a brief struggle which included repeated threats at Alicia. The rest of the unit remained where they stood, an excited murmur rolling across the common area as each inmate watched the excitement unfold like a Sunday matinee. Once the attacker disappeared from the unit, Gonzalez called for Alicia to go to her, which she did.

The guard led Alicia down the hallway to a separate holding cell, where she followed Alicia inside before partly closing the door.

"Not wise for you to be seen talking to me. The rest of the girls will likely target you if they know we're talking. Best to tell them I took you to the medical unit, understand?"

Alicia nodded.

"Good. Now you better listen up, girl," Gonzalez said. She paused, then, sensing Alicia's fear, sat beside her. "This isn't a place where fairytales come true. These people you're inside with, the ones in your unit, they're bad people. They've committed the kinds of crimes you wouldn't wish on your worst enemy, and right now, you have no choice but to live amongst them."

Alicia wiped her tears away as she listened to the guard and found herself close to panic.

"I'm not always going to see what goes on in there, and neither are the rest of my team. You need to toughen up if you're going to survive, you hear me?"

Again, Alicia nodded.

"And by toughen up, I mean exactly that. You can't be putting up with that crap. If someone challenges you, you need to stand up to them, or else they'll walk all over you. Next time that happens, you need to fight back."

"Thank you," Alicia whispered. "I will."

But she wasn't sure how true the statement was.

CHAPTER 14

HENNESSY LOOKED at his watch as Jacinta began packing up for the day. "It's five-thirty already?"

She shot him a wink and wished him a good night as she turned for the door, only to be met by Barry Lockett coming the other way.

"Is he still in?" Lockett's broad Australian accent echoed through the office.

"He's always in. The man never leaves the office. I'm not even sure he has a home to go to," Jacinta laughed as she walked out the door.

Hennessy closed his laptop as he watched the large man rumble into his office. "Bit late for an office call, isn't it?"

"I was in the area and thought I'd take a chance," Barry said as he dropped into the chair opposite.

"It paid off." Hennessy walked over to the cabinet at the side of the room and opened a drawer. He pulled out an unopened bottle of whiskey and two glasses. "I was about to crack this open."

"Orphan Barrel?" Lockett tilted his head a little, but Hennessy could see his lips quiver at the thought of a taste. "Isn't that the same brand as the stolen bottles?"

"It is. I was curious about what a five-hundred-dollar bottle of bourbon tastes like. I received this as a gift years ago from one of the grooms that had their wedding at the vineyard. He was a whiskey man, and he said I had to try it, but I put it in the cellar and forgot about it until this case came up." Hennessy placed the glasses on his desk. "And besides, let's call this professional research."

"I like how you think," Lockett said as he watched Hennessy pour two glasses. When he held one out for him, he accepted the offering with both hands, using one to cradle the glass like an expensive heirloom.

"Bottom's up," Hennessy said, raised his glass, and then took a small sip, letting the flavors roll around his mouth.

The two men were silent as they considered their opinion.

Hennessy noted the musty oak overtones in the smell and the creamy mature richness of an aged bourbon. The 25-year-old whiskey was smooth, beginning with a burst of spice and warming to sweet notes of syrup and fruit. It lingered with a creamy and soothingly sweet afternote, with notes of honey and vanilla. But rather than sound like a whiskey snob, Hennessy said, "That's smooth."

"I agree." Lockett stared into his glass. "That's the most beautiful whiskey I've ever tasted. I could have that for breakfast."

"Sounds like an expensive breakfast," Hennessy laughed and sat down. "Last week, I went to the cellar in the vineyard, feeling a bit down, and Wendy was down there lifting all my whiskey from the bottom shelf to the top shelf. Yep, I can always rely on her to lift my spirits."

"Ha," Lockett laughed and took another sip. He sat with the flavor for a long moment before groaning happily and then smiled. "I've got news for you in the Fenton case."

"Good news, I hope."

"Well, I don't know about the good part, but I guess it's eye-opening. Brock Roberts was the man who entered the apartment when he heard Alicia scream. Do you know much about him?"

"The conveniently located biker? Not really."

"Yeah, well, it turns out he's a known beat-down guy as well. He's a member of the Rebel Sons, and when someone wants someone else beaten, they turn to Brock Roberts. I asked around about him, and apparently, he's connected to some detectives in the police force. And guess what? One of those people is Sean Carver."

"The man who picked up Dennis Fenton from the prison."

"That's right. Both detectives were in bed with the Rebel Sons. Dennis Fenton and Sean Carver had connections to an outlaw motorcycle gang." Lockett leaned forward. "My contact has said they're all connected."

"You're suggesting that Brock Roberts was there to convince Fenton of something?"

"It could've been a coincidence, but I don't think so. Everyone was surprised that Fenton was released after only five weeks. That's got to mean something. I think Brock Roberts was there to beat up Fenton, but his stepdaughter beat him to it."

"But why?"

"That's the question, isn't it? I don't know yet. And the other question is if we even knew the truth about why Brock Roberts was there, would it help with Alicia's self-defense case?"

"It could help establish Fenton's state of mind before the attack."

"All I know is that there are gaps in this story, and we don't know the whole truth yet."

Hennessy leaned back in his chair, his hand cradled around his glass. He took another long sip, letting the flavor roll around his mouth as the thoughts rolled around his head. "Sounds like we need to talk with Brock Roberts."

"Need me to tag along?"

"That's a good idea." Hennessy placed his glass down on the table. "Because dealing with bikers means there's a high chance of violence."

CHAPTER 15

HENNESSY AND Lockett drove out to the one-road town of Grover, South Carolina.

Lockett made several calls to his contacts and found that Brock Roberts spent most of his nights at the Riders Roadhouse, about fifty minutes' drive from Charleston. They took the gamble and drove inland. It was raining as they drove, cooling down the Low Country after weeks of increasing heat.

They found the Riders Roadhouse without any trouble and Hennessy parked out front. He stepped out of his old red truck and was relieved by the hit of cool air.

The roadhouse had seen better days. The dark red building had cracked paint, one boarded-up window, and a flickering sign that pointed to the front doors, saying 'Cold Beer Inside.' The five homes nearby were in the same state of disrepair. None had fences.

According to the reviews, the Riders Roadhouse served average food, average beer, and was guaranteed a fight at least once a week. The place was mentioned in several media articles for being the location of a dozen brutal assaults, and there were statements about it being dominated by bikers from the Rebel Sons.

"This ain't a place for a guy in a suit," a voice said, and when Hennessy turned, he saw a middle-aged man leaning against his Harley Fat Boy. There were ten Harleys, mostly cruisers, parked outside the front door of the roadhouse. "You better keep driving."

Lockett stepped out of the truck, and the man scanned the investigator's broad frame and tattoos.

"I'm looking for Brock Roberts," Hennessy said.

The man sniffed, wiped his thumb on his nose, and pointed to the front door of the roadhouse.

Hennessy led the way, with Lockett a few steps behind. When he stepped inside the bar, the bartender gave him a look, raised his eyebrows, shook his head, and then returned to wiping the glass in his hands. The small bar was dark and narrow, and a stench of cigarette smoke and overcooked meat filled the air. There was little lighting, but that at least covered the dirty floor and tables.

Brock Roberts sat alone at the far end of the bar, his scarred hand wrapped around a Budweiser. He wore a black leather jacket without a symbol, dirty jeans, and well-worn steel-toe boots. He was hunched over, but his size and strength were apparent. He spoke to nobody.

Hennessy approached and sat on the stool next to him. Lockett stayed back, sitting at one of the tables to the side of the room.

Brock Roberts took a moment and then slowly turned to look at Hennessy. "You a cop?"

"No."

"You shouldn't have said that." Roberts took a long sip of his beer. "Because that means I can put you in the hospital and say it was self-defense. Everyone in here will collaborate that story."

"Is that what happened to Dennis Fenton?"

Roberts put his beer down and turned to face

Hennessy. "Is that who you're here for? That scumbag? Man, if this is some sort of revenge act, you ain't scaring nobody."

"I'm a lawyer. I'm defending Alicia Fenton against her murder charges."

"A lawyer? Here?" Roberts chuckled. "You're in the wrong place, buddy."

"You can help me. You can tell me why you were waiting for him and Sean Carver to arrive."

Roberts paused again, scanning his eyes over Hennessy. One of the men at the pool table behind them pointed to Hennessy, but Roberts shook his head. He had the situation covered. "What do you want to know?"

"The truth."

"The truth is that she hit him with a baseball bat, and he died. It ain't nothing more complex than that."

"I want to know why you talked to Sean Carver before it happened."

He scoffed again. "You wearing a wire? Is that what this is? You're trying to catch me out or something? What are you trying to accuse me of?"

"No wire. My job is to get a girl out of prison. I'm not accusing you of anything."

Roberts turned back to his beer and took another sip. He placed it down and rolled the bottom of the bottle over the surface. "If she didn't do it, I'm not sure Dennis would've been around much longer."

"Is that what Sean Carver wanted?"

"I ain't talking to you about him. He's a dirty cop, I'll tell you that much. I wouldn't trust him as far as I could throw him."

"Is he part of the Rebel Sons?"

"You're asking too many questions, lawyer. This

ain't the type of bar where the law matters." Roberts scoffed again. "If you keep asking questions, you could end up with a broken jaw."

The door to the bar opened and light flooded into the darkness. Another man wearing a leather jacket stepped inside. The man grunted to the bartender and then sat down. The bartender placed a beer in front of the man and as the man went to take a drink, he caught sight of Hennessy. He looked twice.

"We can either talk here or in a deposition." Hennessy kept his eyes focused on Roberts. "You've been subpoenaed to testify as a witness, and I want to know why you came to her aid that night."

"I didn't come to nobody's aid. I was walking past, and I heard the girl scream. The door was open, so I stepped inside and that's when I saw the dead body."

"The police report says the door was closed, and you opened it."

Roberts didn't seem bothered by the discrepancy. "You weren't there, old man."

"What did you say to Sean Carver?"

"What's the matter with you? Your hearing aid not up far enough?"

"I know you talked to Carver before you entered the apartment. I've talked to a witness who said that you talked to the person in the car's driver's seat."

"Who said that?"

"You'll find out in court."

"Ain't nobody stupid enough to testify against the people there that day."

Hennessy sat up straighter. "I need to know what you said to Sean Carver before you went in."

Roberts shook his head, stood, and threw a few dollar bills on the bar. He stepped past Hennessy, placed his hand on the lawyer's shoulder, and leaned close to Hennessy's ear. "Man, it's all in my statement. Carver told me exactly what to say, and I ain't changing it."

CHAPTER 16

ON THE drive back to Charleston, Hennessy and Lockett stopped to eat before the day ended.

They stopped at Lewis Barbecue, a legendary barbeque restaurant known for the best brisket in the state. They each ordered half a pound of brisket, pulled pork, a sausage, and a side of collard greens. Hennessy loved the Texas-style barbecue joint, one of his favorite meals in Charleston. The outdoor seating was mostly empty, as it wasn't long before closing time. While they ate, the men barely said a word to each other, hypnotized by the tenderness and flavor of their meals.

"What are we missing?" Hennessy said as he wiped his mouth and finished the delicious meal. "There's a link here that we don't understand."

"I know you love to go in all guns blazing, but we have to step carefully with these guys. The Rebel Sons don't mess around. People who cross them are known to go missing," Lockett paused as he savored his last piece of brisket. "And they're still dangerous, even with half their crew caught up in that drug bust. I wouldn't be surprised if you have a rock thrown through your car window tonight."

"I need to know the full picture of the night Dennis Fenton died."

"Do you? What for? We know that Dennis Fenton

was trying to rape his stepdaughter, and we know she defended herself and hit him with a baseball bat in the back of the head. What more do we need to know to defend her at trial?"

"Sometimes, the details don't become clear until you can see everything."

Lockett shrugged. "You're digging into an area of danger that you don't need to go down. You don't need to stir up the Rebel Sons to prove she acted in self-defense."

A woman suddenly laughed a few tables over, and they both looked up. A young man had chosen that moment to propose. Kneeling on the floorboards beside the table, he held an open jewelry box out, the shimmering diamond big enough for Hennessy to make out.

Fascinated, Hennessy couldn't help but watch as the guy continued his speech, doing his best to make his case worthwhile. It must have worked because when his lips stopped moving, the woman's head bounced excitedly up and down as a few of the closer patrons applauded. Hennessy and Lockett joined in, clapping as the man found himself embracing his new fiancée.

Hennessy was smiling as he stood and walked to the restrooms and would have pushed through the door without seeing the sign if it hadn't been for the warning from a stranger. The stranger pointed to a hand-written sign that read, 'Temporarily out of order.'

"Restrooms are closed, mister. Something wrong with the plumbing. Better off scooting out yonder if you just need to relieve yourself," the man said, pointing toward a tall fence behind the parking lot.

"Sure thing," Hennessy said as the man passed him. "Thanks."

Hennessy walked behind the tall fence, hidden from view from the restaurant, the parking lot, and the road. As he stepped into the dim area, he heard a shuffle behind him, and before he turned and saw what it was, a fist crashed into the side of his head.

He tried to shield his face as a second punch landed in his ribs. He swung around in time to see another fist coming through the air in a wide arc.

He leaned back, easily dodging the punch. He followed with a jab of his own, followed by a crunching right and a quick left hook. His movements were smooth, thanks to years of boxing training, and the man fell to the ground.

A second attacker appeared to his left. The man tried to swing another fist at him, but Hennessy had enough adrenalin charging through his body to react in time. He followed the same combination and ended with another straight right. Punches in bunches, his father used to tell him. The advice had helped him more times than he cared to count.

With a bloodied nose, the first man staggered to his feet and grabbed the second man under the arms. They both got up and hurried away.

"I'm not giving you my wallet," Hennessy said as they turned around the edge of the fence.

Hennessy followed them a few steps behind, watching as they jogged through the parking lot.

As Hennessy's eyes scanned the area, he saw a man at the far side of the lot standing next to a new black Mercedes, a cigarette hanging from his lips.

Detective Sean Carver flicked the cigarette onto

the street and entered his car.

His presence provided Hennessy a clear realization—the men weren't there for his wallet.

CHAPTER 17

HENNESSY DIDN'T report the attack to the police.

There was nothing to say, and he had no injuries. Going through the reporting process would only take him further away from his work. But the attack told him one thing—he was close to finding out something he shouldn't, but he wasn't sure if it was related to the Fenton case.

It was already late in the afternoon when Hennessy arrived back from a meeting with an associate, and he'd come bearing gifts for Jacinta, a distinctive box in one hand as he opened the door with a whole balancing act.

"Whatcha got?" Jacinta asked, her eyes lighting up as she spotted the distinctive logo on the side.

"A man needs to pay his way," Hennessy said, shooting Jacinta a wink.

"And you think—"

"Cupcakes from the Sugar Bakeshop will work," he finished. "Yes, I do."

The cupcakes turned out to be a better late afternoon treat than anyone could have imagined. Neither of them spoke a word until all six were demolished, and even then, they only managed a few noises to show how much they enjoyed them.

Hennessy's cell buzzed on the table, but he

ignored it. The cupcakes were too good.

"Maybe you should grab a dozen next time," Jacinta joked.

"How about I don't?" he quipped and patted his stomach. "Not unless you want Mrs. H on your butt for making her husband fat."

"You're right," Jacinta laughed. "I don't want to turn her against you."

There were piles of folders on the table in front of them, arranged into neat piles by Jacinta. There was a pile of crime scene photos, another for witness statements, and another for expert reports. Hennessy went to the whiteboard at the side of the room and wrote 'Alicia Fenton—self-defense' in the middle. He drew a line and wrote the name 'Dennis Fenton—attacker' on the other side. Around the whiteboard, he wrote several names, including Sean Carver, Brock Roberts, and the OMGs. He wrote the name 'Maria Don' on the board and struck a line through it, and then wrote Edith Chapman's name and a big tick next to it. He stood back and looked at the board, tapping the marker against his top lip.

Jacinta smiled as she opened one of the files. "I love that they call Outlaw Motorcycle Gangs 'OMGs.' It sounds like a text message exchange with a couple of teenagers. 'Like, these guys are totally riding bikes and dealing drugs, OMG.'"

Hennessy smiled. "It's an older name, along with the name, 'one-percenters.' They're called one-percenters because, in the 40s, the American Motorcycle Association stated that ninety-nine percent of motorcycle riders are law-abiding citizens, and one percent are not. And that's how the one-percent patch came to be," Hennessy said as his phone buzzed again. He ignored it a second time. "But there's nothing funny about what they do. They deal drugs and beat people up. Not a lot of comedy there."

"Are you going to keep digging into the OMGs?"

"I have to, no matter how dangerous it gets. I need to know the full picture of what happened that night. That's the only way I'll get to the truth."

"But we're focused on self-defense for the trial?"

"Absolutely. We can't dispute that she hit him and caused his death. The police have made no mistakes in their reports, and we've failed at the only legal pre-trial option available to us. We need to build a profile of who Dennis Fenton was and how he behaved toward his stepdaughter. Edith Chapman's testimony will be a key point in our case. If it makes it to court, we'll open with her. She's an emotional person, and she'll tug at the jurors' hearts."

"And after her, I guess you want some expert witnesses." Jacinta reached across and moved a file closer to her. She picked up a pen and a notepad. "Who shall I contact?"

"I need you to start contacting expert witnesses who will testify that just because an attacker has turned around doesn't mean the attack has stopped. I'll need a few people to drive home that point. I'll also need an expert in domestic violence. There's a brilliant woman in North Carolina named Dr. Julia Owen. If she could testify in this case, it would be a win for us. We'll also need some medical experts to say that excessive force was not used."

Hennessy walked toward the whiteboard and wrote 'Prosecution Witnesses' next to Brock Roberts' name.

"We need to deep dive into every one of the prosecution's witnesses. Anything about their past, their social media, their friends, their careers—I need anything and everything on each one of those witnesses in the discovery file."

"You got it, boss."

Hennessy wrote 'Media' in the blank space on the board. He drew a large circle around it.

"What's the plan with the media?" Jacinta asked as she held her pen ready.

"We need them on our side. There's a public relations company on King Street called SC Media Consulting. Contact them for a meeting, and for the right price, we might get them to guide the media. If we make it a story about an abused teenager standing up for herself, we might be able to build a groundswell of support for Alicia. I'll need you to have prepared several press releases that we can send off periodically over the next two months to keep the story in the headlines."

"On it."

The cell buzzed a third time. Hennessy looked at the missed calls and squinted. He hadn't heard from the caller in years.

"Also," Hennessy turned his attention back to the whiteboard, "I need you to investigate if any local documentary filmmakers would be interested in Alicia's story. If we can gather enough support, their films could be our way to win on appeal."

"We're going all-in on the media and self-defense?"

"It's our only choice," Hennessy said. "There's no disputing that she hit him, and there's no disputing that he died due to that strike. Self-defense is our only option."

For the fifth time, Hennessy's cell buzzed. He answered it. He only spoke to the caller for a few moments, but it might've been the break he needed.

CHAPTER 18

IT HAD been too long since Hennessy had last seen Douglas Bracewell.

Bracewell had been a high-ranking police officer when Hennessy worked as a prosecutor with the Circuit Solicitor's Office. The two men had bonded over their love of the Charleston RiverDogs and the Clemson Tigers. They were friends, more than just men who worked together, but they lost contact after the death of Hennessy's son. Bracewell was there for Hennessy, showing up at all times to check on his friend, but he had a son the same age as Luca, and Joe couldn't bear to think about it. Over the years, they lost contact.

An hour inland from Charleston, Clancy's Bar in the small town of St. George was quiet. The regulars preferred it that way. It was dark inside, and the only sound seemed to radiate from the television at the end of the bar playing a college football game. The pool tables and jukebox weren't being used. The bar was a popular mid-week watering hole for people who just wanted to be left alone to contemplate their future, forget about their lives, or stew about their past. No flashy distractions, no comical wait staff, just serenity and beer.

When Hennessy stepped through the doors of the bar long after the sun had set over South Carolina, he found his old friend quickly enough, sitting alone at a table near the far wall.

Douglas Bracewell had put on a lot of weight since Hennessy had last seen him. A proud cop, he was shot in the leg during a traffic stop five years ago and had been assigned to desk duties ever since. He transferred to a small town near his home in St. George, a place with seven officers and little action. Sitting behind a desk, he turned to food for comfort, and the pounds piled on. His stomach hung over the top of his belt, and his shirt was too tight. His face looked bloated and he'd lost a lot of hair.

Bracewell saw Hennessy the second he walked in and gave him a casual wave, then held up his glass, which had already been drained down to the final third. Hennessy gave him a thumbs up, went to the bar and ordered a fresh round.

Once Hennessy set the beers down on the table, the two old friends embraced. Over the next forty-five minutes, they laughed and smiled and chatted. They talked about their children, about their wives, and about their careers. Hennessy spoke about the vineyard, and Bracewell talked about being a cop in a small town. Hennessy spoke about the wines, and Bracewell talked about his growing craft beer obsession. They laughed about past stories, chuckling about the situations they found themselves in, reminiscing about their much younger selves. They chatted, slapped each other on the back, and felt like they hadn't missed a day together.

"I knew the bullet to the leg was lucky, and I told myself it was the cost of protecting my community, but gee, some days, I wish I could get back out there," Bracewell said after he returned with the fifth round of beers. "I'd love to run again."

"Is it holding up alright?"

"It's going ok. This extra weight," he patted his stomach. "It doesn't help."

"Ok, old friend, put me out of my misery," Hennessy said. "You didn't call me here to find out when Luca's Vineyard is releasing its next Merlot."

Bracewell chuckled a little, but Hennessy could sense the underlying nerves. "You were always one to turn the conversation to business."

"It's in my blood."

"Too right," Bracewell lifted his beer. "Ever heard of the name Sean Carver?"

"I've heard his name a lot over the past few days."

"Well, he's familiar with Dennis Fenton as well, or at least he was before his demise. They were former partners in the police force." Bracewell took a long sip of his beer. "Fenton and Carver were both connected to the Rebel Sons. There was a major drug bust by the Feds last year, and a lot of people fell victim to it. Carver escaped any conviction but was ordered by the Feds not to have any contact with the gang for two years. Now, he has Internal Affairs watching his every step. He's been warned to stay well away from the Rebel Sons."

"Carver was also the person who picked up Fenton when he was released."

"And that's not a coincidence. Now, you didn't hear this from me, but Fenton secured his early release in return for a testimony. And this is where it gets interesting—rumor has it that Fenton snitched on one of the main guys from the Rebel Sons. That's why he was released so early. There's nothing official on file because it's a federal drug case, but I've heard it from a few different sources. If it's true, then the Rebel Sons would've wanted to teach Fenton a lesson the second he stepped outside the prison walls."

"Fenton turned into a snitch?"

"That's right. He did it to save his own butt from another year in prison. He did five weeks behind bars and decided that was enough." Bracewell drew a long breath. "And if I found out that information, you can be sure the Rebel Sons would've known that information."

"You're suggesting that Carver set Fenton up? He picked up Fenton to drive him somewhere to be beaten?"

"Carver wouldn't have beaten Fenton, but the man outside the door would."

"Brock Roberts."

"He provides a lot of muscle for the Rebel Sons. It wasn't a coincidence that he was outside the door just after Fenton was released from prison. And if his daughter didn't get to Fenton first, Brock Roberts would've beaten him to a pulp."

"Stepdaughter," Hennessy said a little too defensively.

"Sorry, stepdaughter." Bracewell noticed and held a hand up in apology. "But remember, you didn't hear this from me."

When Hennessy finally left the bar a little before midnight, he had a broader picture of the case, but it only made the case harder.

Corrupt cops had a way of creating much more danger than anyone else.

CHAPTER 19

THE MCDERMOTT'S home in Mount Pleasant was exactly as Hennessy expected—a large two-story red brick home with an RV in the driveway and the American flag hanging over the porch.

In the front yard, flowers were aligned in neat rows, surrounded by a green lawn that was bordered by a freshly painted white fence. The trees outside the home were plentiful, providing shade and privacy, and the street was quiet. The Saucer Magnolia tree dominating the side of the yard drew the eyes to the pinks and purples of its flowers, which matched the trim and curtains of the house behind it. It was clear that this was a home, not just another building. It was a place where lifelong memories were made.

Hennessy hadn't crossed halfway through the front yard when the smell of something bread-like and buttery filled his nose, and when a warm smile greeted him through the open door, Hennessy wondered whether he had walked into a 1960s sitcom.

"Mr. Hennessy," Brandon McDermott said as he held a hand out and practically pulled Hennessy inside.

McDermott didn't waste time to introduce his wife, Helen, and their two twin twenty-year-old daughters, Sissy and Kayla, who still both lived at home. Hennessy greeted each of them with a smile and a handshake, including the dog, Buster, with a scratch behind the ear. The house was filled with the aroma of fresh gingerbread, the distinct scent of cinnamon lingering just behind the warmth of baking cookies.

The meeting didn't begin immediately, with the proud father showing the lawyer around his home. Hennessy knew what was going on. The man wanted to show Hennessy his life for one reason, and that was to make him aware of what he would lose if his legal counsel failed to protect him. Hennessy understood a presentation when he saw one, which included ten minutes of idle chit-chat over iced tea and freshly baked ginger snaps, apparently a timeless recipe from Helen's German-born grandmother. Hennessy couldn't help but be surprised at how well the tang of the lemon in the tea worked with the still-warm cookies.

After Helen insisted on Brandon taking his guest to the den for a bit of privacy, Hennessy followed his host into a room he'd already been shown earlier in the visit.

Brandon closed the door and offered Hennessy one of the two bar stools. "I read about your other case in the news this morning. A murder trial. Was the girl really defending herself?"

"She was."

"Good for you. I took one look at that girl's picture and knew she wasn't a bad kid." McDermott sat down and sighed. "I'm sorry for taking up a bit more time than I should have. I'm just so nervous about the case, and I wanted you to get a sense of who I really am and everything that I could lose over such a minor charge. The truth is, I'm terrified, Mr. Hennessy. If I lose this case, I lose my reputation, and twenty people lose their jobs."

"I understand," Hennessy said. "And I wish I could be more helpful, but I've looked over the details more than a few times, and the potential outcome is always the same. If we take this to trial, it's likely that we'll lose. The evidence is against you. The prosecution also knows this. You were found with a bottle of whiskey on you, and even though you didn't have the other bottles with you, a reasonable person would assume that you took them."

"Tell me straight," Brandon said, as his eyes sank to his fingers nervously wrestling with each other on the bar. "Do we have any chance at all?"

"If you're asking for my honest opinion, my suggestion would take a plea deal."

McDermott took a long deep breath and sighed. "It's just that Phil Pickering isn't exactly a down-to-earth kinda guy, if you catch my meaning. He's about as Catholic as the Pope and runs the school with the same moral code. He's strict and sticks to his guns. He knows about the charges, but I said the cops have got it wrong. He said he won't cancel the contract until it's all resolved, but I can tell there's some doubt in his voice about my innocence."

"I get it," Hennessy said, "But other than taking a plea deal, I don't see any other way out of this for you. We won't win a trial."

A silence fell between them as Hennessy leaned back a little to give his client a moment to comprehend the situation and allow the reality to sink in. McDermott muttered under his breath to himself.

"Taking a plea deal isn't going to help with

Pickering," he whispered. "It just won't. A court case is a court case, and if found guilty, it's over for me."

"That's what I wanted to talk to you about. How long until the project is finished at the Catholic school?"

"Fifteen months. And then a two-month buffer."

"We'll have to plan it carefully and file a lot of motions, but we can stretch the court case past that date, and that will give you time to finish the project. After that, you'll already be onto the next project, and we can quietly take a plea deal for a suspended sentence. You'll be done with Phil Pickering and nobody else is going to care about a minor charge," Hennessy stated. "We'll present new evidence at regular intervals and file requests for extra time to investigate the material. The prosecution isn't chasing this conviction hard, so it's likely they'll agree with any requests to put this off. The issue with that is that it'll take time and money."

"Do it." McDermott's eyes opened with a glimmer of hope. "I'll finish the project at the Catholic school and then take a deal for a suspended sentence. That's the best I can hope for."

"I'll call my investigator and begin the ball rolling," Hennessy said. "And we'll start gathering new evidence to present to the court at regular intervals."

For the next fifteen minutes, Hennessy took McDermott through the finer details of his plan to stretch the case out. By the time he left the home in Mount Pleasant, McDermott had a smile on his face. He had a solution to his problems, and while it wasn't perfect, it allowed him to keep his business going and keep his staff employed.

Ten minutes after leaving the family home,

Hennessy was driving to Charleston over the towering Arthur Ravenel Jr. Bridge, complete with a postcard-perfect sunset over the Cooper River.

Built in 2005, the bridge had become a part of the landscape of South Carolina, a well-photographed symbol of the area. When officials revealed in 1995 that the former bridge scored a 4 out of 100 for safety and integrity, retired US Congressman Arthur Ravenel Jr. ran for the South Carolina Senate, intending to solve the funding problem for a new bridge. More than five hundred million dollars and ten years later, South Carolina had a new bridge named in his honor.

After navigating the lanes of traffic on the bridge, Hennessy called Barry Lockett.

"What's up, mate?" Lockett answered.

"The Brandon McDermott case," Hennessy said. "Unlike most cases, Mr. McDermott isn't in any hurry to see this case through just yet."

"Got somewhere else to be, does he?"

"The opposite." Hennessy explained the man's position at a local Catholic school and how the principal wasn't a fan of alcohol-induced stupidity. "We're not desperate for information on the matter yet, but we need a steady supply of new evidence coming in."

"How long do you think you can stretch this out for?"

"Years, if I have to," Hennessy said. "Which will be long enough for him to get his project done at the Catholic school."

"What's the angle? I mean, didn't he break the only working camera in the place?"

"That he did, and unfortunately, he effectively killed his defense in the process, but it gives us an opportunity. I need you to try to find some local video footage first."

"The street the liquor store sits on is quite a busy one. I'll contact local cabs and Ubers and see if I can't get my hands on a few dash cams and see if there's any evidence of Mr. McDermott that night. Might take me a while to get them all back, though."

"Can we go for anything else? Is there anything that will confuse the prosecution so that they also request time to investigate?"

"We can also look into GPS data of the newer cars."

"Go on."

"New cars like BMWs and Mercedes have a central storage center for GPS data. If I can access that, I can see what cars were around that location at the time of the robbery. If we can locate the cars around that time, we can see if they have any dashcam footage that could identify what was happening when the alarms went off."

"Sounds difficult."

"I have a contact at Mercedes head office. If you can draft a legal letter stating the day and time and the event, I might have a chance to access the data. And then we can go about contacting the owners."

"That's perfect. That will confuse the prosecution, and they'll request extra time to investigate," Hennessy said. "We've got time, but make it happen. If you come across anything incriminating, I don't want to see it for the next couple of weeks."

CHAPTER 20

AS HE arrived back at the office, Joe received a phone call from someone he wasn't expecting to hear from. The second he saw the number, he felt undeniable guilt. It was his brother, Matthew, a man he hadn't spoken to in more than a year and someone he hadn't seen in more than two.

"Matt, how are you?" Joe said, hoping he sounded friendly enough for his brother.

"Joe, hey man. Just thought I'd see how the big brother was doing."

"I'm doing fine," he said. "You?"

"I'm good. I know it's been a while, but I'm in town and thought it would be great to catch up if you have time."

"Tonight?"

"Yeah, man. I know it's sudden, but how's seven at Red's Ice House in Shem Creek? There should be a game on."

Joe looked at his watch. "Seven sounds good. See you then."

He hadn't heard from Matt in quite some time, and the saddest part was that it didn't appear to be anyone's fault. "Life just has a way of moving along," he had put it to Wendy one night back when the distance between the two brothers became much more pronounced.

Matt, his wife Bella, and their two children had moved to New Orleans five years earlier. Aside from the initial visit when they first moved into their new home, Joe and his family had only returned once. Despite both wives doing their best to try to keep in contact, life just got in the way. Between Matt's work as a financial advisor, Bella's work as a high school teacher, and the commitments of two sports-mad teenage boys, their lives were hectic.

When Wendy once asked whether something had happened between the brothers, Joe shook his head and avoided the subject. But deep down, he knew why the distance between them grew. Seeing Matt's teenage boys grow, who so closely resembled Luca in looks and personality, hurt in ways he couldn't explain. He was happy for his brother, proud of him, but a little piece of him broke every time he saw the boys.

Joe went into the office, made several case notes on the McDermott file, and then closed up for the night. Pulling into the parking lot of Red's Ice House twenty-five minutes later, Joe grabbed a mint and headed inside.

Shem Creek was a locals' hangout, with the river flowing through the heart of Mount Pleasant and spilling into the Charleston Harbor. Known for its glorious sunsets, the area was used as a base for boating, fishing, kayaking, and paddle-boarding. Waterfront bars and restaurants stretched along one side of the river, with a boat tie-up in the front of the restaurants, inviting thirsty sailors inside after a day on the water.

Red's Ice House was one of the main bars seated along the creek. It was a laid-back bar, with cold beer and fresh seafood, that had stunning views over the marsh. It was quiet that night, and Hennessy preferred it that way.

"Matt," he said as he neared the section of the bar where his brother sat. The younger Hennessy rose, and the pair hugged, finishing with the all too familiar backslap.

"Well, you don't look like a man working eighty-hour weeks." Matt's sense of humor had always been dry. "Did you get yourself a rejuvenation serum?"

"Nothing other than beer, whiskey, and some good Low Country cooking."

"The diet of champions." Matt laughed and ordered a beer for each of them. "I love the food of New Orleans, but there's something about Frogmore Stew that always feels like home."

"So, what brings you to town?"

Matt's hesitation told Joe everything he needed to know. This hadn't been his idea. "My company is looking at opening an office here, and they asked me to check out some potential sites."

"Is that right?"

Despite his tone not being suggestive, Matt's guilt somehow peaked. "You don't believe me?"

The bartender placed two beers in front of them and Joe drank deep, downing half the glass in one breath.

Matt paused as he watched his brother. "Thirsty?"

"It's been a long week," Joe said and, as he set the glass back down, decided he'd had enough of the charades. "And I know you didn't call me just because you were in town. How about leveling with me?"

"What are you talking about?" Matt asked, his posture changing to match the defensiveness in his tone.

Joe could see the color rise in his cheeks and felt his anger rise because of the continued denial. The younger Hennessy must have seen something in his brother's face that he hadn't contemplated, a look of confusion that seemed to hit just the right note. Joe watched him as his shoulders slumped down a little, a sure-fire sign he was about to come clean.

"Alright," he whispered, "but you can't tell Wendy I told you."

Joe pursed his lips and nodded his acceptance.

"Listen, she's worried about you, that's all. She says you're down here in the city for weeks on end, alone, working all the time, doing seventy-five-hour weeks just to save the vineyard. I know how much that vineyard means to you, but maybe you can ease off a bit. You're not a young man anymore. You're entering prime heart attack age."

Joe took a deep breath and sighed. He couldn't be angry, not when the purpose of the visit had been his welfare. "I'm ok," he whispered. "I'm doing fine."

"You sure? 'Cause from what I've heard, it sounds like you've been isolating yourself quite a bit. Throwing yourself into work and forgetting about everything else. I've seen you do that before."

"I know it's not healthy, but I can't let the banks take the vineyard."

"How much are you behind? We're doing well financially and if you need some money, just ask."

"Thank you, but no. I have to do this myself. I owe it to Luca to fight for the place. I'm getting lots of work down here, and we're almost getting in front of the banks. Another few years in Charleston as a defense lawyer, and we'll be back in front. Then I can go back to the vineyard and spend my years with the vines. That's the dream, anyway."

"Wendy hinted you might've discovered information about what happened to Luca."

"Maybe. I don't know yet." Joe stared into his beer. "Time will tell if I can get the information I need."

"I know you're too proud to accept my help, but really, if you need it, I'm here. Financially, or emotionally. I know we haven't talked a lot over the last few years, but I'm still your brother."

"I appreciate you." He smiled at his brother, reached out, and patted him on the back. "And I won't tell Wendy you told me as long as you tell her I'm doing great."

They laughed, and the ice had been broken. For the rest of the night, the two men joked, drank, and told great stories about their lives. They laughed at long-forgotten memories, talked about the vacations they remembered from decades before, and smiled when telling stories about their own children. They talked about the dramas of the Low Country, how everyone was seemingly connected, and how there were no secrets in small cities. They chatted about their old adventures and how the stories had become exaggerated over the years.

By the time they exited the bar some five hours later, just after midnight, Matt had invited Wendy and Joe to his home in New Orleans, and Joe promised he would make it happen.

Despite the years pulling them apart, the bond between the two brothers remained strong.

CHAPTER 21

Five weeks later.

THE HOURS turned into days, and the days into weeks, and the date of Alicia Fenton's judgment approached.

The media had loved the regular press releases from the Joe Hennessy Law Office. With assistance from a public relations company, Jacinta sent out weekly statements that were ready-made to fill the headlines, and at times, the news outlets printed the press releases word for word.

Alicia's case had developed an outpouring of support, the perfect case for the moral crusaders. Her supporters posted their thoughts on social media, attacked anyone who dared to suggest she was a murderer, and sent thousands of emails to politicians, both State and Federal. Many people asked how far a woman could go to defend herself against a rapist, and whether women had any rights in the court system at all. Hennessy never mentioned the attempted rape in the press releases, but the action was implied enough for the media to create their own version of events.

The prosecution tried to push the trial date out, and Hennessy kept working to find a break, but he also had to focus on his other cases. He had to work with his paying clients.

On the books, he had a DUI, a minor theft charge, and a fraud charge to defend. Brandon McDermott's case had stalled as well, pushed down the list thanks to a motion to dismiss based on faulty evidence, and after it was considered for several weeks, it was rejected, but it achieved the goal of delaying the case. Hennessy requested grand jury transcripts, he disputed new evidence, and wrote a number of lengthy briefs. The progress was slow, but that was by design. Hennessy enjoyed flexing his legal muscles, confusing the prosecution at every turn. When he lodged several more motions to delay, he received no objections from the prosecution team.

The weather had heated up, and South Carolina was in the grip of a sweltering hot and humid summer. It was hard to move fast when temperatures pushed close to one hundred.

Hennessy worked long into the hot summer nights, many times working until he fell asleep at his computer. He was in Charleston to work and earn money, and he found little comfort in sitting in his apartment alone.

Hennessy had talked to John Cleveland twice, and both times the prisoner refused to say anything more until his daughter was released from prison. He gave Hennessy nothing.

When the date for Alicia's case was settled to begin trial, Hennessy wasn't convinced they could win.

"I see we have several motions and requests on the docket today, and we're due to start this trial next Monday?"

Judge West sat at the front of the courtroom,

looking at the lawyers from over the top of her glasses. The courtroom's air-conditioning was working overtime, pumping in cool air from the vents above the judge, but it was fighting a losing battle. Even in the windowless courtroom, the heat was still coming in through the door.

"That's correct, Your Honor." Hennessy stood behind the defense table. "May I suggest we start with the motions and requests that have been agreed upon between the defense and the prosecution?"

"We can." Judge West lifted several files on her table and opened the first one. "I see the defense has lodged a motion for the defendant to remain unshackled during the trial. Any objections from the State?"

Garrett stood behind the prosecution table. "No objections from us, Your Honor."

"That's good, gentlemen. This motion is granted." She closed one folder and moved to the next. "Next, we have a request for a general questionnaire of the potential jurors to be completed before they have entered the voir dire. I see we have the wording here. Any objections to the wording from either party?"

"No, Your Honor," Hennessy responded. "We worked together to settle on those questions."

"No objections from the State."

"Good. The questionnaire is approved. And the next motion." Judge West moved another file in front of her. "I see this one will be quite important to the trial. Mr. Hennessy, we have a notice from the defense that states the defendant intends to assert that she acted in self-defense. Any issues with the notice, Mr. Garrett?"

"No, Your Honor."

"The court accepts the notice." She closed the file and moved to the next one. "Ah. Now, I imagine this one will cause a little more concern. Mr. Garrett, I see you have lodged a motion to suppress any reference to Mr. Fenton's time in prison?"

"That's correct, Your Honor." Garrett stood. "We believe it will be highly prejudicial against the victim to allow the defense to reference any time Mr. Fenton spent in prison on an unrelated matter. His imprisonment has no bearing on this current case."

"I argue it does, Your Honor," Hennessy responded. "The victim was in prison for drug charges, which speaks to his frame of mind. But more importantly, the defendant's home is the first stop the victim made after five weeks in prison. It speaks to his intent, it speaks to his actions, and it speaks to what happened that day. It would be highly prejudicial against the defendant not to include it."

"Agreed, Mr. Hennessy," Judge West said.

"Your Honor—" Garrett argued, but Judge West held up her hand.

"I don't believe we can even begin to consider this trial without speaking to the victim's state of mind. The defendant's home was the victim's first stop after spending five weeks in prison. We have to talk about his actions on that day during this trial. The motion is denied." She moved another file over the desk. "Mr. Garrett, I see you've also lodged a motion to suppress any reference to a potential sexual assault. Care to explain your motion?"

"Yes, Your Honor. We believe that the defense will try to assert that Mr. Fenton was attempting to rape the defendant, however, there's zero evidence of this happening. We cannot let this court be led on a ridiculous story that has no basis in fact."

"Your Honor," Hennessy began. "There's evidence from a nurse to say that Mr. Fenton had raped the defendant previously, and we—"

"And Mr. Fenton was found not guilty in a court of law!" Garrett argued.

"We must tell the truth in this court. This is what happened to the defendant, and it paints a very clear picture of their relationship. She submitted to a rape kit at the hospital and it shows she was sexually assaulted. Minimizing the extent of the sexual assault is not unusual for this prosecution team, but it's important to this trial."

"We do no such thing!" Garrett slapped his hand on the table. "The victim was found not guilty of the rape charge by a jury of his peers."

"It doesn't mean he was innocent. He was found not guilty because there wasn't enough evidence to convict him, not because he didn't do the actions. The rape kit presented in the trial was clear—Miss Fenton had been sexually assaulted. That fact was indisputable and accepted by the prosecution at the time. The only thing that saved Mr. Fenton was that they didn't have enough evidence to prove it was him. This is a part of the defendant's past, and this is her truth."

"It's not the truth in a court of law!"

"Enough." Judge West stated. "Having reviewed the motion earlier and listening to the arguments, I will grant part of this motion. There will be no reference to the alleged sexual assault of the previous court case, however, if there's further evidence of a history of sexual assault outside what was alleged in the previous trial, I will allow it. If any reference is to be made about sexual assault, I need that to be presented to the court first, understood?"

"Your Honor, I must object," Garrett argued. "There's no evidence that a sexual assault occurred on the date of the murder."

"Your objection is noted, Mr. Garrett, but my decision is final." Judge West looked at her files.

They spent the next two hours arguing for various motions in limine. A motion in limine was a request for the court to refuse to admit unrelated, inconsequential, defective, or unduly prejudicial evidence. Hennessy argued that including the defendant's high school record was irrelevant, that including teachers who testified about Alicia's mental health was prejudicial and untrustworthy, and including evidence about her personal relationships was inconsequential. Hennessy won on several motions, dismissing five pieces of evidence from being mentioned in court.

After the hearing, the judge wished them well and told the lawyers to be prepared for the trial, starting in only a few days. The pre-trial hearing had gone well for the defense. They had several small wins, but Hennessy knew they were still on the back foot.

He needed a break, something that would blow the case wide open.

And he wasn't sure if he could find it in time.

CHAPTER 22

PRISON TIME is something else.

The hours of boredom, the hours of watching the days slowly pass, made the minutes feel like hours, the hours feel like days, the weeks like months, and yet, when looking back, it all felt like the same moment. Alicia sat on her bunk alone in her cell, staring out the window at a near cloudless sky. The weeks hadn't been easy for her. After her run-in with Deb, some of the other inmates had made her a target. Alicia did her best to stay out of their way by remaining in her cell.

But as the weeks passed and her time inside increased, it also brought the upcoming case closer, with the countdown at just a few days. Her nerves had steadily climbed and now felt as if they had taken control of her, the familiar sick feeling in her stomach bad enough to affect her physically. She had already vomited that morning and felt as if she was about to again.

It was the helplessness that she found so difficult to handle. The feeling that she was nothing more than a passenger on a train, unable to have any input on where it went, while others whom she had never known were now contemplating her fate. The feeling was bad enough to strangle her with despair.

Throughout her life, she'd been at the mercy of

others, and the hope of a nursing career had been the one saving grace, giving her something to look toward. In the blink of an eye, that hope had been torn from her and with it, any chance she had of finally escaping her own private hell. It was as if even in death, her stepfather had ensured her misery would continue.

Since being locked up, she lost her job as a cashier at the local grocer. They didn't want a potential criminal on their books. She had no idea how the apartment was going. She had asked the court-appointed lawyer to check on it when she was first locked up, but heard nothing back. She didn't want to ask her new lawyer, not with all the work he was doing for free.

Dennis had transferred the property into her name to avoid having to sell it after his conviction. He then declared bankruptcy before his trial. He told her it was a common tactic for those who knew they were going to lose. It provoked sympathy from the judge when it came to sentencing.

She didn't miss him. Not the man he'd become since her mother's death, anyway. She had no good memories left of him. She didn't swing the baseball bat hard that night, only enough to hurt him. She just hit him in the right spot, and he fell hard. She'd thought about that night a lot, but she didn't regret it.

He surprised her, coming home from prison fourteen months early. He stunk of whiskey. It was always worse when he had whiskey. He told her to drink, and when she refused, he pushed her into the kitchen. He tried to reach under her skirt, but she slapped him away. He asked for sex, told her that he wanted to make love to her, and when she said no, he hit her. Then he said he was going to rape her anyway. As soon as he said that, his face relaxed. She'd seen that look on him before. It was the moment the morphine kicked in. He must've had a hit just before he went into the apartment. When the morphine kicked in, he turned around.

She told the police that he was turning around to lock the door. Was that true? She didn't know. But she knew that he calmed so much when he had a hit of morphine.

Had the threat ended? Was he still thinking about raping her after the morphine hit kicked in?

She didn't know. She couldn't be sure. And she didn't care.

The man had taken so much from her, he'd stolen every ounce of innocence from her life. She hated that it happened, she hated that she killed someone, but she didn't regret the moment.

She'd received letters from all over the country supporting her. There was a lot of media attention, and as her lawyer said, it was the right time to have the case. Domestic violence was constantly in the news, and the questions about whether she was allowed to defend herself filled the airways.

"Hey, you ok?"

Alicia looked up and saw Jada standing in the doorway. Unsure of how long she'd been watching her, she didn't bother moving, simply offering a forced smile. Seeing that her friend wasn't in the best of mindsets, Jada entered the cell and sat next to Alicia.

"I feel so helpless," she said, continuing to look out the window as Jada slid up with her back against the wall.

"I know, right? Kind of how I expect they want you to feel in this place. Like a passenger watching your fate unfold before your eyes, and you're nothing more than an onlooker."

"At least I've got a good lawyer," Alicia said. The thought of Hennessy was enough to bring a faint smile to her face.

"He good?"

"From what I've seen, he knows his stuff. He's got a plan, too."

"So, why the long face? You could be out of here soon."

Despite knowing Hennessy was fighting for her, Alicia couldn't help denying the unmistakable feeling that the battle was far from a winnable one. "What if this self-defense angle isn't enough?"

"Not enough?" Jada looked at her. "Girl, if he attacked you and tried to rape you, then that's reason enough to defend yourself. There's no doubt in my mind that you did the right thing. Us girls have gotta have a way of dealing with men like that."

"I know, but what if? What if, no matter what my lawyer does, the court ignores the facts and just sees me killing him? I could be in here for a very long time."

"Ten years. Isn't that what they already offered? Sounds to me like that might be the top of their sentence. It ain't so bad. You're still young."

"I can't sit in here for ten years."

She was close to tears, and Jada sensed she needed to back off a bit.

Alicia turned her attention back to the window to watch a helicopter soaring through the sky before disappearing from view.

"I don't think I've ever been this nervous before."

"I get it." Jada leaned sideways and rested her head on Alicia's shoulder. "Unfortunately, the system has always been against the vulnerable and weak. Most of the girls in here are poor. No money means no defense, and for the city, that can mean quick cases."

"He raped me once, and I wasn't going to let him do it again." She paused as she struggled to speak without the emotion taking over. Jada sat quietly beside her, giving her friend time to get herself back under control. "He was a horrible man, and when he forced himself on me, I snapped. I wasn't thinking straight, and when I picked up that bat, all I could think of was stopping him from hurting me again."

"I'm sorry that happened to you," Jada said and put an arm around her. The gesture was enough for the first few tears to finally break free.

"I didn't mean to kill him," she sobbed. "Honestly, I just wanted to stop him from hurting me again."

They sat like that for a long time, Jada holding Alicia close in a way she hadn't felt in years.

CHAPTER 23

HENNESSY WOKE on Monday morning with the weight of the world on his shoulders.

His head was thumping from the stress, and his back was sore. He hadn't slept well in weeks. The air-conditioner in his room was struggling to keep the humidity away. He looked in the mirror and splashed water on his face. He looked tired—bags under his eyes, dry skin, hair going grayer.

Preparing for the stressful day ahead, he'd already laid out his suit, shirt, and tie the previous evening, just as he always did before the first day of a trial. He preferred to have everything ready in advance so he could focus his mind.

He didn't feel like eating but forced himself to eat a slice of toast and an apple. He had two cups of coffee and two aspirin, and then stepped out into the street, toward his old red pickup truck.

It was hot. Even before 8am, the sun was baking the city. The street in front of his apartment was slightly flooded due to the high tide and a small amount of rain overnight. As a low-lying city, there was no escaping the flooded streets in Charleston when rain was met with high tide. He looked at the sky. Gray clouds flanked the eastern horizon, which meant the forecast rain was likely to hit before midday.

Hennessy rolled into the parking lot almost fifteen minutes later. The truck's engine was sputtering, and he knew he'd have to spend a weekend finding the problem. That would have to wait until after the trial.

As Hennessy walked toward the Charleston Judicial Center off historic Broad Street, he saw five patrol cars parked near the front. His stomach tightened as he walked across the road toward the front entrance of the courthouse. Ten officers were waiting, with every eyeball on him.

As Hennessy passed the first officer standing on the street, he noticed their conversations stop. One of the older officers stepped into the middle of the path, blocking the lawyer's way.

"Watch where you step, son," the officer lifted his chin to look up at Hennessy's towering figure. "I wouldn't want you to get hurt before such an important case."

Hennessy went to step around the older man, but another officer stepped up. They bumped shoulders, but Hennessy didn't react.

The media pack watched every moment, but no cameraman was brave enough to film the interaction. They knew it wasn't worth the trouble.

Hennessy's tactic of involving the media had worked well. There was a groundswell of support for Alicia from all over the country, including a female Senator from North Carolina who made many comments on television about the case.

"Mr. Hennessy," one of the reporters called. "Do you have anything to say before the start of the trial?"

Hennessy stopped and looked back at the police officers.

"Good morning," Hennessy said as he turned back

to the media. "I'm happy to answer several questions."

The questions came thick and fast, and Hennessy did his best to answer most of them. He spent ten minutes with the mob of reporters. He repeated the essential parts of his case several times—Dennis Fenton assaulted his stepdaughter, and Alicia defended herself the only way she could manage.

After he thanked the media, he walked through the courthouse security, greeting the guards by their first names. He paused in the courthouse foyer and looked past the statue of Englishman William Pitt to the words etched in marble behind him, 'Where the law ends, tyranny begins.' He let that statement sink in for a moment and then continued toward his destination.

Walking toward courtroom five, he found Aaron Garrett waiting for him.

"I know what you're trying to do," Garrett began, stepping close to Hennessy. "If you plan to turn this trial into a media circus, let me dissuade you from such a course. Trial by media isn't how cases are won, especially when they involve an open-and-shut murder."

"Alicia Fenton was acting in self-defense."

"She was not. She's a vengeful, determined killer, and we don't let killers walk free in this country, no matter how many bleeding hearts are out there calling for her to be released. This is a trial in court, not a Netflix special." Garrett pointed his finger at Hennessy. "And I'll only warn you once—if you suggest to the media that my office is chasing this case for the benefits of political influence with the police department, we will sue you for defamation. You'll lose a lot of money, and even if we don't win, you'll be tied up in litigation for a very long time. Are we clear on that?"

Hennessy didn't respond. He glared at the prosecutor, stepped around him, and then entered the courtroom.

The stage was set, the pressure was on, and the intensity was at breaking point.

CHAPTER 24

INDICTMENT

STATE OF SOUTH CAROLINA
COUNTY OF CHARLESTON
IN THE COURT OF GENERAL SESSIONS
NINTH JUDICIAL CIRCUIT
INDICTMENT NO.: 2023-AB-05-255
STATE OF SOUTH CAROLINA, V. ALICIA
JANE FENTON, DEFENDANT

At a Court of General Sessions, convened on 25th of April, the Grand Jurors of Charleston County present upon their oath: Murder.
That in Charleston County on or about the 15th of April, the defendant, ALICIA JANE FENTON, with malice aforethought, did kill and murder DENNIS ANDREW FENTON by means of blunt force, and DENNIS ANDREW FENTON died in Charleston County as a proximate result thereof on or about 15th of April.

COUNT ONE
S.C CODE SECTION 16-3-10. MURDER
That in Charleston County on or about 15th of April, the defendant, ALICIA JANE FENTON, did murder with malice aforethought. To wit: ALICIA JANE FENTON did murder DENNIS ANDREW FENTON per violation of Section 16-3-10 South Carolina Code of Laws (1976) as amended.

FINDINGS
We, the Grand Jury, find that ALICIA JANE FENTON is to be indicted under Section 16-3-10 South Carolina Code of Laws (1976) as amended.

*****

AS HE sat down, Hennessy stared at the American flag standing at the side of the courtroom, with the flag of South Carolina next to it. He drew a deep breath and tried to settle his nerves. He opened his laptop, organized his files, and read over his opening statement, fine-tuning his delivery.

Aaron Garrett and his team entered fifteen minutes later. They laughed as they entered the room, sharing jokes and stories about their weekend and feeling confident about the trial ahead. Garrett greeted Hennessy with a handshake.

They had spent the entire previous day in voir dire, the process of selecting the jury. It was a process of elimination. Garrett and Hennessy asked questions of the potential jurors. What were their views on convicted felons, what were their views on domestic violence, and did they believe a person had a right to defend themselves in their own home? What did they think of police officers? Did they believe that good people could do bad things, and what were their current religious views? After seven hours of elimination, the lawyers had settled on the final twelve.

The selected members were a broad mix of ages, outlooks, and careers. Two people under thirty, three over sixty-five. The rest were in that broad cohort of middle age. Six women, six men. There was a construction worker, a road worker, and a hairdresser.

One was a college professor, and another was a high school teacher. There were four government workers and three retail employees. Hennessy felt confident with the group, but Garrett appeared happy as well. That worried him. What hadn't he seen?

The courtroom seats filled steadily during the morning until there was standing room only. There were media, podcasters, police officers, and interested citizens. There was a hushed silence in the crowd as the bailiff escorted Alicia into the room. Once at the defense table, the bailiff nodded to Hennessy and then unlocked her handcuffs.

Alicia rubbed her wrists in relief. She was shaking slightly, and Hennessy pointed to the glass of water. She sipped it, but it did little to ease her nerves.

Five minutes later, the clerk called for all attendees to rise. Hennessy organized his notes and then rose to his feet with the rest of the courtroom.

The Honorable Judge Nancy West entered through a private door at the side of the room, followed by her assistant. She sat down, opened her laptop, and moved it to the side of her bench. The assistant left her laptop open in front of her.

Judge West welcomed the parties to the court and invited the bailiff to bring the jury into the room. Alicia was taking deep breaths as they walked to their seats, trying to calm herself.

Once the jury was seated, Judge West swore their oath and spoke to them about their responsibilities. "Ladies and gentlemen of the jury, the laws of the State of South Carolina do not permit me to comment on the facts of the case. It's your duty, as jurors, to be the sole judges of the facts. That is your role in this court. My role is to give you the law, and you must accept and apply the law as I give it to you. Not only are you the sole judges of the facts in this case, but you, as a jury, are the sole and exclusive judges of the effect and value of the evidence, as well as the credibility of all the witnesses who will testify. I wish you well." Judge West then turned to the prosecution team. "You may begin your opening statement."

Garrett stood, buttoned his suit jacket, and walked to the lectern.

*****

"Your Honor, ladies and gentlemen of the jury, my name is Aaron Garrett, and these are my colleagues, Michelle Saltmarsh and Maxwell Smith. We're here to present the charge of murder against the defendant, Miss Alicia Fenton. In this opening statement, I'll provide an overview of the evidence we'll present in this trial for you to consider.

As an Assistant Solicitor, I represent the ninth judicial district in the great state of South Carolina. Along with my colleagues, we serve to make our state a better place, and we do so with pride. Cases like this are tough, but we take pride in serving our community and ensuring the justice system works.

In this case, the facts are simple.

Miss Fenton struck her stepfather Dennis Fenton in the back of the skull with a baseball bat. That is an indisputable fact in this case. Miss Fenton held a baseball bat in her hands and swung it with such force that it instantly killed her stepfather.

Mr. Fenton had returned to his home after five weeks away, and when he arrived, he'd barely been in the home ten minutes before Miss Fenton struck the fatal blow that killed him.

Over the coming weeks, we will present witnesses to you, and they will provide the evidence in this case. You'll hear from Mr. Brock Roberts, the first person to arrive at the scene, and he will tell you he found the victim moments after the strike, and the victim was lying face down on the carpet.

You will hear from Detective Sean Carver, who was the first detective to arrive at the scene of the crime, and he will testify about what he saw. He will also testify about what he saw Miss Fenton do after the incident.

You'll hear from Deputy Coroner Dr. Garry Wilson, who performed the autopsy, and he will tell you that Mr. Fenton died as a result of the blow to the back of his head.

You will hear from crime scene experts, and they will detail the evidence that was found at the scene and how this evidence will point to murder. These experts will describe the evidence at the scene, and they will leave you with no doubt that Mr. Fenton was struck in the back of the head. They will tell you that Mr. Fenton was walking away from his stepdaughter. They will tell you he was moving away from her when he was struck.

You will hear from body position experts and other forensic experts who will talk about what was found at the scene of the crime. They will all tell you that the evidence points to one fact—that Mr. Fenton was walking away from his stepdaughter when he was struck and killed.

Let me repeat that for you so it's clear—Mr. Fenton was walking away from his stepdaughter when he was struck and killed.

You will hear from witnesses who will make it clear that Miss Fenton had a motive to murder her stepfather. These witnesses will tell you that Mr. Fenton suffered terribly from PTSD, and when it all became too much, he would lash out at his stepdaughter. That's not acceptable behavior, and we in no way approve of it. However, this behavior did not continue and was not occurring during the night of April 15th. The witnesses you'll hear from will establish that this past behavior motivated Miss Fenton to exact brutal and callous revenge on her stepfather.

Now, during this case, you'll hear fanciful stories from the defense about what happened that night. Do not be fooled by stories that have no basis in fact. Remember, you're here to assess the facts, not make guesses about what happened.

You must assess the facts, and you must apply the law.

No matter what your personal opinions are, no matter how you feel about a situation, you must apply the law.

Once we arrive at the end of this case, once you have heard all the evidence, I have no doubt that you will have enough evidence to convict Miss Fenton of murder in the first degree.

It was her intent to kill her stepfather that night, and she must be punished for this inexcusable crime.

As jurors, you have been tasked with great responsibility. You're tasked with assessing the evidence in this case. You're tasked with evaluating the evidence that is presented to you. As jurors, you're tasked with making a decision based on the rule of law. Remember that you must look at the evidence, not the stories. You must apply the law, not feelings.

At the end of this case, I'll address you again and ask you to consider all the evidence we have presented and conclude that Miss Fenton is guilty beyond a reasonable doubt.

Thank you for your service to the court."

*****

During Garrett's opening statement, juror number five stared coldly at Alicia, not taking his eyes off her once. He was a lifelong government worker who appeared to have no respect for anyone younger than him. The older man was dressed in a blue shirt and a red tie. He rolled his eyes and scoffed loudly when the word 'self-defense' was mentioned. Hennessy wondered how the man slipped through the selection.

When Garrett finished his opening statement, he looked at the jury and nodded. Juror five nodded back. He worried Hennessy. The man had brought his biases into the room, and he was going to present a problem for the defense.

After he was asked to open by Judge West, Hennessy took a moment, read over his notes, and then stood. He moved to the lectern, studying the faces of the jury, and then began.

*****

"May it please the court. Ladies and gentlemen of the jury, Your Honor, my name is Joe Hennessy, and I'm the criminal defense attorney representing the defendant, Miss Alicia Fenton.

This is a case of self-defense.

Plain and simple.

Let me be clear on what the law states—a person is allowed to defend themselves from the threat of death or serious bodily injury. That's the law. Plain and simple. Miss Fenton was defending herself from an attack. That's all this is.

Miss Fenton has no history of violence. She has no history of drug use. She has no history of alcohol use. This was not an incident where someone lost control. This was not a moment of revenge. This was not a planned event.

Her actions were in self-defense, plain and simple.

Alicia Fenton was in her home on Logan Street in Downtown Charleston, where she had lived alone for more than five weeks. Because she was in her home, Miss Fenton was under no legal obligation to flee from her attacker.

You will hear from witnesses who will testify that Mr. Fenton had only been released from prison hours earlier, and this was his first stop. They will tell you that Mr. Fenton still had fourteen months left on his prison sentence. He did not tell Miss Fenton that he was being released fourteen months early. Miss Fenton was surprised to see him when he arrived at the house that she owned.

You will hear from witnesses who will testify that

Mr. Fenton was drunk and high on drugs when he arrived at the home listed in his stepdaughter's name. The Deputy Coroner will tell you that Mr. Fenton had high levels of alcohol and morphine in his system when he died.

You will hear from witnesses who will testify that they saw Mr. Fenton strike his stepdaughter many times in the past. Mr. Fenton's own sister will testify that she wanted to take Alicia out of Mr. Fenton's care because she had seen him physically abusing her.

You will hear from a nurse at the school where Miss Fenton attended, and she will testify that she was afraid that Miss Fenton was being abused by her stepfather.

You will hear from a witness who will say that there is clear evidence that Mr. Fenton physically attacked his stepdaughter that night. Her blood was found on the kitchen wall, and she had a large cut above her eye.

Let me repeat that for you—you will hear from a witness who will testify that Mr. Fenton attacked his stepdaughter that night. Her blood was spattered on the kitchen wall.

Because Miss Fenton has claimed self-defense, there are four things that the prosecution must prove, and they are as follows:

Firstly, the defendant must be without fault in bringing on the difficulty. She must not have provoked the attack. You will hear from a witness who will testify that Miss Fenton was in her own home and was not even aware that Mr. Fenton had been released from prison.

Secondly, the defendant believed she was in imminent danger of being killed or seriously injured, or actually was in imminent danger. You will hear from a witness that will testify that Mr. Fenton had struck his stepdaughter only moments before the incident.

Thirdly, if based on the belief of imminent danger, a reasonable person would've had the same belief as the defendant. That will be clear to you by the end of this trial.

And lastly, there was no probable means of avoiding the danger. Miss Fenton was cornered in her own home, where she lived alone. She had no other choice than to defend herself.

On his first night since being released from prison, Mr. Fenton attacked his stepdaughter.

In response to his attack, Miss Fenton defended herself.

Remember, the burden of proof remains on the prosecution, and if they fail in the obligation, you must find Miss Fenton not guilty. The law does not require any defendant to prove his or her innocence of a crime. The law requires the State to establish a defendant's guilt by evidence and must do so beyond a reasonable doubt. And a reasonable doubt is the doubt that a reasonable person would have.

Alicia Fenton acted in self-defense. If you agree with that, and by the end of this trial, the evidence will say so, then you must find Miss Fenton not guilty.

When you are asked to make a decision in this case, you can only conclude that Miss Fenton is not guilty.

Thank you for your time."

CHAPTER 25

DUE TO the consistent media coverage, the interest in the case was high.

Spectators filled every available chair in the gallery. Media filled the space to the side of the room, each reporter with a lanyard around their neck and notepads ready. The five cops from the first hearing were standing at the back of the room, arms folded and not a smile to share between them. The bailiffs stood at the front of the room, searching the crowd for any movements. The smell was stuffy, mostly due to the old overhead air-conditioners. The air-conditioners were struggling in the heat. They were loud and inconsistent, but mostly their low hum filled the room with white noise.

The intensity of the opening statements had left the court unsettled. The atmosphere in the crowd was tense, full of anticipation about the coming witnesses.

Aaron Garrett moved to the lectern, looked at the jury, and then called his first witness. "The State calls Dr. Garry Wilson."

As the doctor walked to the stand, Hennessy could feel the nerves radiating off Alicia like a fever. Her leg bounced up and down, and she clutched her hands over her stomach. Hennessy wrote a note on his legal pad and showed it to her. 'Remember to breathe,' he wrote. She took several deep breaths as the doctor swore his oath.

Deputy Coroner Dr. Garry Wilson walked to the stand full of confidence. He was balding and didn't try to hide it. His remaining hair was gray, and he wore a plain black suit without a tie. His shoes were unpolished.

"Thank you for coming to the court today. Can you please tell the court your name and occupation?"

"My name is Dr. Garry Wilson, and I'm employed as a Deputy Coroner with the Charleston County Coroner's Office. I'm a proud member of the South Carolina Coroner's Association, and I've previously served as a private medical doctor. I have over fifteen years of experience with the Charleston County Coroner's Office. At the Coroner's Office, we conduct independent investigations into certain types of deaths within our county limits. These investigations are conducted to determine the cause and manner of death, and to ensure that the circumstances surrounding it are completely understood."

After Garrett established the witness's name and professional qualifications, he submitted the doctor's report into evidence. "Dr. Wilson, did you examine the body of Mr. Dennis Fenton?"

"I did."

"And what did you find?"

"Mr. Fenton died as a result of blunt force trauma. When you're a coroner, you see a lot of blunt force trauma cases that cause deaths, and this is because it happens in a wide variety of circumstances, such as motor vehicle accidents, pedestrians being struck by vehicles, jumping or falling from heights, blast injuries, or being struck by a firm object, such as a fist or a bat. In this case, I determined that blunt force trauma caused a diffuse axonal injury, or DAI, which is an injury in which scattered lesions occur over a widespread area in white matter tracts of the brain. DAI is the main cause of unconsciousness in patients with blunt force trauma to the head, and the outcome of the trauma is frequently coma. In most instances of severe DAI like we have with the victim, the person never regains consciousness."

"Where did this blunt force trauma take place on the head?"

"To the back of the skull, where the head and neck meet. This is called the craniovertebral junction. This is a very complex area of the body as it's where the brain transitions to the spine. In this area is a range of complex nerve and vascular structures. If this area is impacted heavily, as I have observed with the deceased, it can cause instant death."

"To the back of the head known as the…" Garrett paused and pretended to think about the answer, but it was just a show to focus the jury's attention on the detail. "Sorry, Doctor, what was the area at the back of the head called again?"

"Objection," Hennessy said. "Asked and answered."

"Your Honor," Garrett looked across at the defense table. "The back of the head is a complex part of the body, and I'd like to be sure that the court is clear on what the back of the head is called."

Hennessy scoffed. One of Garrett's trial tactics had become crystal clear—he was going to use the term 'back of the head' as much as he could throughout the trial, so the jury had no doubt about where the victim was struck.

"Overruled," Judge West said. "Because of the complex nature of the answer, you may answer the question, Dr. Wilson."

Dr. Wilson nodded. "The area at the back of the head is called the craniovertebral junction."

"The craniovertebral junction at the back of the head," Garrett repeated. "Was there any sign of what caused this blunt force trauma to the craniovertebral junction at the back of the head?"

"The impact was consistent with a rounded object, such as a baseball bat, or a similar type of object, like a pole."

"And to strike someone with enough force to kill a person, where would the assailant have to be?"

"For this amount of force, the person would've been behind the deceased."

"Was there anything unusual about this blow to the back of the head?"

"Unusual? No."

"And what time of death did you record?"

"Due to the body's temperature when the forensic team first found it, we calculated the time of death to be between 9:35pm and 9:45pm on April 15th."

For the following fifty minutes, Garrett guided Dr. Wilson through his report. The statements were all factual, full of the smallest details, and Garrett mentioned the term 'back of the head' at least another twenty-five times.

When Garrett finished his questioning, Judge West looked at her watch. It was 4:35pm, almost the end of the first day. "Your witness, Mr. Hennessy," Judge West declared.

"Thank you, Your Honor." Hennessy turned to a file on his desk, opened it, and removed a piece of paper. He spoke as soon as he stood, not waiting to arrive at the podium. "Dr. Wilson, thank you for coming to court and testifying today. Can you please tell the court if you conducted a toxicology report on the deceased?"

"We requested one. The toxicology report was provided by the South Carolina State Law Enforcement Division Forensic Services Laboratory."

"And what was found in the toxicology report?"

"The deceased had both alcohol and morphine in his system. His blood alcohol reading was high at 0.15, which is usually associated with a high level of intoxication. His morphine level was medium, suggesting that he was under the effects of the substance."

"How does alcohol interact with morphine?"

"Not well. Because alcohol and morphine are both depressants, combining them can result in drowsiness, motor skill impairment, delayed responsiveness, and poor decision-making abilities."

"Poor decision-making abilities," Hennessy reiterated and looked at the jury. When he saw one of the juror's heads nod, he continued. "Other than the blow to the back of the head, did the deceased display any other injuries?"

"There was recent bruising on the knuckles of Mr. Fenton's right hand."

"Was the bruising consistent with someone who has hit another object or person with a clenched fist?"

"That's correct, although I can't say what he hit."

"Is it possible, from your studying of the bruising on his knuckles, that he struck another person?"

"From the bruising on his knuckles, yes, I would say that's possible."

Hennessy paused again, allowing time for the information to sink into the minds of the jurors. "And can you please tell the court how heavy the deceased was at the time of his death?"

"He weighed 215 pounds."

"And his height?"

"He was six-foot-two."

"Would you describe him as a large man?"

"Absolutely. He was certainly well above average in height and weight, yes."

"Intimidating?"

"Objection," Garrett called out. "Mr. Hennessy is asking the witness to speculate."

"Sustained."

"Let me rephrase." Hennessy paused for a moment. "In this drunken and high state, do you believe, in your medical opinion, this larger-than-average man would have been capable of hurting someone?"

"Yes."

Hennessy nodded and turned to the witness. "Thank you, Dr. Wilson. No further questions."

When the judge called an end to the first day, the case was evenly poised, and the atmosphere was buzzing.

The court was heating up, and it was all on the line.

CHAPTER 26

"THE STATE calls Detective Sean Carver."

The crowd turned to watch as the detective entered the room to begin day two.

Right from the start, he eyed Hennessy with distinct aggression. He had dressed in a suit for the occasion, but it did nothing to hide his unhealthy appearance. He had the skin of a lifelong smoker, eyes tinged with the yellow of a heavy drinker, and the teeth of a man who cared little for his appearance.

His walk, his demeanor, and the tone of his affirmation to the bailiff were filled with arrogance. Carver was a man set in his ways, and the last thing he wanted was people questioning him. He preferred the streets, where he ruled, and people followed his direction.

"Thank you for coming to court today, Detective Carver. Can you please begin by telling the court your name and profession?"

"My name is Detective Sean Carver, and I've been a member of the Charleston Police Department for over three decades. I've served with honor and great pride, and it's been my privilege to serve this great city."

"And how did you know Mr. Fenton?"

"Mr. Fenton was a former detective, and we were partners in the police force once. We started as partners around ten years ago. In total, we were partnered for five years. During that time, after spending many hours on the road together, we became close personal friends."

"And why did the partnership as detectives end?"

Carver looked down and then drew a long breath. "We both witnessed something horrific in our duty as detectives, and as a result of that event, we both suffered Post-traumatic-stress-disorder, or PTSD, as it's more commonly known. Fenton took some time off, but I just kept working through it."

"Post-traumatic-stress-disorder," Garrett repeated. "And how did this affect Mr. Fenton?"

"Terribly. His personality changed after that day. It was like a switch. That can sometimes happen, apparently. The psychologist explained that what we saw was so horrific that it couldn't leave our brains. It was like it was a permanent mark there. I really struggled with it, and so did Mr. Fenton."

Garrett was attempting to build sympathy for Dennis Fenton by painting him as a good man caught in a bad situation.

"And what was the event you and Mr. Fenton saw that caused both of you to suffer from PTSD?"

"Objection," Hennessy called out. "This question has no relevance to this case."

"I argue there is, Your Honor," Garrett responded. "This event permanently changed the victim and speaks to his mental state before this day."

"I agree," Judge West nodded. "The objection is overruled. You may continue."

"Detective Carver," Garrett was soft in his tone to the detective. "Can you please tell the court about the event that you and Mr. Fenton saw that caused both of you to suffer from PTSD?"

"We got a call one night about a horrific single-vehicle accident involving a baby. We were two minutes away from the location, and given that the accident involved a baby, we turned quickly to the scene, knowing that we would arrive before the paramedics or uniformed police officers. We turned to see if we could help them."

"And could you?"

The tears welled up in Carver's eyes. "No."

"Why not?"

Carver struggled to hold back the tears. His lip was quivering, and he avoided eye contact with Garrett. He grimaced and looked down. This was no act. The tough exterior was broken.

After a few moments, Carver took a deep breath and looked back at the prosecutor. "When we arrived at the scene, the car was a mangled mess. The small car had crashed into the side of a parked truck. The small car hit it head-on. It was clear that she had been speeding from the damage. We raced to the car and found... and found the mother had been decapitated by a piece of metal. It was horrific. Then we tried to save the baby, but she was a mangled mess." He fought back the tears again. "We tried to save her, but she died later in the hospital."

"Take your time, Detective Carver," Garrett said. Carver took a few moments to calm himself, dabbing at his eyes with a tissue. There was nothing fake about his performance, nothing put-on, and nothing exaggerated. It was a horrific event that the detectives saw in the line of duty, and it had affected them for a long time. "And can you please tell the court what happened to Mr. Fenton after that day, five years ago?"

"He…" Carver sighed and shrugged. "He really struggled. We both did. Dennis turned to the drink after that, and he later turned to drugs."

"Were you aware if he was ever violent toward his stepdaughter?"

"When she was young, maybe fourteen years old, I went to his home, and she answered the door. It was during school hours, and she had a black eye. I knew something was wrong by the way she looked at me. I asked Dennis about it, and he denied he hit her at first, but later, after I kept pushing it, he broke down and told me the truth. He told me that he was drinking a lot to forget the accident. And that when he got drunk, he became violent. He hated himself for it. I forced him to book himself into rehab, and he went for five days. At first, rehab was successful. He stopped drinking, which was a win. But soon, he found another outlet. He turned to drugs. Morphine. It helped him escape and eased his mind. Morphine was the only thing that calmed him down."

"That must've been hard to watch your friend go through," Garrett said. "Did you see him beat Miss Fenton again?"

"I don't think so. He told me he didn't and that the morphine chilled him out, while it was the alcohol that made him violent."

"Thank you, detective. I understand it must've been hard to talk about." Garrett walked back to the prosecution desk and opened a file. He took the piece of paper back to the lectern. "Can you please tell the court what you saw on April 15th?"

"I drove Dennis Fenton home to his apartment on Logan Street, on the Peninsula. I parked the car across the road, and then Dennis said he'd like a few moments to himself in the apartment. I agreed, and I waited there for around five to ten minutes before I heard the screaming. I got out of my car and approached the screaming woman, who had run out onto the street. That woman was Miss Fenton."

"What did you do next?"

"I tried to calm her down to try and get an understanding of what happened."

"And how did she seem after she ran out onto the street?"

"Objection to the word 'seem,'" Hennessy said. "It calls for speculation."

"Sustained," Judge West said. "Please choose your words more carefully, Mr. Garrett."

"Yes, Your Honor," Garrett stated. "Detective Carver, what do you think she was—"

"Objection to the word 'think.' Again, it calls for speculation."

"Again, the objection is sustained."

"How did it feel—"

"Objection to the word 'feel.' It calls for the witness to characterize the events."

"Sustained," Judge West agreed. "Mr. Garrett, I've asked you to choose your words more carefully. The witness is allowed to talk about what they saw that day, but is not to make assumptions or characterizations."

Frustrated, Garrett exhaled loudly and turned back to the prosecution table. He picked up another file and then carried it to the lectern. "What did you see Miss Fenton do when she ran out of the building?"

"She was crying and upset. She was also angry, but I tried to calm her down. That's when she told me that she'd just killed her stepfather."

"Were those her exact words?"

"Yes. She said, 'I've just killed my stepfather.'"

"What did you do then?"

"I saw someone run into the apartment, so I followed them. I went through the open front door and found Mr. Fenton on the ground. The other man in the room, Mr. Roberts, had turned him over. I checked for a pulse. There was none. I called it in and knew I had to create a crime scene. I secured Miss Fenton in the back of my car for further questioning and waited for the arrival of the support cars."

For the next two hours and fifty-five minutes, Garrett launched into question after question about the night and the subsequent investigation, rattling each off with rehearsed precision. Every question had a direct answer, but Hennessy objected where he could to break Garrett's rhythm. As the lead investigator into the crime, Garrett used Carver to introduce a lot of evidence to the court, including the murder weapon and pictures of the crime scene. The jury watched Garrett's display of what happened with the murder weapon with keen eyes.

Garrett put on a performance worthy of an Oscar nomination, hooking the jury with his actions, rises in tone, and simple questioning.

"Your witness, Mr. Hennessy," Judge West said after Garrett finally ended his questioning and relinquished the witness after a short lunch break.

Hennessy took his time reviewing his notes and then stood and walked to the lectern. He stared at Carver for a long moment before he began. "Detective Carver, could you tell the court when you last saw the deceased?"

"As I said earlier, I drove him home."

"But you didn't tell the court where you drove him home from, did you?"

"I probably just forgot to mention it."

"Can you please tell the court where you picked Mr. Fenton up from?"

"I picked him up from the Lieber Correctional Center."

"And can you please tell the court why Mr. Fenton was at the Lieber Correctional Center?"

"He'd just been released."

"Just been released. How long had he been released before you picked him up?"

"Only fifteen minutes."

"And were you the first person he saw after he had just been released from prison?"

"I believe so."

"And did you make any stops before you arrived at the apartment owned by Miss Fenton on Logan Street?"

"No. The apartment was our first stop. It took around forty-five minutes to drive there from the prison."

Hennessy pretended to be surprised for the sake of the jury. "Can you please tell the court why Mr. Fenton was serving time in prison?"

"The Feds convicted him of buying drugs from the Rebel Sons."

"And are the Rebel Sons an outlaw motorcycle gang?"

"That's correct."

"Was he charged with any other crimes?"

"He was charged with criminal conspiracy but wasn't convicted of that crime."

Hennessy nodded and took a few moments before continuing. "And did Mr. Fenton talk about his stepdaughter after you picked her up?"

"Yes, but I don't remember his exact words. He didn't say much. He just said how much he hoped she was doing ok."

Hennessy paused for a long moment, thinking over the situation, and then nodded to himself. "No further questions for now, however, we reserve the right to recall this witness as a defense witness."

Carver's stare told him everything he needed to know—he was pushing the right buttons.

CHAPTER 27

"THE STATE calls Mr. Brock Roberts."

Brock Roberts walked to the stand with his head held high. He wore clean blue jeans, a black shirt, and steel-toe boots. The clothes were tight on his broad frame. The end of a tattoo was visible from under the sleeve of his shirt. And no matter the quality of the clothes, he still looked like a biker underneath.

Silence enveloped the courtroom as the bailiff swore the witness in, and Roberts agreed to tell the truth, something Hennessy suspected would not happen.

"Thank you for testifying, Mr. Roberts." Garrett began seated behind his desk. "Can you please describe to the court where you were on April 15th?"

"I was walking along Logan Street in Downtown Charleston. I'd been told that Dennis Fenton was released from prison, and I went to see him to wish him a happy release. It ain't easy being released from prison—I should know. I've done it a few times."

He smiled at the jury as if it was some kind of great joke. Nobody smiled back.

"What happened when you arrived at the apartment, Mr. Roberts?"

"As I was about twenty yards from the apartment, I heard someone scream. It was definitely a girl's voice that screamed, so I ran toward it, thinking someone might be in trouble."

"And what did you find?"

"Alicia Fenton, the woman sitting over there, ran straight past me, screaming. I thought something real bad must've happened, given the way she was screaming."

"What did you do next?"

"I looked in the open door where she'd just come from and thought I saw someone on the ground."

"And did you?"

"I did, so I went further into the apartment. He was lying face down on the carpet, so I turned the man over, and that's when I saw it was Dennis Fenton. I tried to find his pulse, but there was none."

"And what time was this?"

"Around 9:30pm, maybe a bit after."

"And what else was around the scene?"

"There was a baseball bat beside him, but there wasn't much blood. There was a little bit, but not a lot. On the other side of him was a whiskey bottle, which I think was in his hands as I turned him over."

"What happened next?"

"A detective showed up at the door and started swearing a lot. He checked for a pulse as well, and he couldn't find one either. I think it was clear he was dead."

"How long had you known Mr. Fenton?"

"I'd known him for around two years. We met through a mutual acquaintance."

"And did he ever talk to you about his stepdaughter?"

"Sometimes. He talked about how he did her wrong a few years earlier but was working to make up for that."

"'Did her wrong.' Did he elaborate on what that meant?"

"He said he hit her in anger a few times. The alcohol used to get to him, and he'd get real angry."

"And were you aware he was taking a lot of morphine?"

"I knew he took some morphine. I'd seen him take it a few times."

"How was he after he took the morphine?"

"Calm. It just seemed to calm him down. Take the edge off, you know? He was pretty angry a lot of the time, but when he had a hit of morphine, he relaxed. It was like it eased his brain."

Garrett looked to his first assistant. He provided the junior lawyer a nod, and she typed a few lines into her laptop. A picture appeared on the court monitor. "Mr. Roberts, these are the crime scene photos that were ordered by Detective Carver. Can you please take the court through your activities in the room and what you saw, step by step?"

For the next forty-five minutes, under the guidance of Garrett's questions, Roberts painted a clear picture of what he walked into.

It was clear to Hennessy that the prosecutor was avoiding one key aspect of the witness's testimony and, as he continued listening to the questions, almost predicted that the all-important question wouldn't be asked. By the end of the testimony, he was proved right.

"Mr. Roberts, thank you for coming in today," Hennessy began, staying seated behind his desk. "You mentioned there was a whiskey bottle next to Mr. Fenton. How much of the whiskey bottle was filled?"

"I'd say it was about half full."

"Or half empty." Hennessy turned a page in his files. "You said he'd get angry when he drank, is that right?"

"Yeah. He used to."

"And there was a half-drunk bottle of whiskey next to him?"

"That's right."

Hennessy paused and shrugged his shoulders. "Would you please tell the court if you heard any words being screamed out before you entered the apartment?"

Roberts didn't answer immediately. He instead glanced over to Alicia, and the pair exchanged a brief look while the rest of the court sat silently around them. He finally cleared his throat and said what Hennessy had been hoping for all along.

"There was a scream, and someone yelled, 'Not again.' Then, about ten seconds later, there was another loud shriek."

"'Not again,'" Hennessy repeated. "Just like that. 'Not again.' those were the words you heard?"

"That's right."

"And when you saw Alicia Fenton, did she have a fresh cut blood above her eye?"

"I didn't get a good look at her. She was running too fast past me."

"Thank you, Mr. Roberts," Hennessy said. "No further questions."

CHAPTER 28

THE TESTIMONY of the next-door neighbor, Mr. Steven Manson, went as expected. Yes, he heard the scream that night. No, he didn't see anything else. Yes, he knew Mr. Fenton lived next door. All very accurate and sound, but nothing that would sway a jury.

The next witness, family friend Mrs. Denise Campton, was much the same. Yes, Dennis Fenton's personality changed overnight after the incident five years earlier. Yes, she had seen the bruises on Alicia. And yes, she found that morphine calmed Dennis down. She said he was almost placid after any hit and could barely raise his voice.

Decent witnesses, but nothing that pointed to the fact that Alicia wasn't acting in self-defense.

Garrett called Dennis' ex-girlfriend next.

Ms. Gemma Briggs walked to the stand with her head down. She wore jeans, a white shirt, and some jewelry, but all her clothes were loose on her large frame. She had her brown hair tied back into a ponytail, and she wore too much makeup.

"Ms. Briggs," Garrett began after the witness was sworn in, "can you please explain to the court how you knew Mr. Fenton?"

"We dated for two years but broke up last year. At his heart, he was a good man, but I couldn't take all the morphine use. I didn't like it, and I told him that many times. Eventually, we broke up because he wouldn't stop trying to find hits of morphine, and I was trying to get clean after a few mistakes in my life."

"How did he react to morphine?"

"He calmed down. He was always edgy and jumpy, even when we went away on weekends. He never seemed to switch off. But when he took the morphine, he calmed right down."

"Had you ever seen him be violent?"

"Sometimes he would get really, really angry and punch things, but never on morphine. If he got a good hit, he would just sit down and stare into nothing with a smile on his face. He was so relaxed on morphine."

"And did you also know Miss Fenton, his stepdaughter?"

"I'd met Alicia quite a few times."

"And when was the last time you saw Miss Fenton?"

"About a year before she murdered him."

"Objection," Hennessy called out. "The answer assumes facts not in evidence. The word 'murdered' implies that Miss Fenton acted in a certain way."

"Sustained," Judge West stated. She turned to look at the witness. "Ms. Briggs, during your witness testimony, you are to talk about your personal knowledge of events, and you're not to make claims about anything else. Is that understood?"

"Yes, ma'am," the witness replied.

"While you knew Mr. Fenton," Garrett continued, "how would you describe their relationship?"

"Objection," Hennessy said. "The question calls

for speculation."

"Sustained," Judge West replied.

"Let me try another question," Garrett paused and gathered his thoughts. "Had you ever talked to Miss Fenton alone, just the two of you?"

"I picked her up from sporting events some days when Dennis was busy. One day, she was really angry at her stepfather. I don't know why. I didn't ask, but she said she wanted him out of her life. I asked what she meant by that, and she said she wished he was dead, and if she had the chance, she would do it."

One jury member gasped and then covered her hand over her mouth. Once Garrett heard this, he turned to Judge West. "No further questions."

Hennessy waited a few moments before he started. He glanced over his files and then stood, waiting next to the defense table as he began.

"Ms. Briggs, were you friends with Miss Fenton?"

"Friends? No. She was a teenage girl, and I'm an adult woman. We weren't friends."

"Then how would you describe your relationship with Miss Fenton?"

"Strained."

"Strained," Hennessy repeated and then looked down at the file on his desk. "Two years ago, last April, did you post on a Facebook discussion board that you, 'Hate your boyfriend's daughter,' and, 'I'd do anything to make sure she went to juvenile detention.'"

"That's taken out of context."

"Really? In what context would a statement like that be appropriate?"

"I was…" She shook her head, trying to buy time. "Look, we didn't get along. That sometimes happens with new girlfriends and kids."

"Would you lie to this court to ensure she went to prison?"

"Objection!" Garrett called out. "The defense is accusing the witness of lying."

"Given the witness's previous statements that she would do 'anything' to ensure the defendant is locked up, I argue it's a very appropriate question." Out of the corner of his eye, Hennessy saw one of the jury members nod. "But I'll withdraw the question, and I'll ask another one—did you also take hits of morphine with Mr. Fenton?"

"Objection. Relevance."

"It's very relevant, Your Honor," Hennessy responded. "It demonstrates the relationship between the witness, the victim, and the defendant."

"Overruled. Ms. Briggs, you may answer the question."

"Ah, yeah. We got high together sometimes."

"In fact, you took other drugs as well as morphine, didn't you?"

She shrugged. "But I'm clean now. Been clean for ten months. I've put on fifty-five pounds, but I'm not getting high anymore."

"Please answer the question."

"Yeah, ok. Sure. I took some heroin at times, but it's all in the past."

"Is it true that one night when Mr. Fenton was out of town, Miss Fenton reported your drug use to the police when you were supposed to be looking after her?"

She exhaled heavily through her nostrils, trying to maintain her anger. "Yes."

"And you were fined a large amount and given a

misdemeanor charge for this, weren't you?"

"Yes."

"Were you also high when Miss Fenton allegedly threatened her stepfather?"

"No, come on. I wasn't high then."

"Really?" Hennessy scoffed. "Then can you please tell the court the words Miss Fenton used?"

"It was something like—"

"Something like? Ms. Briggs, we deal in facts in a courtroom, not 'likes.' Can you please tell the court what Miss Fenton said?"

"I don't know the exact words. All I know is that she's a little brat."

"And you would do anything to put her away," Hennessy sighed and shook his head. He heard a 'tsk tsk' from one of the jurors. "No further questions."

It was a win for Hennessy, and he wasn't finished yet.

CHAPTER 29

OVER THE following days, Garrett kept piling on the indisputable facts of the case, leaving little doubt that Alicia had struck her stepfather in the back of the head with a baseball bat.

Body position experts came to the stand to talk about the position Alicia had to be standing in to strike Dennis Fenton in the back of the head. Crime scene experts spoke about how the body had landed. And forensic experts talked about every aspect of the crime scene. By the time they arrived at the court on Friday morning, the jury was clear about how the scene looked, where Alicia had been standing, and what had happened in the heat of the moment.

When Garrett called medical expert Dr. Cynthia Caldwell, his trial tactic had become abundantly clear. He was going to push the fact that Fenton was too high on morphine to attack his stepdaughter.

"Thank you for coming to court today, Dr. Caldwell." Garrett stood behind the lectern. "Can you please tell the court your occupation and your expertise?"

"Hello," Dr. Caldwell stated. "My name is Dr. Cynthia Caldwell, and I'm a doctor and researcher at the University of South Carolina, and my research has specialized in the study of the effects of so-called opioid drugs, including the two types of opioid drugs.

There are those that occur naturally and come from the opium poppy, for example, codeine, morphine, and heroin. And there are those that are created synthetically, such as fentanyl."

"And how long have you studied this subject?"

"Over two decades," she responded. "During that time, my work has been published in many medical journals, and I've spoken at many conferences. I've also been called to testify in over fifty court cases."

"Impressive." Garrett nodded. "Can you please describe to the court what happens to the body when morphine is administered?"

"Morphine attaches to proteins called receptors on nerve cells in the brain, spinal cord, gut, and other parts of the body. The receptors communicate pain through the body. For instance, if I hurt my foot, these receptors spring into action and tell my brain that there is a pain in my foot. Morphine blocks that pathway, and my brain doesn't receive the message. In short-term use, this is very effective at pain relief. However, it's also highly addictive."

"And what happens to a person after they take morphine?"

"Morphine looks for delta, kappa, and opioid receptors. This drug produces most of its analgesic effects by binding to the receptors within the central nervous system and the peripheral nervous system. This inhibits pathways in the central nervous system as well as the nociceptive afferent neurons of the peripheral nervous system. This causes an overall reduction of nociceptive transmission, and this process can cause effects such as euphoria, pain relief, sleepiness or drowsiness, reduced anxiety, false or unusual sense of well-being, or a calm, relaxed feeling."

"Would someone with PTSD take a medication that blocks physical pain signals?"

"Absolutely. By directly impacting a person's central nervous system, morphine can decrease anxiety and produce feelings of euphoria. This effect can be highly addictive to someone suffering from reoccurring and intrusive thoughts. It can provide them great relief from their own troubled mind."

"In your professional opinion, do you believe someone with his level of morphine could be violent?"

"It's possible, but at that level, it's unlikely."

"It's unlikely," Garrett repeated. "Thank you, Dr. Caldwell. No further questions."

When called, Hennessy stood for his cross-examination. He waited a moment, running his hand over a line of notes, and then lifted his head to look at the witness. "Dr. Caldwell, for someone with a high tolerance of morphine use, would the drug have the same effect as someone taking a first dose?"

"No. The body adapts to what it's given, and tolerance is a very well-known result of prolonged morphine use. In fact, it's one of the first signs that someone is addicted."

"And for someone with a high tolerance of morphine, is it possible, or not possible, that they could act violently?"

"Yes, it's possible."

"Thank you, Dr. Caldwell," Hennessy said. "No further questions."

The jury was losing focus when the next witness of the day, Crime Scene Forensic Analyst Dr. Frank Wagner, walked to the stand after lunch.

For fifty-five minutes, Garrett questioned Dr. Wagner about his analysis of the crime scene, painting a very plain description of the room. Dr. Wagner explained the photographs he took, where the body was found, and the likelihood that Dennis Fenton was walking away from his stepdaughter at the time of the attack. Even Hennessy struggled to keep focused during the lengthy testimony delivered from a monotone voice.

Once all the presented evidence from Dr. Wagner was boiled down, it came down to one simple point—that Dennis Fenton was walking away from the defendant when she struck him with the bat.

When that point was drummed in, Garrett turned the witness over to Hennessy, and rather than get up immediately, the defense lawyer remained sitting and reading his notes.

"Mr. Hennessy? Do you wish to cross-examine?"

Hennessy looked up and met the judge's gaze but still hadn't had any positive sign of which direction to take. He could sense Alicia's nerves beside him, her apprehension rising with each passing moment.

"Mr. Hennessy?"

"Yes, thank you, Your Honor," he finally said and rose to his feet.

Trying to buy himself a few more precious seconds of thinking, he slowly walked toward the witness stand, stalling a single second at a time with each step. Only when he closed the distance to just a few feet did he realize his time had come.

"Mr. Wagner," Hennessy began, "did you study the entire apartment in your analysis of the crime scene?"

"That's correct."

"And you're quite an experienced blood spatter expert, would you agree?"

"I've studied blood spatters in the past, yes."

"In fact, you've even delivered papers on blood spatter, correct?"

"That's right."

"How many years have you studied blood spatters?"

"Perhaps over twenty now."

"And how can you tell whether the threat had ended from your blood spatter evidence?"

"The blood spatter can't prove or disprove that."

"Right. Were there any other traces of blood in the apartment?"

"Yes."

"And where was that?"

"Near the far wall of the kitchen room."

"And was it determined who this blood belonged to?"

"Yes. It was determined that the blood belonged to Alicia Fenton."

"And how was the spatter against the wall? Was it consistent with a strike across the person's face?"

"It could've been from any part of the body, but yes, the spatter is consistent with a fast strike across someone, and given the height of the spatter, it's most likely the blood came from someone's face."

"And could this blood on the wall have come from the cut above the defendant's eye?"

"It's possible. She didn't have any other cuts on her, so it's possible that the strike came from the cut above her eye."

Hennessy looked at the twelve members of the jury. One was busy writing on her pad, and another was nodding his approval.

"No further questions."

CHAPTER 30

THE SECOND week of the trial felt longer than the first.

The prosecution pushed witness after witness, question after question, consolidating a mountain of facts that Alicia Fenton had hit her stepfather in the back of the head. Garrett was right from his opening statement—those facts were indisputable.

Garrett called the second police officer to arrive at the scene to the stand. She testified about what she saw when she arrived. Next, a character witness came to the stand to testify about the effect that PTSD had on Dennis Fenton. After that, a psychiatrist came to the stand to testify about the effect PTSD can have on an individual's personality.

The prosecution was doing their best to paint Dennis Fenton as an angel, a good man who suffered from an incident at his job. The testimonies were all very accurate, all very reliable, but there was nothing in the testimonies that pointed to the out-and-out guilt of Alicia.

While each day continued to drag on with repetitive monotony, Hennessy noticed the toll it was taking on his client. For the first few days of the trial, she appeared strong, but with each passing day, her demeanor worsened.

Hennessy, Lockett, and Jacinta sat around the

conference table late in the second week after another day in court. Hennessy was exhausted. The heat was baking the streets, and he could feel the humidity sap his energy.

He couldn't escape the way he'd left Alicia at the end of day ten in the murder trial, just a frail shadow of the confident girl she had been at the start of the week. The days had worn her down faster than he could've imagined, and the way she looked as the guards escorted her out of the courtroom was sad. Seeing her shoulders slump, the legs barely rising enough to move from one step to the next, her whole body just kind of running on empty as she walked between the guards.

"We're losing," he whispered more to himself than the others.

Lockett had been scrolling through his cell phone, and he looked over to Hennessy. "It's too early to call it."

"He's right. It's too early for that. All they've established is the act, not the intent," Jacinta tried.

"We're losing," he repeated with more conviction. "I saw it in the faces of the jury, and I saw it in the face of the judge. They've poured on the facts, and they've dulled the jury into submission. If I hear one more expert witness say she hit him in the back of the head, I'll scream. And Garrett is close to doing cartwheels in that courtroom."

"But you've been doing good with the witnesses. I mean, from where I've been sitting, it sounds to me like you've been getting your point across. She was defending herself. That should be obvious to the jury."

"They're not convinced. There's not enough

oomph behind our case," Hennessy said as he rose from his chair and walked to the window. "Apart from the cut on her eye, there's no evidence she was threatened. And a small cut on the eye is not enough legal cause to strike someone with enough force to kill."

He looked out across the street below as the sun slowly dipped from view. Life outside the office continued as normal, with most people heading home for the weekend.

"You know what you can do?" Jacinta said softly.

"I know. We can call her to the stand, but that's got to be the very last resort. Garrett will tear her apart up there. He'll question how the sexual assault progressed and why she had no further injuries. And that's not to mention the questions about why she hit him in the back of the head. She'll be destroyed up there and lose any sense of credibility. The jury won't believe a word she says, and they'll doubt our entire self-defense claim."

"So what do you do?"

"We pin our hopes on Edith Chapman's testimony that she knew about the abuse."

They discussed strategies for the next hour. They talked about the witnesses still to come and reviewed the statements of the ones that had come before. They looked for one small crack in the prosecution's armor but found none.

Soon, they finished up for the week, and Jacinta said she would check in on him the next day. As she packed up, she asked, "You heading back to the vineyard tonight?"

He wanted to, yes, wanted to more than anything. But given how the case stood, he couldn't justify leaving the city to spend a couple of days ignoring the facts. If Alicia had to suffer through the weekend, then so did he.

"No, not this weekend," he said.

There was too much work to do, too many holes in his case, which he still needed to fill with evidence he didn't yet have.

After Jacinta and Lockett had left, Hennessy sat in the office alone, staring at the pages.

He tried to focus on the update from Brandon McDermott's case, but his mind kept drifting back to Alicia. He read line after line, studied law reference after law reference, until he looked up to the clock and realized it was after 10pm.

Hennessy stood and walked to the window of his boardroom, tapping his forehead against the glass, frustrated the case was slipping away.

CHAPTER 31

ALICIA FENTON waited in line with twenty-five other women for their dinner.

She'd already skipped several dinners during the past week because of her severe anxiety, but Jada convinced her to line up for this one.

Not that she was hungry, quite the opposite. But even she had noticed the change in her face these past few days, a surefire sign of how much the stress was affecting her. The glow of her skin, which she used to pride herself on, was gone, replaced by a dull sheen reminiscent of dust. Even her fingernails had cracked, each riddled with brittle lines as if all the life force was being sucked from her.

She hated the person she had become. All her ambitions were gone, and her drive to succeed was faded out by the system. Her once infectious laugh hadn't come forth in weeks, another victim of her circumstances. Her essence was gone, replaced by a derelict shell of a person.

"Your lawyer given you any sign of how things are going?" Jada asked.

"He doesn't need to," she said. "It's pretty obvious from where I'm sitting."

"I don't get it," Jada said as she took a step forward with the rest of the line. "I thought people had a right to protect themselves in their own home?"

"They do, but we just have to prove it," Alicia whispered as Deb passed them, carrying a dinner tray. She shot Alicia a look, grimaced weirdly, and fed off the laughter from the woman following her. Together, they headed for the nearest table where, thankfully, Deb turned her back to them.

"I hate that woman," Alicia whispered even lower.

"Tell me about it."

They got their meal trays and took seats on the opposite side of Deb and her group of followers, who had turned their attention to another unfortunate victim. Alicia felt relieved seeing it and sat with her back to the group to lessen the chances of them spotting her and coming for another go.

They ate in near silence, more so because the surrounding noise from the boisterous inmates would have made conversation next to impossible. Plus, the serving of mac and cheese was the first time she had it warm since going inside, and Alicia shoveled in spoonfuls once her stomach reminded her it needed more than just a passing meal occasionally.

As the food dwindled and more and more inmates finished their meals, the noise elevated even further. One group had some sort of communal drug party earlier in the afternoon, and the effects of the meth remained, causing many to run around like crazy folk, laughing and screaming at the top of their lungs.

"Think it's time to find cover," Jada said once she finished, and Alicia agreed as she ate the last of her meal. "I'll meet you in the cell. Just gotta grab something from my bunk."

Jada didn't wait for an answer, and Alicia didn't hesitate to return her tray before making her way back up the stairs to her cell. The cellmate she had that morning had been released during the day, and a replacement hadn't been brought in yet. That meant she would more than likely enjoy a night alone, which would be her first since arriving. The prospect of a single cell was more appealing than ice cream at that point, not that she told anybody.

Once back in her cell, Alicia dropped onto her bunk while she waited for Jada. It felt good having someone she knew in the unit with her, and she figured Jada was probably the only thing keeping her sane. She heard approaching footsteps, and as they rounded the doorway, she opened her mouth to ask Jada if she had some spare shampoo.

It wasn't her friend, and she snapped her mouth shut almost as fast as the two women came into her cell. Right from the start, she knew she was in trouble, with both intruders looking at her like hungry stalkers who had found their prey.

"Thought we'd come by for a chat," the first one said, a brutish forty-year-old woman named Tasha.

"What do you want?" Alicia asked as she sat up. She felt a shudder run down her spine as a third woman entered the cell.

"Need to teach you a lesson," the second one said.

Alicia didn't know her name and was about to ask them why when an open hand launched in her direction. Alicia lunged to her right, but the woman's arm caught her around her throat, the weight and speed dragging the weaker woman back down onto the bed. The other two joined the first and rained blows across Alicia's body while the first held her tight.

She screamed, but even a new inmate like Alicia knew the rules, and nobody would come to her aid.

This was a prison-style message, and anybody interfering in the delivery of it would suffer the consequences. All she could do was try to protect herself as much as possible and hope her attackers didn't go too far.

Alicia tried curling herself into a ball, a tough task when being held down. She turned a little sideways and brought her legs up enough to shield her middle while her arms covered her face as best she could. It didn't work perfectly but deflected most of the blows to areas of her body where it didn't matter as much. They didn't touch her face.

After a run of punches, the two women halted their assault, their heavy breathing sounding as if they had run a four-hundred-meter sprint. Alicia kept her arms up as the final one let her go. Tasha kneeled next to her.

"Take the offer, you hear me? You got people digging around the wrong parts. My ex-boyfriend wants you to know that it's not appreciated."

"Who's your ex-boyfriend?" Alicia whispered.

"Who's my ex-boyfriend?" Tasha laughed. "My, ain't you got a mouth on ya!" Tasha leaned closer to Alicia. "My ex-boyfriend shared a cell with your stepdaddy. Dan Coleman is his name. And he said your stepdaddy said he wanted to rape you many, many times. That was the first thing he needed to do when he got out of prison."

"Why does he want me to take the deal?" Alicia grimaced.

"Why?!" Tasha laughed again. "Why? 'Cause you got all sorts of people sniffing around the Rebel Sons, and they don't like it. They don't like it at all." Tasha's face turned serious. "Take the offer and put an end to the case." As if needing to annunciate the message, the woman leaned closer, grabbed a handful of Alicia's hair, and whispered the last part directly into her ear. "Stop the case and take the deal. Brock was going to kill him, anyway. You just saved him the work."

The last part of the message was still ringing in her ear as the attackers left the cell again, leaving her to ride the pain from her injuries. Alicia didn't move, remaining as still as possible on her bunk as the throbbing railed across her body. The point which hurt the most felt alive with fire, the outer part of her left thigh numb with pain. She knew the bruises would already be forming.

Jada never showed up that evening. Alicia spent the night alone in her cell. The voices always came out after lockdown. They tormented her that night, calling for her to abide or die.

Alicia didn't sleep.

A guard popped his head into her cell briefly at lockdown. He called for a sign she was alive and she gave him a wave. He didn't linger. He simply closed the door and moved on.

All she could do was ride the pain as best she could. Despite her fears about spending ten years behind bars, she knew she had little choice now. The message had been delivered, and if scaring her into submission was their intention, it worked. In the morning, she would call her lawyer and…

Alicia sat up in the darkness, freezing her thoughts in place as she reconsidered them.

Could she agree to accept the deal and spend the next decade here?

One of the first things she had been told about

prison was not to show weakness. If she did, then she would be a target forever.

While it scared her to go against what the message had told her, she feared the consequences of remaining behind bars more. Choosing prison over freedom wasn't going to end well for her.

She needed to get out of there.

CHAPTER 32

SITTING AT the far end of the White Point Gardens at the very tip of the Charleston Peninsula, Hennessy looked out to the water, taking a moment to center himself. The morning sun glistened off the water, simmering as boats sailed past. Looking out at the river had always calmed him. It had a magical way of settling the nerves that seemed to be constantly building.

After a while, he pulled out his cell to scroll through the day's news, but as his hand moved, he forced himself to stop. He didn't want to know about the horrors of the world. His mood was just right, the sun the perfect companion for him. Why would he want to open himself up to the terrible stories? Murders, wars, scams. Every story that dominated news sites seemed to be the same dreary depression as the rest.

He put his phone away, but then it buzzed in his pocket. He took it out and looked at the number. It was the Sherriff Al Cannon Detention Center. He sighed and answered the call. The guard on the other end of the line only talked for a minute, but she said all he needed to know.

Alicia wanted to meet, urgently.

He sighed. The peace of his quiet morning had already been broken.

The roads were busy on the way to the detention center and even busier in the parking lot. Prisons were always busier on the weekend, especially for those families trying to gain entry, and Hennessy found himself at the back of a considerable queue once he arrived. Before him, countless families stood in small groups, lined up with hopes for a quick procession inside. More fell in behind him as the line moved forward, and it wasn't long before he found himself surrounded.

"Mr. Hennessy," a voice suddenly cried from somewhere near the back, and he turned to see a face smiling back at him. The woman walked toward him, and while he knew he should have known her, her name remained hidden in the shadows. "Wow, I thought I recognized you," she said as she neared him, and that's when it hit him.

"Erica Linderman," he said in an almost relieved tone and then felt himself tense as she leaned in and hugged him.

Erica Linderman had been a brief client of his several months before, the victim of a theft which saw her vehicle used in a deliberate hit-and-run incident. She had been facing ten years in prison, and with no vision on hand to prove her innocence, she looked certain to be convicted of a manslaughter charge. Her saving grace was a homeless person who saw her passed out drunk in the same park she called home.

"What are you doing here?" Hennessy asked. "I thought I saved you from this place?"

"Friend of mine got himself into trouble. His ex is using his children against him, and he kind of flipped out."

"That'll do it," Hennessy said as he continued.

"Maybe I can give him your card," she suggested, but Hennessy shook his head.

"Unfortunately, I don't really dabble in family law and—" he said with a distinct tone of empathy, but Erica cut him off mid-sentence.

"Oh, of course." She slapped her forehead and chuckled to herself. "What a klutz."

Rather than turn her away, Hennessy took out his notepad and pen and scribbled something. When he finished, he tore a sheet from the pad and held it out.

"Take this," he said. "This woman is a friend of mine. Martha's a brilliant lawyer, and she'll be able to help your friend."

Erica took it and thanked him again before returning to her spot in the queue. Hennessy watched her for a bit before turning back toward the building as he smiled contently. Seeing one of his clients out in the wild always gave him an extra bounce in his step.

The brief distraction was enough to bring Hennessy almost to the front of the line, and he entered the prison foyer just a couple of minutes later. After giving over his ID and following the usual checks and instructions, he whizzed through the process. The guards worked with a fierce determination to get through the line, most of whom had deadlines to enter the facility.

Once through the process, Hennessy was led to one of the interview rooms. Alicia joined him fifteen minutes after he took his seat. When he saw her, he knew something had changed, even without paying attention to the fresh bruise beneath her right eye.

"What happened?" Hennessy asked the moment after the guard closed the door and sealed them inside.

The change was evident, but given the evidence of a physical altercation, it wasn't the change he expected to see. When he'd watched Alicia leave the courtroom the previous afternoon, she was a shadow of her former self, withdrawn and suffering from a distinct lack of life. She was down, depressed, with the weight hanging heavily on her shoulders. A slight wind would have blown her over, and the guards looked as if they were preparing for it with each step she took.

The woman who had walked into the interview room could have been Alicia's much more confident twin sister. She walked in with a purpose, sat confidently upright, and met his gaze as he asked his question. This wasn't the same girl he had left the previous afternoon.

"They attacked me yesterday," she said, her words sounding matter-of-factly, her face devoid of emotion.

"Are you ok?"

"I'm fine," Alicia said. "Save for a few bruises here and there, but that's not the point. They attacked me because they wanted me to take the deal."

"So, they were put up to it," Hennessy muttered, more to himself than his client. He tried to think of who would set her up like that, but too many names sprang forth, and none felt right. "The question is—by who?"

"I know who."

Hennessy squinted. "Go on."

"The Rebel Sons don't like people sniffing around their business, and they see me as the reason why you're out there asking questions about their operations."

"How'd they get a message to these girls?"

"A man named Dan Coleman is the ex-boyfriend of one of the girls in here."

"And is Dan Coleman a member of the Rebel Sons?"

"No. I asked around this morning." She leaned forward. "The Rebel Sons run drugs through a lot of prisons, and they're connected to the Royal Nation. Dan Coleman is a member of the Royal Nation."

"The Royal Nation are a black prison gang."

"That's right. The Rebel Sons and the Royal Nation help each other out, if you know what I mean."

Hennessy studied her confident demeanor. "So, why do you look happy about that?"

"Because Dan Coleman is also the former cellmate of my stepfather. They said that Dennis told him he was going to rape me. Dennis told him what he was going to do to me. That's evidence. That's going to get me off."

Hennessy sat back. "Only if he testifies."

"Then you have to make Dan Coleman testify." Alicia's voice was desperate. "You have to make him testify about what he heard. That's my way out. Don't you see it?"

Hennessy looked at her, contemplating the new information.

"Did you hear me? My stepfather told Dan Coleman that he was going to rape me. If Dan Coleman says that in court, then the case is over. I can walk out of here."

"What do you know about this Dan Coleman?"

"Other than he's part of the Royal Nation—

nothing. Not a thing. You have to get up there and talk to him. I'm sorry to make you do this on the weekend, but this is my ticket out of here."

Hennessy wasn't as convinced.

"I'll try to talk to him," Hennessy said, and then he changed his tone to one a little more paternal. "In the meantime, you make sure you keep your head down. If they came for you once, they'll do it again. And next time, you won't be so lucky."

CHAPTER 33

THE LIEBER Correctional Institution was located near Ridgeville, an hour from Charleston.

Hennessy called ahead, arranged a meeting with a prisoner named Dan Coleman, and started the drive. The lack of traffic surprised him as the day turned into the afternoon, and he arrived ahead of time. Everyone was at the beach, he figured.

Initially taking the interstate, Hennessy turned onto Route 78 at the major interchange and continued northwest. He could've taken the interstate almost all the way to the prison, but there was something about country roads and small towns that appealed to him more, even if the trip took a little longer.

He passed the Christ Temple Deliverance Church a little after twelve and knew it to be one of the mental markers he'd picked out when checking his route to the prison. It was only half a mile or so further up the road that he would need to turn left, a small indiscriminate intersection he'd need to pay attention to. When he got close, he spotted a small house which, at some point in the past, had been somebody's pride and joy, a place to call home. Now, it suffered a fate of natural reclamation, with an abundance of overgrowth looking as if it had a mission to swallow the home in its entirety and return the materials back to the earth. Great tufts of greenery had broken through the roof in several places, with more poking out through the windows. Perhaps the most damning part of the home was the line of plants that grew where the roofline met the walls as if trying to force them apart at the seam.

Hennessy turned at the intersection, then glanced back at the house, wondering how long it would remain standing. Surely somebody owned the land. "Renovator's delight, with great views of the nearby prison," he whispered as he centered himself in the seat and, a hundred yards down the road, found the first signs for the prison.

Hot country air filled his nose as he stepped out of the truck once he'd pulled up in the parking lot. If he closed his eyes, he could almost have imagined himself standing in the middle of a field, with a slight breeze blowing some much-needed relief into his face. The high barbed wire fences, sharp enough to kill, dispelled that thought. They were a blatant reminder that this was where society's forgotten men were kept under lock and key.

It might've been in the country, but that didn't change the fact that the same procedures needed to be followed, and once Hennessy got to the front of the queue to gain entry, he went through the same checks as always. It took him a little longer to gain entry because this wasn't one of his usual prisons, but the on-duty guard came from one of the city jails, and he recognized him. He still had to remove his shoes and belt, walk through a metal detector, be sniffed by a drug detection dog, and then got patted down for good measure.

From only the first steps, it was clear that the

Lieber Correctional Institution was no vacation club. The first thing he noticed was the screams of the mentally ill echoing down the halls. The second thing he noticed was the lack of clean floors. The third was the potent smell of sewage. It seemed prisons were the same everywhere.

A guard led Hennessy through to an interview room, where he sat and waited patiently for the prisoner serving thirty-five years for murder.

It seemed to take forever for the guards to bring Coleman to the interview, with Hennessy getting to his feet to stretch his legs half an hour after arriving. He was close to popping his head out into the corridor to ask someone if they had forgotten about him but resisted, reminding himself that weekends were normally some of the busiest days in any prison.

His patience paid off, and not five minutes later, a tall black man entered the room. The guard instructed him to sit and then chained him to the hook on the table. At first, the guard appeared like he wanted to remain behind when he took up a post next to the door and simply stood there. Hennessy turned to look at the guard and the pair exchanged a look before he took the hint.

"I'm outside if you need me," the guard said and closed the door.

"Do I know you?" Coleman snapped at Hennessy.

"Dan Coleman, my name is Joe Hennessy. I'm a lawyer representing Alicia Fenton. She's the stepdaughter of Dennis Fenton."

He didn't appear to follow. His face scrunched up into a mass of confusion. "Why you talking to me then?"

"Because you were his old cellmate. I want to

know what Dennis Fenton said to you about his stepdaughter."

He stared at Hennessy and then nodded. "You got a smoke?"

"No."

"Money, then? Ten dollars goes a long way in here."

"And what do I get for that money?"

"Everything I know."

"We're being watched." Hennessy nodded to the camera in the corner of the room. "They'll take it from you the second I give it to you."

"Then you be all smooth, like. You take that money out of ya wallet, and you drop it under the table, near my foot. I'll do the rest. I done it before."

Hennessy considered his options and then nodded. While pretending to talk to the prisoner, he moved his left hand into his trousers pocket and fished out a bill. He didn't know how much it was, but he knew he wasn't carrying any more than a twenty. He shifted his body toward the camera and flicked the money under the table. Dan Coleman nodded and then pressed his feet together. He angled his back toward the camera, slipped off one shoe, and picked the money up with his toes. He then slipped his shoe back on.

Dan Coleman nodded. "I knew Dennis." He rolled his tongue over his lips and then played with it in his mouth for a moment before he continued. "Yeah, I got transferred down here from Lee Correctional after the last riot. I wasn't part of it, but they thought I was. Gang connections and all that. They put me in a cell with Dennis Fenton."

"Go on."

"He told me he was going to rape her the second he got out of 'ere. Told me that he'd done it before as well. The man was a pig. The way he used to talk about her, like she was some girlfriend he had on the outside. He talked about her sexy little butt and how he owned it because she was his stepdaughter. He told me that he would beat her if she didn't behave. Nasty man. I would've beaten him myself if he wasn't connected to the Rebel Sons."

Hennessy squinted. "He told you that he was going to rape her the day he got out of prison?"

"He sure did."

"Did he talk about her often?"

"As often as ever. Guy was always talking about her. Man used to boast how he had been with her and was gonna make her his again once he got out." He paused, then added, "Guess she didn't think the same way, eh?"

"No, she didn't." Hennessy considered the man for a moment, knowing that all the information in the world wouldn't matter unless he could use it. Even with Coleman's repeated revelations, none of it mattered unless it was made public.

Hennessy dropped the next statement like a bomb, not bothering to sweeten it up in any way.

"I need you to testify," Hennessy said, and just as he thought he would, caught Coleman off guard.

"What?"

"Testify," Hennessy repeated. "Get up on the witness stand and tell the jury what you told me."

"I don't think you understand what you're asking me to do."

"I know exactly what I'm asking," Hennessy said. "The information you have would be enough for the jury to learn the truth about what Dennis Fenton had intended. Your information would prove premeditation of his attempted rape, and that alone would exonerate an innocent girl."

Coleman looked nervous. It wasn't fear, yet Hennessy could see the man trembling at the thought of getting up on the stand.

"I don't know if you've ever served time, but in here there are rules, ya know? If anybody finds out I ratted out another inmate, I'd be dead in a week. Nobody does that. They'd get me within a week."

"Dennis Fenton was a cop. That's all you have to tell anyone."

"A cop with connections to the Rebel Sons. There ain't no way I'm testifying."

Hennessy tried again, rewording his request over and over.

It didn't work.

No matter how many times he asked, or how he changed the words, Hennessy couldn't convince Coleman to agree to testify, and eventually, he had no choice but to accept the man's answer.

He'd found the break he was looking for, but without a testifying witness, the information was as good as useless.

CHAPTER 34

HENNESSY'S HAND shook as he held onto the steering wheel. The truth was so close, within touching distance, but he couldn't quite grasp it.

He drove in silence back to Charleston, barely able to think about anything else. As he rolled into the peninsula, he slid his car window down for a hit of fresh air and called his investigator.

"Barry," Hennessy said. "You in the area, by any chance?"

"About five minutes away. Want me to drop by?"

"Might be easier," Hennessy said, and Lockett acknowledged him before canceling the call.

He was close to the truth, and Hennessy knew the more times he went fishing for information, the more chance he had of hooking something. Hennessy parked his truck, entered his office, and sat at his desk. He switched the computer on, running the conversation with Dan Coleman back through his mind as he watched the starting screen flash into view.

He was reading through his emails when Lockett turned up a few minutes later and, after a quick handshake, pushed himself a little back from the desk.

Hennessy began by sharing his meeting with Alicia and the beating she had received. He also mentioned how she had been told to take the deal, but more importantly, what one of them had told her as an afterthought.

"So I went and visited Dan Coleman at Lieber Correctional. I didn't think I'd get anything. You know what these guys are like. They want nothing to do with authority." Hennessy drew a long breath. "I should've taken more time before I met with Dan Coleman, but I didn't think it was worth it."

"What did he say?"

"Everything we needed him to say. He said that he was a cellmate of Dennis Fenton and that Fenton had often talked about how the first thing he was going to do once he got out of prison was rape his stepdaughter."

"He said that?"

"He did, which means I have a new mission for you. I need you to look into Dan Coleman's past and see if there's anything we can leverage to convince him to testify."

They sat opposite each other for a few moments as Lockett considered the request. "What's Coleman in for?"

"Murder. He's been locked up for ten years now. He was in Lee Correctional until the prison riot a few years ago and then moved down to Lieber. His first cellmate in Lieber was Dennis Fenton."

Lockett grimaced. "That's going to be hard to get information about him, Joe. The first few years after someone goes away, people still care and have memories of their time together, but life has a way of moving on. All the inmates say the same thing. People come to visit in the first few years, but after a decade in the slammer, you'll be lucky to get a phone call once a year. A lot of the people he used to know won't want to revisit his past. They would've long forgotten about him."

"I need you to try. And I need you to do it quickly."

"Ok. No promises, but I'll get on it straight away."

"Thanks, Barry."

Lockett left the office, and Hennessy spun his chair around and looked out the window as he thought about the latest developments. He had a chance, a sniff, to have the case thrown out. Hennessy looked out the window toward the church steeple and felt himself relax enough to smile.

For the next five hours, Hennessy's afternoon disappeared under the weight of investigation, trying to find anything about Dan Coleman that could change his mind. Coleman was locked up at twenty-one, still just a kid in the wrong place at the wrong time. He had killed another kid the same age in a dispute about drugs. He had no wife, no children, and no surviving parents. He had no past to speak of and nothing to come back to. Coleman's life was in prison, locked up behind the sharp wire fences of Lieber Correctional. If Coleman made it to his release date, Hennessy wondered how he would see the world with nothing left for him.

After his eyes became blurry staring at the computer screen, he called it a night. The heat had eased as he walked back to his truck, but the air was still thick with humidity. Hennessy's phone buzzed in his pocket. It was Lockett.

"You find anything?"

"I have," Lockett said, sounding proud of himself. "Your friend John Cleveland?"

"What about him?"

"Turns out he's a member of the same prison gang, the Royal Nation."

"I'm not following," Hennessy said.

"Cleveland and Dan Coleman belong to the same prison gang, Joe. They spent a lot of time together at Lee Correctional. That's your way in. Talk to John Cleveland and tell him to convince Dan Coleman to testify."

CHAPTER 35

WHEN HENNESSY awoke Sunday morning with the sunshine streaming in through his window, the gentle ding of church bells rang in the distance. It was impossible to avoid the ring of church bells on a Sunday morning in Charleston.

He climbed out of bed and looked out his window to see a group of well-dressed worshippers, with suits and bow ties for men and long, summery dresses and hats for women, walking to their nearest church. As he made a coffee, the church bells continued to echo through the still air like a choir on Christmas eve. Sunday mornings always felt like a celebration in Charleston, but how everyone awoke so early and with so much energy always surprised Hennessy.

He hadn't been to church in over twenty years, ever since he carried his ten-year-old son's casket out of one. He didn't know if he still had faith. Maybe he did, maybe he didn't. All he knew was that there was something bigger than him, a heartbeat in the world that he couldn't understand.

Feeling the presence of something greater than himself, he looked up to the blue sky out of his window and then made the sign of the cross. "No harm in trying," he whispered to himself.

After two coffees and a fry-up of bacon and eggs, he drove out to the Lee Correctional Institution, the third different prison he'd visited that weekend. He cruised the two-hour drive, listening to the gentle sounds of country music as he rolled through small towns and past long flat areas of farming land. He had the window down, arm resting on the door, singing badly to his favorite tunes. He passed lonely houses, overgrown yards, and busy churches.

He arrived at the prison just minutes before a bus load pulled up to the entrance. The on-duty guard sped him through the security sequence and then phoned for someone to escort him through to the interview room. According to current rosters, Cleveland was still in with a visitor at that moment, but they would bring him through the second it was over.

Hennessy found himself again waiting in an interview room with only the sounds of the prison for company. The clanging, the banging, the yelling—it was the same in every prison. He sat waiting for close to an hour before the familiar rattle of keys and bootheels on concrete grew louder as they made their way toward him.

Cleveland looked surprised when he walked in and found Hennessy sitting at the table but kept quiet until the two men were alone. At first, they sat and stared at each other as if sizing the other up before speaking. Cleveland broke the silence first.

"I haven't heard from Alicia to say she's free, so I'm guessing you haven't come to gloat about your victory."

Wasting little time, Hennessy fired off the first question. "I need you to get a message to the Royal Nation members in Lieber."

"Why?"

"Because it will help the case with your daughter."

"What's the message?"

"There's a man in there for murder—Dan Coleman. He's a member of the Royal Nation, just like you. He used to be here before the riot." Hennessy kept his glare on Cleveland. "When they moved him to Lieber Correctional, he was a cellmate with Dennis Fenton, who admitted that he wanted to rape Alicia as the first thing he did out of prison. That's the evidence I need to get your daughter off these charges. I need you to convince Dan Coleman to testify."

"Need or not, you know that isn't going to happen any time soon."

"Why not? This is your child we're talking about here. The girl whose life you abandoned but wanted to save. She's about to go to prison for murder unless we can prove she was defending herself. Dan Coleman's testimony will do that."

"I can't help you."

"Why not?"

"Because it'll connect me to the case."

"You're already connected."

"Not as far as anyone knows, they don't." Cleveland's face softened. "And it needs to be kept like that. Alicia is a Fenton, not a Cleveland. Most people in here don't even know I have a daughter." He leaned forward. "And nobody must know, you hear me? They'd go after her if they knew she was my daughter."

"I hear you, but why?"

"Because I've done some bad things back here. You have to, if you want to survive. I'm here for life, anyway. What are they going to do? Put me here for two lifetimes? No. I'm not scared for me. Let them pricks come after me. But her? Yeah, I'm scared for her. No one in the gangs knows Alicia is my daughter, and it has to stay that way."

"Which gangs?"

"I'm part of the Royal Nation—"

"Which is connected to the Rebel Sons."

Cleveland nodded. "You do your research." He sighed. "And I've killed and hurt some people in the Supreme Brotherhood. One of them was the child of one of the main guys."

"A white supremacist prison gang."

"That's right. They've got connections everywhere, and if they find out Alicia is my daughter, she'd be dead in a week. An eye for an eye, and all that."

"She'll die behind bars if we lose this case. She's putting up a tough front, but she's not hardened like you. She won't last a year behind bars, let alone thirty." Hennessy pressed his index finger into the table. "I need you to make up a story, call in favors from your gang members, and convince Dan Coleman to testify."

There was another moment of silence as each man considered the conversation. Cleveland again broke it with a little more of a revelation for Hennessy.

"Nobody knows the link between her and me. And nobody knows why you took the case. They'd find out if they dug a little under the surface, but it isn't common knowledge. Right now, nobody behind these bars knows."

Hennessy tried one final time. "John, this is your chance to do the right thing."

With a final head shake, Cleveland turned his head and called for the guard.

A second later, the door opened, and a few seconds after that, Hennessy found himself alone again.

The meeting was over, and he was no closer to the truth.

CHAPTER 36

THE DRIVE home from the Lee Correctional Institution was long.

At the end of the weekend, the traffic was a lot heavier than he'd expected, and two accidents had effectively slowed the traffic heading south down to just a crawl. He didn't mind, not now that he had a much clearer picture of the events surrounding the case.

Hennessy wound the window down as the afternoon South Carolina heat choked the interior of his truck, the sweat feeling as if it was running down each side of his body. The breeze was barely noticeable, and he leaned toward the window a little more to take advantage. Moving at less than ten miles an hour wasn't going to come close to cooling him down, but it was better than nothing.

His cell phone buzzed on the seat beside him, and Hennessy answered without checking the number first. He had assumed it would be one of two people—Wendy to tell him about that weekend's wedding at the vineyard or Lockett with another piece of information he couldn't wait to share. It was neither. Brandon McDermott sounded like he was hiding in the back of his bathroom, the voice barely audible, yet each word came through with a stark echo.

"I can't do this anymore, Mr. Hennessy," McDermott whispered, the desperation choking his words. "The stress is killing me. Phil Pickering keeps asking me when this is all going to be resolved, and I have to lie to him about what we're doing. I keep telling him that I'm pleading not guilty, but I know that's not the truth. What if he finds out before then? What if he finds out our plan and cuts my contract anyway?"

"Brandon," Hennessy said. "Calm down. I know it isn't easy, but it won't be long before this is over. We've got a plan, and we need to stick to it."

"But for how long?" the man's voice was laced with desperation. "Having this hanging over my head feels like a death sentence. I can't do it. Every night I worry that they'll withdraw the building contract and I'll have to fire twenty people. I can't sleep."

"We can get through this."

"Maybe this is easy for you, but this is strangling me. I can't eat. I can't breathe. Whenever my wife looks at me, I feel like I'm failing her. Every time my daughters hug me, I feel like I'm about to let them down." And then, with intense annunciation, "It's driving me insane."

"I understand, but we've already discussed that stretching things out is the best course of action for you right now, remember? This is how you save jobs. This is how you ensure you get through to the end of the building contract. We keep pushing it out and stalling the case."

"I didn't think it through when we discussed it, though. I honestly didn't think it would be this difficult. Can't you do something now? Can't you get it thrown out on a technicality?"

"Unfortunately, the law doesn't work like that."

"But there must be something that will see this through sooner?"

"And risk you losing the construction project? I thought we already agreed that—"

"I don't think I can wait that long," McDermott whispered. "This is killing me."

"I understand. Right now, I'm in the middle of a trial, but I can get my investigator to do another sweep of the evidence and see if he can find anything we may have missed. Maybe he's found something new to have the case thrown out. I've told him to hold off on the information, so maybe he's got something new for us. I'll talk to him tomorrow."

McDermott hesitated to respond as the traffic ahead of Hennessy picked up again. The wind coming in through the open window felt much cooler.

"Thank you," McDermott finally said. "But you'll call me if you find anything? Anything at all?"

"Of course," Hennessy confirmed. "I promise. Have a good afternoon. Take some deep breaths and enjoy the company of your family."

Hennessy watched the traffic pass by and cleared his mind as best he could, hoping that the less stress in his mind, the more chance he had of getting home before the headache began. The stress, along with the rising humidity, was getting to him.

His drive took almost fifty minutes longer than expected, but the heat had eased. There was rain forecast, although Hennessy wasn't sure if it would eventuate.

He turned into his street. His foot eased off the accelerator.

Parked in front of his home were five Harleys,

with large, hairy men standing next to them. They were all dressed in vests with the emblem of the Rebel Sons on their backs.

Hennessy considered not stopping, but that would only delay the inevitable.

He parked on the opposite side of the street and leaned across to his glove box. He took out his Glock 19 and holster and put it on. He stepped out onto the sidewalk.

All the members of the Rebel Sons kept their eyes on Hennessy as he walked toward his home.

"Joe Hennessy."

Hennessy turned and saw Detective Sean Carver leaning against his new Mercedes, parked next to the five Harleys.

"What do—" Hennessy began as he closed the space between them, but Carver cut him off.

"Shut up and listen, Counsellor, because I'm only going to tell you this once. Stop trying to get information out of the likes of John Cleveland and Dan Coleman, you hear?"

"Coleman? Cleveland? What interest are they to you?"

"I said shut up and listen," Carver puffed hard on a cigarette and then flicked it to the gutter. He stepped forward to face Hennessy. "I know that's hard for you loud-mouthed lawyers to comprehend. The Royal Nation has sent me here to give you a friendly warning."

"The Royal Nation?" Hennessy looked at the members of the Rebel Sons. They all wore the same expression—grumpy, angry, and annoyed.

"They're a prison gang, Hennessy. Both Cleveland and Dan Coleman are members."

"And why would you get messages from them?"

"You think that cops just stumble across the information? You think we just sit in our offices and wait for information to come to us? No, boy, we're all connected. Everyone in this state is connected by just a few degrees of separation."

"You certainly seem to be connected to a lot of people, Carver. From what I hear, the Royal Nation and Rebel Sons are linked very closely. Close enough to run drugs through the prisons."

Carver raised his eyebrows and pulled back his jacket to expose his weapon in its holster. "Stay away from the Royal Nation, or the next message ain't gonna be so friendly."

"If I prove that you have strong links with members of the Royal Nation and members of the Rebel Sons, what would that do for your career?"

"I don't like what you're suggesting, lawyer."

"I know you're skating on thin ice with Internal Affairs." Hennessy nodded to the bikers standing a few feet away from them. "I've seen the reports where they've told you to stay away from the Rebel Sons."

"I can talk to whoever I want."

"The report states that you've been ordered to stay away from their clubhouse, or you could face criminal conspiracy charges. One stop at their clubhouse would see you behind bars for a long time. You could get to know the Royal Nation quite well."

"If you have any evidence of that, I suggest you burn it."

"Or I'll present it in court. I'm sure the Office of Internal Affairs would be very interested in it."

Carver stepped forward. "If you link me with

those gangs, it won't be me you'll have to deal with."

With both hands, he shoved Hennessy back. Carver looked to be taking another step toward him, but Hennessy threw a left hook.

The fist found its mark, connected with the side of Carver's jaw, and sent him to the ground. Hennessy stood over him, but Carver decided fair-fight-time was over. He pulled his gun.

"Give me a reason," Carver said. "I ain't playing with ya." As if to show how much he disliked the lawyer, he stood and spat at Hennessy's feet. Before he could react, Carver lowered the pistol a little and said, "Consider this your only warning," before he turned and entered his new Mercedes.

The bikers remained for a moment before they roared into the night.

CHAPTER 37

ALICIA HAD trouble pushing her lawyer's face from her mind.

While she said nothing to him directly, his demeanor had frightened her. He looked tired. Almost defeated. The once confident lawyer she relied on for her confidence appeared gone, having faded out fast during the previous few days. His face was weary, lacking any sign of the winner she first met, and she wondered whether she had placed her hopes in an acquittal that would never happen.

She thought about how to prepare for the inevitable verdict ahead of time as the guard led her and two others back to the unit from the medical wing. If she began now, maybe she could get her mind right, and then take the failure in her stride as she began what would be a ten-year sentence.

Ten years, she thought to herself as she walked back into the unit ahead of the others. Up on the top landing, Jada leaned on the railing and waved for her to join her. Alicia returned the wave and headed for the stairs. Someone shouted something at her, but she ignored it.

"How was the meeting?" Jada asked as they turned for her cell. Alicia still hadn't been given a cellmate, a good thing and something she wasn't about to complain about.

"Same as always," Alicia said, trying to sound nonchalant.

"That exciting, huh?"

She shrugged.

Jada moved closer to her and kept her voice low. "Listen, you didn't hear from me, but people have been asking about you."

"Who?"

"Girls who are linked to men in the Royal Nation. They're a prison gang, mostly out at Lee Correctional, but they have ties everywhere. They've been talking about you."

"Why?"

"I don't know, but I can't say anything more."

Jada looked away to make sure no one was listening.

Fear, doubt, and uncertainty all circled inside Alicia, and at times, it was bad enough for her to feel nauseous. The thought of spending any more time than she had to in prison was enough to frighten her beyond anything she had ever felt, and yet, it was a very real possibility.

"What if it all went to hell?" she said as they sat on her bunk. "Like it all fell apart."

"What do you mean?"

"I mean, what if I was found guilty and ended up in here, anyway? What if the judge ends up sentencing me to a higher sentence than what's already been offered? He might sentence me to fifty years." She shook her head a few times and then continued. "Maybe I should take the ten years."

"Then that would blow big time," Jada said.

Alicia looked down at her hands, saddened by the state of her skin. Working in the laundry had dried them out. Her nails, normally manicured and topped with fake ones adorned by cute designs, now looked sad and worn, with a couple snapped at the edges.

"Is this my future?" Alicia looked over at her friend. "I mean, what if this is what I actually deserve? I killed him. I hit him with a baseball bat. Maybe I deserve this."

"Don't say that."

"Why? I hit him from behind, after all. I killed a man. I should be punished for that, right?"

"I said don't say that," Jada repeated. "I mean it. I don't want to hear that from you."

Alicia could see her friend didn't like hearing it, but her feelings were almost overwhelming.

"Tell me you'd stay with me if I accepted the deal," she asked, her tone close to begging. Jada looked at her but frowned. "Please. I don't think I could do this alone. At least if I knew you were here, then I would have someone to lean on."

"I told you to stop talking like that," Jada said. "I can't hear you talking like that."

"But I did it. I hit him, and he died. I'm a murderer. I hit him with a baseball bat in the back of the head."

Rather than stay and argue, Jada shook her head and slid off the end of the bunk. When she reached the door, she looked back at Alicia, who met her gaze. "Take the deal or don't. That choice is yours. But don't sit there calling yourself a murderer when you know that's the last thing you are."

She left Alicia alone, and by then, the girl could no longer hold her emotion.

Tears spilled in two neat streams down her face. Feeling disgusted by the sensation, Alicia buried her face deep enough into the pillow to ensure her cries weren't heard out in the common area.

She had a choice to make—and she didn't think she could survive either option.

CHAPTER 38

THE START of the third week of the trial was much the same.

The prosecution piled on the expert witnesses, laying down the facts that Alicia had hit her stepfather in the back of the head, suggesting the threat to her life was over and that she had no legal right to hit him.

Garrett filled the days with an abundance of boring experts and specialists, most from specific scientific fields, who combed over every inch of crime scene evidence. As the days edged past, the answers became monotonous. The experts all came to the same conclusion—Dennis Fenton had been walking away when Alicia Fenton hit him from behind. They theorized that the threat to her life ended when Dennis turned his back. Hennessy did well in some cross-examinations, but it was of little use.

The procession continued until 5pm on Wednesday before Garrett rested the prosecution case.

Their argument for murder was over, and the jury appeared convinced.

The jurors nodded when he nodded, smiled when he smiled and shook their heads in disgust whenever Garrett mentioned Alicia's past. His story convinced the jurors. How could a man who was high on morphine threaten a girl as he was walking away?

Hennessy could barely remember blinking through the hours of Wednesday, but when he saw Alicia's face that afternoon, he saw the undeniable thoughts running through her mind, and despite not wanting to admit it, he felt the same way. He could never prove her innocence if Dennis Fenton's intent to rape his stepdaughter wasn't established.

Alicia was days away from being found guilty, and Hennessy was about to lose the chance to find the truth about his son.

Once Judge West called an end to the day and left the courtroom, Hennessy remained sitting at his table longer than usual. He explained to Alicia that when their case began the next day, they would present the facts as she knew them, but he could see the defeat on her face, and he didn't try to change her mind. There was no point. If he did, then he would effectively be lying, not only to her but also to himself. And so, he had simply watched her leave the courtroom under escort.

Once she was gone, Hennessy turned his attention to the paperwork lying before him, reading what he had already read a thousand times over. The names, the evidence, the background, none of it mattered in a one-sided case. He could sense his frustrations build and, surprisingly, didn't try to stop it. What he really wanted to do was scream.

"Want me to get you anything?"

He turned and saw Jacinta standing just behind him. For a moment, his brain refused to kick into gear, and for a split second, he felt panicked as he forgot where he was.

It's just stress, he thought to himself and smiled at

Jacinta. But was it just stress? He couldn't be sure. He couldn't be sure of anything at that moment.

"Can you meet me in the conference room in five minutes?"

"Sure thing." Jacinta agreed. "Want me to take your briefcase?"

He thanked her, dropped the rest of the paperwork into it, snapped the lid closed, and handed it over.

"Thank you," he said. "I won't be long."

Hennessy headed for the restroom. Once in the only place in the entire building where he could be alone, Hennessy looked at his reflection in the bathroom's mirror and tried to see what others could. He felt exhausted. To him, the case appeared all but lost, pulled from his grip by repetitive assaults from the prosecution, and it seemed as if he was powerless to do anything about it.

His head throbbed, his back was sore, and he missed his family.

"What the hell are you doing?" he asked himself, eyes fixed on his reflection. He wanted to answer himself but couldn't.

It wasn't until he sat in the courthouse conference room with Jacinta that he felt himself let go of the strong facade he'd been hanging onto for the entire week. It took Jacinta about two seconds to notice it, and not one to keep quiet, she commented almost immediately.

"It's not the end, Joe," Jacinta said. "We still have to present our case."

"It might as well be the end," he whispered. "How am I supposed to turn things around from here? Edith will be a great witness, but you saw the face of those jurors. They're convinced that because Fenton was high on morphine and walking away, the threat was over. She won't win on self-defense. We should've tried a different tactic."

"It's not lost yet. We can still win this."

"I don't see it. Usually, I can see a way out, but with the morphine and the strike to the back of the head, any reasonable person would say she used excessive force. Manslaughter is the best we can hope for."

He could see the worry on Jacinta's face and felt guilty for the poor attitude he had.

"I'm sorry," he said, rubbing his temples as he closed his eyes. "This week is just getting to me."

"You could put her on the stand," she suggested. "She could tell her story."

"It's a terrible idea. Garrett will tear her apart," he whispered. "But maybe we should prepare her. It might be our last hope."

CHAPTER 39

"THE DEFENSE calls Edith Chapman."

Hennessy opened the defense case with his big gun. This was it. He had to lay the groundwork for everything to come. The jury was comfortably in the prosecution's favor, and it was time for Hennessy to change that.

Edith Chapman entered the courtroom with her head bowed forward. She avoided eye contact with everyone in the room. She wore a blue dress with a white cardigan and bright yellow glasses. She didn't have a hair out of place, and she held herself confidently. After swearing her oath, she sat in the witness stand and waited for the lawyer to begin.

"Thank you for coming to court today, Mrs. Chapman." Hennessy walked to the lectern and began his questioning. "Can you please tell the court how you know the deceased, Mr. Dennis Fenton?"

"Dennis was my brother, and Alicia is my niece, or step-niece, I suppose. I don't know, but I always considered Alicia as a part of my family."

"And how would you describe the relationship between Dennis and Alicia?"

"When Dennis first met Shauna, that's Alicia's mother, they were great together. Alicia never had a father figure in her life, so she adored Dennis. They would play and dance together, and he would take her to ballet lessons on Saturday mornings. It was beautiful, and I was really happy for Dennis. He couldn't have kids of his own, so having Alicia in his life full-time was a blessing. They were wonderful for the first five years together."

"Only the first five years?"

"Unfortunately, yes."

"And what happened that changed their relationship?"

"After five years of being together, Shauna passed away. We were all devastated, and Dennis legally adopted Alicia. He said he would take care of her because she had no one else. She had no other family. And then, only a few months after he lost Shauna, he went through an incident at work that caused him great mental distress. He was later diagnosed with PTSD, but his personality seemed to change overnight."

"How did his personality seem after the incident?"

"He was angry all the time. He drank a lot and swore a lot and was never home. Poor Alicia had just lost her mother, and then she also lost her stepfather. Dennis was a good guy, but he became a raging bull, always angry and blaming everyone else for his troubles."

"Was Mr. Fenton violent after that?"

"Very. I saw him punch Alicia many times. My husband, who's a doctor, and I tried to get her taken out of his care, but he refused. He said he owned her. She would stay with us sometimes when Dennis had to work weekends, and she would always come over with bruises on her body. I'd ask about the bruises, but she would say that Dennis said it was an accident and that he was sorry." Edith blinked back a tear. "It was horrible to watch."

"Did Alicia disclose any other types of abuse?"

"Objection," Garrett rose to his feet. "Relevance. We've discussed this in the pre-trial hearing."

"Approach," Judge West waved them forward.

The two lawyers walked to the side of the judge's bench and lowered their tone. Judge West turned off her microphone and turned on the white noise in the speakers above the jury box to ensure the jury members didn't hear their discussion.

"Is this question regarding the court case where Mr. Fenton was found not guilty of rape, Mr. Hennessy?"

"No, Your Honor," Hennessy explained. "The witness will talk about a separate discussion that she had with Alicia where the abuse happened."

"We're stepping into dangerous territory," Garrett argued. "I don't think the witness will answer the questions without talking about the rape."

"She'll be able to, Your Honor," Hennessy said. "I've discussed with her what can and can't be said."

"Then the objection is overruled for now, and you may proceed, but be careful with the questioning, Mr. Hennessy. The second you stray near the previous court case, I will uphold the objection."

The lawyers returned to their tables, with Garrett shaking his head the entire time. Hennessy checked his notes and then returned to the lectern. "Mrs. Chapman, did Alicia disclose any details of the abuse to you?"

"Objection," Garrett stood. "Hearsay."

"Mrs. Chapman is talking about the behavior of the defendant and the victim," Hennessy argued. "This line of questioning is establishing the defendant's mental state over the years before Mr. Fenton's death."

"The objection is overruled for now." Judge West's tone was slow and cautious. "But don't stray too far into hearsay, Mr. Hennessy."

"Thank you, Your Honor," Hennessy said and refocused on the witness. "Mrs. Chapman, did Alicia disclose any details of the abuse to you?"

"She did."

"And can you please tell the court about what she disclosed?"

"She talked about how Dennis used to watch her shower."

"And how old was she at this time?"

"Fourteen."

"And did Alicia tell you she was comfortable with this behavior?"

"She said she was very uncomfortable with the behavior. She hated it, but she knew if she argued with him, she would be beaten." She lowered her head and dabbed her eye with a tissue. "I wish I could've saved her. We tried everything. Child services, the courts, the police, but the issue we had was that Dennis was a very well-connected man. Nobody did anything."

"Was there any other abuse that Alicia disclosed to you?"

"She talked about how he would often rub his hands over her…" she paused and sighed. "Over her bottom and breasts. She would spend the first day crying about the abuse whenever she came to our house. She hated it, but she couldn't do anything about it. Even if she tried to do anything, he would beat her."

"And your brother Dennis, did he ever talk to you about this abuse?"

"When I visited him in prison, he said he couldn't wait to get his hands on her. It was disgusting, and I told him as much, but he was so high, he didn't even think twice about it."

"Do you remember his exact words?"

"He said, 'I can't wait to get my hands on that sweet piece of tail.' And then he said that he 'owns her.' It was disgusting." She shook her head several times, staring into nothing. Hennessy gave her all the time she needed. "And another time, when he picked her up after a weekend at our house, he said he was so happy to have his 'little plaything back in his hands.'"

"Those were his exact words?"

"Yes, but I think he was high at the time."

"Were you aware of what he was high on?"

"After he tried to kick the alcohol, he got addicted to morphine. He said he had a legal prescription for it, but I doubted it. Every time I saw him over the past two years, he looked high on something."

For the next forty-five minutes, Hennessy asked question after question in rapid fire, painting a clear picture that Alicia had grown up in an abusive household. But while it painted a picture of the past, it provided no evidence of what happened to Alicia on the night of April 15th.

When Hennessy finished questioning, Judge West invited Garrett to begin.

"Mrs. Chapman," Garrett asked, still seated behind his desk. "Can you please tell the court if you ever witnessed the alleged sexual abuse?"

"I witnessed the mental effects of it."

"But you didn't witness the alleged sexual abuse, or are you just relying on the word of a sulky, vengeful teenager?"

Edith shook her head and then sighed. "I didn't directly witness any sexual abuse."

"Thank you, Mrs. Chapman. Nothing further."

And with just two questions, Garrett destroyed any progress the defense had made.

CHAPTER 40

AFTER EDITH Chapman's convincing opening testimony, Hennessy called several witnesses to consolidate the defense case.

He called the paramedic who attended to Alicia's wound at the crime scene. The young woman was very factual in the delivery of her testimony. Yes, Alicia had a cut above her right eye. Yes, Alicia stated her stepfather had hit her. Yes, Alicia appeared to be terrified and confused.

Next, Hennessy called an expert in prisoner analysis. Yes, Dennis Fenton had a letter addressed to the Lieber Correctional Center. Yes, Fenton was due to be residing there for another fourteen months. Yes, he would consider Fenton trespassed on Alicia's property as he had no legal right to be there. Then came a property law expert. Yes, Alicia's name was on the title of the property. Yes, the title was in her name. No, Dennis Fenton was not paying rent. The expert concluded that Dennis Fenton was not a resident at the time of his death.

Next came the nurse from the school Alicia attended. She was an older lady with a caring smile. She had noticed Alicia's bruises and had reported the physical abuse to the authorities. After a while, she became scared for Alicia's well-being. She read from her detailed notebook, which clearly stated she was worried there was also sexual abuse at the home.

To start the third day of the defense case, Hennessy called domestic violence expert Dr. Julia Owen. She explained the pattern of behavior that abusers used and how, given all the evidence available, it was likely that Alicia had suffered regularly at the hands of her stepfather.

Hennessy called medical experts to state that excessive force had not been used in the single strike. One medical expert said the strike to the head didn't crack Mr. Fenton's skull and could not be considered excessive. It didn't take much force to impact the craniovertebral junction, the expert explained.

On the afternoon of day three, Hennessy called Bloodstain Pattern Analyst Mr. Tony Cross.

"Can you please tell the court why blood pattern analysis is important?"

"The analysis of bloodstain patterns can return useful information in a criminal case. The general role of the Bloodstain Pattern Analyst is to assist in reconstructing the events of an alleged incident. Individual bloodstains and bloodstain patterns become useful when analyzed because the information is descriptive of the events that could have produced them. Bloodstain pattern analysis evaluations are conducted to determine what action or sequence of actions could have happened. This information may include, for example, the position of the individual when the blood was deposited, were they sitting or were they standing, the relative position of individuals at the time of bloodshed, the possible type of weapon used as well as possible mechanisms that could have produced the blood staining on a surface."

"And does blood have the same properties as other liquids, such as water?"

"No. It behaves very differently." Cross scoffed. "And because blood behaves in certain ways, trained analysts can draw conclusions about how the blood may have been shed. It may appear random to the untrained eye, but we can gather information from spattering patterns, transmissions, spaces, and other marks."

"And how is that done, exactly?"

"The analysis looks at the principles of biology, physics, geometry, distance, and angle to assist investigators in answering questions about the scene."

"Interesting," Hennessy nodded. "Mr. Cross, did you analyze the pictures of the blood on the kitchen wall?"

"I did."

"And did you determine where the blood in the kitchen came from?"

"The police report states it was Alicia Fenton's blood on the wall."

"What caused the blood to land on the wall?"

"A strike to the face. As you can see in the crime scene photos, the pattern created by blood drops is because of its motion, in this case, from right to left. This is called the Cast-Off Pattern. And given the height of the blood, it would've come from someone around five-foot-five."

"And could you determine which direction Alicia was wounded?"

"She would've been struck by a force higher than her, and that striking motion would've come from a downward direction."

"From the blood stains, can you determine how

Alicia and her attacker were positioned?"

"They were both in the kitchen, and the attacker was at the doorway. Alicia was in the corner."

"Her attacker was blocking her exit?"

"Possibly."

"And from the crime scene analysis, could you tell how long the blood stain was there?"

"You can see from the crime scene report it was a very recent stain."

"Thank you, Mr. Cross. No further questions."

Garrett declined to cross-examine, and Judge West called an end to the day. Once the judge and jury had left the room, Garrett stepped closer to Hennessy.

"I really hope you're going to put Alicia on the stand." Garrett looked over the top of Hennessy, who remained seated. Garrett eyed the defendant. "I'm going to enjoy questioning you on the stand."

"Is intimidation now part of your tool kit?" Hennessy stood, towering over Garrett and blocking his view of the defendant.

"I'm just saying I'm looking forward to it." Garrett smiled and raised his hands. "Because no matter how many experts you put up there, it doesn't change the facts. The only option you have left is to put her on the stand."

Garrett turned back to his desk and packed up his items. Hennessy turned to Alicia and told her not to worry. The guards collected her a moment later and led her through the side door.

Hennessy sighed as he sat at the defense table in the almost empty courtroom. He stared at nothing as he tapped his finger on the edge of the table. Garrett was right. They didn't have many options left. He would have to call Alicia to the stand, but that opened her up to all sorts of danger. Garrett would focus on her lack of injuries, the lack of ripped clothes, or even bruising on her hands. He would make a mockery of her statements, and the jury would have no choice but to find her guilty.

No, he had to find another way.

As Hennessy left the courthouse, his cell phone rang.

When he answered it, the voice alone stopped him in his tracks, but what the caller said next changed everything.

CHAPTER 41

JUDGE WEST walked into the courtroom on the third day of the defense case. The seats in the public gallery were half-filled, but the same five police officers stood at the back of the room. Before Judge West could call for the jury to enter the room, Hennessy stood.

"Yes, Mr. Hennessy?" Judge West asked.

Hennessy looked at Garrett, who eyed him with suspicion.

"Your Honor, the defense would like to lodge a motion to adjust the witness list."

"It's a bit late to bring in new witnesses, don't you think, Mr. Hennessy?"

He took a breath and pinned his hopes on the change. "I apologize for such a sudden introduction, but unfortunately, the information this witness has presented to the defense has only just come to light. We had no control over the timing of this issue."

"The State objects to calling new witnesses at this time, Your Honor," Garrett said as he rose to his feet. "We've almost finished this case, and the defense is only looking to stall the decision."

"Noted. Mr. Hennessy, who is the new witness?"

"Mr. Dan Coleman," Hennessy stated. "He was the cellmate of Mr. Fenton before he left Lieber Correctional. I had previously asked this witness to testify, however, he only stepped forward last night. This is the first opportunity we've had to present his statement to the court."

"And do you have a written statement there?"

"We do." Hennessy walked forward and handed one piece of paper to the bailiff, who passed it onto the judge and then gave a second copy to Garrett. "As you can see from this statement, his testimony is essential in uncovering the truth in this case."

"Your Honor," Garrett argued, "this is ridiculous. This is an unreliable witness, a convicted felon, who has suddenly stepped forward when he had months to come forward before this. We can't allow this person to take the stand."

"As I mentioned, the witness only came forward last night."

"And the witness is here?"

"He is."

Judge West expressed her surprise at the end of the statement, raised her eyebrows, and said, "Ok. I will allow it. The prosecution can have the morning to prepare for the witness testimony, and we will reconvene after lunch. If the prosecution would like to question the witness under deposition, they can do so this morning. If additional time is required to investigate the claims made in his testimony, then we can discuss that after lunch. Any problems with that, Mr. Garrett?"

"I would like the State's objection to this decision noted."

"It's noted," Judge West said and then banged her gavel. "We will see you all after lunch."

The morning passed quickly. Hennessy and Jacinta spent most of their time waiting in the conference meeting room of the Charleston Judicial Center. They saw members of the prosecution team hurry past the door several times, desperate to prepare for the new witness. After lunch, the lawyers returned to the courtroom, and when Judge West received nothing further from the prosecution, she instructed Hennessy to call the new witness.

"The defense calls Dan Coleman."

Judge West called for the witness to be brought in, and two guards escorted Coleman from the door Alicia normally emerged from. Still dressed in his prison gear, he looked uncomfortable as all eyes turned on him. He looked at Hennessy. The lawyer gave him the slightest nod before Coleman turned his attention to the witness stand.

Once the bailiff did his duties and swore the witness in, Hennessy took over and rose to his feet.

"Thank you for coming to the court today, Mr. Coleman," Hennessy began. "Can you please begin by telling the court how you knew Mr. Fenton?"

"I was his cellmate for the whole time he was at Lieber. Five weeks of listening to that pig of a man." Coleman kept his voice low. He looked nervous outside the secure walls where he'd spent the past decade. "He talked a lot about everything. You couldn't shut the guy up."

"And have you been offered anything to testify today?"

"What'ya mean?"

"Have you been paid to be here?"

"No," he looked confused.

"Then why have you only come forward with this testimony today?"

Coleman's eyes darted over Hennessy's shoulder

to where Garrett sat watching him. Hennessy saw the moment he brushed his fear aside and took control of himself as he leaned closer to the microphone.

"I listened to my conscience. I didn't want to get involved, you know? I got plenty going on in my own life already."

"I understand," Hennessy said. "And we appreciate your willingness to speak with us to tell us the truth in this court. Tell me, Mr. Coleman, did Dennis Fenton mention his stepdaughter, Alicia Fenton?"

"All the time."

"What did he say about her?"

"Objection, Your Honor. Hearsay."

"I argue that it's not hearsay, Your Honor," Hennessy responded to Garrett's objection. "The witness spent five weeks with Mr. Fenton, and his knowledge of their conversations speaks to the state of mind of Mr. Fenton when he was released."

"Overruled. The witness can talk about what was said to him directly, but only to speak about Mr. Fenton's state of mind. He can't characterize what was said."

"What did Mr. Fenton say about his stepdaughter?" Hennessy repeated the question to the witness.

Coleman didn't hesitate. "He used to tell me how beautiful she was and how much he longed to get with her again."

"Are you telling us that Dennis Fenton told you he was attracted to his stepdaughter?"

"That's right. One of his favorite subjects was telling me what he wanted to do to her when he got out. He said whiskey and sex with her would make the perfect match."

The crowd behind Hennessy gasped, and the judge gave her gavel a quick tap, calling for the court to come to order. Only once the silence returned did the judge gesture for Hennessy to continue.

"Did Mr. Fenton tell you exactly what his plan was?"

"Exactly?"

"Yes. Did Mr. Fenton tell you precisely what he wanted to do the day he got out?"

"Just like I said, he told me he was going to blow off steam and then go to his stepdaughter's house and rape her. He was very detailed about what he was going to do to her."

"Mr. Coleman, are you saying to us, in this court, that Mr. Fenton intended to go to his stepdaughter's apartment to 'blow off steam and rape her?'"

"That's what he said. And he told me he'd done it before as well. He spoke about it as if he was proud of it."

Hennessy turned his attention to the jury and saw the change he'd been hoping for in their faces.

Gone was the look of doubt, replaced by disgust and repulsion.

When Hennessy looked a little further around and saw the prosecutor with his head in his hands, he finished his questioning.

With the new witness, Hennessy was one step closer to the truth.

CHAPTER 42

GARRETT DIDN'T move when first asked to cross-examine the witness. His eyes remained downcast, focused on his writing pad.

Judge West asked a second time, and when Garrett finally stood, the first person he looked at was Hennessy, sending the man a subconscious message that the defense attorney received loud and clear. Hennessy didn't respond, sitting in anticipation, along with everyone else.

"Mr. Coleman, you testified that Mr. Fenton had been your cellmate for five weeks. Is that correct?"

"That's what I said."

"And during that time, it's your claim that Mr. Fenton often spoke about assaulting his stepdaughter. Is that correct?"

"Yeah, I said that."

The prosecutor had been approaching the witness stand at a slow pace, with Garrett mostly looking down to the floor as if that was where the answers to his questions lay.

"How did that make you feel?"

"How did that make me feel?"

"Yes," Garrett confirmed. "You say he spoke about raping his stepdaughter repeatedly. How did you feel about that?"

"It made me sick to my stomach. The man was a

pig. No doubt about it."

"So, he disgusted you?"

"Yeah, he disgusted me," Coleman said, his eyes briefly looking toward Hennessy.

"If you were so disgusted by this man, why didn't you come forward earlier?"

"I already said I didn't want to get involved. Life is different behind bars."

"You didn't want to get involved to help an innocent woman who risked yet another attack from a man you claimed told you he enjoyed raping his stepdaughter?" As if to highlight the question, Garrett turned back and looked in Hennessy's direction, only his eyes focused on the defendant sitting next to him.

"Fenton was an ex-cop. You don't want to get involved with court cases and cops. If I did, I could get beaten."

"You mean by other prisoners? Why would they care? Don't your morals demand a higher sense of duty to the innocent?"

"Objection, Your Honor," Hennessy said. "Relevance."

"Sustained," West returned. "Keep the questions relevant to the current case please, Mr. Garrett."

"Do you think he could've been lying to sound tough?"

"Objection. The prosecution is asking the witness to speculate."

"Sustained. The witness is only here to talk about what he heard, not the meaning or connotation behind it."

Garrett nodded. "Mr. Coleman, can you please tell the court how Mr. Fenton sounded when he talked about his stepdaughter?"

"Objection to the word 'sound.' It calls for characterization."

"Your Honor, the witness is testifying about what he heard." Garrett's tone was frustrated. "That's why he's here."

"He can testify about what he heard but no opinions on it," Judge West said. "Only what was spoken."

Garrett grunted loudly. Judge West stared at him, daring him to do something else that she could hold him in contempt for. He didn't. He returned to his desk and looked over a piece of paper.

All eyes were focused on the prosecutor. From the judge to the crowd in the gallery, to Coleman, sitting upright like a man on the edge of a cliff.

"No further questions," Garrett said but remained standing. "Your Honor, the prosecution would like to request a short recess."

Judge West looked at Hennessy. Hennessy nodded, and the request was approved. The jury was escorted out, and then the bailiff called the court to rise, and the judge left the room. The second the door closed behind her, Garrett walked over to Hennessy and spoke just two words.

"Let's talk."

CHAPTER 43

AS HE stepped out of the courtroom and into the hallway, Hennessy's cell buzzed. He looked at the number. It was Barry Lockett.

"The GPS location data came back for the Brandon McDermott case," Lockett began. "And it's very interesting. I've got the locations of cars around the liquor store when the alarm went off. We've—"

"Sorry, Barry, but I'm about to head into a meeting with the prosecution in the Fenton case. This could be all over in fifteen minutes."

"Joe, you'll want to listen to this."

Hennessy squinted and then listened to Lockett provide an update on the information he'd received from his contact.

"That's brilliant. You're a genius."

"Thanks, mate," Lockett replied. "I'll email it to you and Jacinta."

Five minutes later, Hennessy was called into the meeting room near the entrance of the building. He entered the room with Jacinta by his side. Waiting inside the room were Aaron Garrett and his two assistants. They didn't smile.

When Hennessy and Jacinta sat down, Garrett walked to the door and closed it. He walked to the middle of the room before stopping and turning around. Hennessy noted the man's apprehension as he paused for a brief moment, time enough to consider whether he was doing the right thing.

"I think we both know where this might end up," Garrett began. "So, how about we try to sort this out right here and now?"

"You heard the witness. Alicia was acting in self-defense. Fenton intended to go there and rape her."

"The witness is a murderer who is spending his life behind bars. Hardly a reliable witness that the jury warmed to."

"We'll see. What's the deal on the table?"

"She pleads guilty to voluntary manslaughter. Two-year sentence. One year in prison, the rest suspended."

"Still a year in prison?"

"What else do you want from me, Joe?" Garrett stood and paced the room. "I can't go lower than that. She killed a cop. You've seen the police in the courtroom every day. They're not there for you. They're there to intimidate me. They're there to remind the prosecution that we need to keep on the good side of the police department. A year is as low as I can go. You should encourage your client to take it. All you have is the hearsay testimony of a lying murderer. If this goes to the jury decision, then the case is still a fifty-fifty call. It can still go either way, and she'll spend the best years of her life behind bars. Just take the deal."

"I'll talk to my client."

Hennessy went to stand, but Garrett held out his hand. "I get the feeling that you're not going to encourage her to take the deal. Joe, this is the best chance she'll ever get. She hit him in the back of the head with a baseball bat, for crying out loud! She killed a man. She's got to do some time!"

Garrett rubbed his hand over his brow.

Hennessy slowly stood and held his glare on Garrett. "Like I said, I'll take the offer to my client."

"You're unbelievable," Garrett stated. "What more could you possibly want?"

"We still have one more card to play, and trust me, you won't like it."

Hennessy turned and walked out of the room, with Jacinta following a few steps behind.

As he walked, Hennessy wondered how much his desire for information about his son's death influenced his decisions. This wasn't just about Alicia doing one year instead of ten. For him, this was about Luca, a boy murdered two decades before, a boy who deserved justice. This was about a father finding the closure he so badly needed. It was about giving his son the opportunity to finally rest in peace.

Hennessy opened the door to the meeting room next to the cells and allowed Jacinta to enter first. They said nothing as they waited. They were in the room for five minutes before the guards escorted Alicia inside.

"Is everything ok?" Alicia looked up as the guards closed the door.

Looking from Jacinta to Alicia, Hennessy continued rolling through the possibilities he now had to contend with. For his client, a decision would need to be made, depending on what information he gave her. This was the point he had been hoping for, for weeks, and it all came down to how he gave her the news.

"They've come back with an offer," Hennessy said as he clasped his hands on the table.

"And?" Alicia looked genuinely scared, and Jacinta placed a hand on her shoulder in a maternal gesture.

"If you plead guilty to voluntary manslaughter, they'll give you two years with one year suspended. From today, you'd be out in nine months, given the time you've already served."

"Nine months," Alicia said, thinking about the possibility. "I can do nine more months."

"Think about it long and hard," Jacinta said. "This isn't just about another nine months. This will affect you for the rest of your life. You'll be a convicted felon when you leave prison. That will affect everything that you do. It'll affect the jobs you can have, the travel you can do, and how people treat you. It's not just nine months. It's a life sentence as a convicted felon."

Alicia's face lost its initial happiness when she saw Hennessy wasn't smiling. Her relief faded out as she looked at his serious face. "Why do I feel this isn't the news you were hoping for?"

Hennessy wanted to answer, but something kept him from telling her what he really thought. In his mind, he kept wondering whether the real reason behind his hesitation wasn't for the sake of her, but for himself. Was he being selfish by thinking of himself and Wendy and the information regarding Luca? In a way, he felt he had a right to be. They'd suffered enough, and this had been the first chance at redemption in twenty years.

"My advice is to not accept the deal," Hennessy whispered. "We can still win this. We can still get you out of here."

"Why wouldn't I take this? It's a year. I've already been in for almost three months, so we're talking nine months, max. I can—"

"We still have one more play to make, and if it goes well, the jury will have no choice but to find you not guilty by reason of self-defense."

It must have been something in his eyes, or perhaps his tone, but no sooner had the words left his lips when Alicia slowly nodded.

"He was trying to rape me, and I was acting in self-defense," Alicia confirmed. "I shouldn't go to prison for that. I have a right to defend myself."

Feeling apprehensive, Hennessy muttered a subdued, "Ok then," before rising back to his feet and walking to the door. He called in court security, who took Alicia back into custody. She exchanged a look with him as she passed by on her way out, and he could see the message in them loud and clear. Don't fail me now, her look said.

When Jacinta stood near him, she whispered, "I hope you know what you're doing, Joe Hennessy."

CHAPTER 44

FIFTY-FIVE MINUTES and numerous phone calls later, Hennessy returned to the courtroom. The crowd sat under a hushed silence.

Judge West entered the room, and the bailiff led the jury in a few moments later. The media was ready. They expected the prosecutor to stand up and declare a deal had been reached. Hennessy looked over his shoulder and saw the surprise on their faces when the judge invited him to continue his case.

"Are you ready to call your next witness, Mr. Hennessy?"

"We are, Your Honor." He paused and looked over to Garrett. "The defense recalls Detective Sean Carver, Your Honor."

Garrett squinted at Hennessy and then turned to look at the courtroom doors. When they opened, Carver stepped back into the courtroom. He made his way to the witness stand and took a seat. Hennessy could see beads of sweat on the man's brow as he approached him once he was handed over to the attorney. For a few seconds, the silence returned as the two men eyed each other as if sizing their opponent up.

"Thank you for returning to the court, Detective Carver." Hennessy walked to the lectern and then looked to the jury. They looked at him with puzzled faces. "During your previous testimony, you told the court that you picked Mr. Fenton up from the Lieber Correctional Institute. Is that correct?"

"That's correct."

"And what vehicle did you pick him up in?"

"My private vehicle."

"And what is the make of that vehicle?"

"It's a Mercedes sedan."

"Is it new?"

"That's correct. Only five months old."

"Are you aware if it has GPS monitoring?"

Carver squinted at Hennessy.

"Detective Carver, can you please answer the question?"

"It has anti-theft GPS monitoring, yes."

"Anti-theft GPS monitoring," Hennessy confirmed. "Are you aware that this monitoring occurs at all times and is stored by the Mercedes head office for twelve months, protected by privacy protocols?"

"I don't know the exact details, but sure, that makes sense."

"And are you aware that if subpoenaed, Mercedes would have to present those records to the court?"

Carver stared at Hennessy. "That would make sense."

"Knowing this," Hennessy walked to the defense table and picked up a folder. He held it aloft for a few moments and then placed it back down. "Knowing that Mercedes would be required to release that data under subpoena, can you please tell the court where you drove Mr. Fenton on the night of April 15th?"

Carver sat back slightly, his mouth hanging open. He sat in stunned silence for a few long moments.

"Your Honor, can you please instruct the witness to answer?"

"Detective Carver," Judge West leaned closer to the witness, "are you able to answer the question?"

"Yeah," he whispered, trying to buy himself enough time to get his story straight. "I... I drove him to his apartment."

"Did you stop at all?"

Carver nodded.

"Detective, can you please answer verbally?"

"Yes, we stopped."

"And where was that stop?"

"Just off Market Street."

"Outside the Whiskey and Vine Liquor Store?"

"Objection," Garrett called out. "Leading the witness."

"Withdrawn," Hennessy responded. "What was the store that you stopped outside of?"

"Ah," Carver shook his head. "Dennis said he wanted to get a drink after being locked up for so long. I stayed in the car. I don't know where he went."

"Interesting." Hennessy placed the folder back on the defense table. "And did Mr. Fenton return with something to drink?"

"Yeah, he did. He returned with four bottles of expensive whiskey."

"How expensive?"

"He said they were around five hundred dollars a bottle."

"And how did he pay for those bottles?"

"I didn't ask."

"And do you remember the brands of those whiskey bottles?"

"One was Orphan Barrel. I remember that."

"And did he drink a lot of that whiskey?"

"He drank half the bottle very quickly. Said it was the best whiskey he'd ever tasted."

"Detective Carver, have you ever been investigated by Internal Affairs?"

"Objection. Where's the relevance here?"

"I'll withdraw the question," Hennessy said, but the shot had been fired. The shocked look on Carver's face said he understood where the questioning was headed. Hennessy drew a breath and picked up the folder again. He stared at the witness, but Carver avoided eye contact. "Of course, Mercedes would also have every location you went before you picked up Mr. Fenton. All we want is the truth, Detective Carver. I'm not interested if Internal Affairs are investigating you, but I'm very interested in exactly what Mr. Fenton told you before you dropped him off at Alicia Fenton's address."

"What do you mean?" Carver whispered.

Hennessy placed the folder back down and deliberately put another folder on top.

The movement indicated that Hennessy was happy to bury the information. The message was clear to Carver, and he nodded.

"All I want is the truth, Detective." Hennessy calmly moved back to the lectern. "Did Mr. Fenton talk about his stepdaughter after you picked her up?"

"Yes," he whispered, desperate for Hennessy not to release the details of his movements before he arrived at Lieber Correctional. "Dennis talked about his stepdaughter."

"And what did he say in the vehicle with you?"

Carver looked at Hennessy and then at the folder.

Carver raised his eyebrows. Hennessy nodded back.

"He said he was going to rape her," Carver stated.

"Can you be clearer and tell the court who said that?"

"Dennis Fenton said he was going to rape his stepdaughter when I parked outside his apartment, but I didn't think he was serious."

Nobody moved, the moment encased in a bubble of tension.

After a few moments, Garrett leaned back in his chair, mouth wide open. Hennessy sat down and the shocked crowd began to talk with each other. A loud murmur covered the room. Garrett tossed his pen on the table, unable to hide his disappointment. He declined to cross-examine the witness.

When Judge West instructed Hennessy to continue, he stood and announced, "The defense rests, Your Honor."

CHAPTER 45

"THEY HAVE to find me not guilty by reason of self-defense," Alicia said as she paced the meeting room in the Charleston Judicial Center. She had been pacing the room for fifteen minutes since Judge West called a recess before closing statements. "They've all said it. They've all stood up there and admitted the truth. He was trying to rape me. I was acting in self-defense."

"We're close," Hennessy agreed. "We'll go back into court, present closing statements, and leave the decision with the jury."

"But sometimes the jury can be unpredictable," Jacinta noted, seated at the far end of the table. "We can never tell what they're thinking. You need to be prepared that it might not go the way you want."

"How can they find me guilty after that?"

"They can still find you guilty of the lesser charge of voluntary manslaughter," Hennessy noted. "There's no evidence that you didn't use excessive force. There's only hearsay evidence that Dennis intended to rape you. The jury will have to decide whether they believe that threat was over or not, and whether or not you used excessive force."

Alicia slumped into the chair at the end of the dark wooden table, arms folded across her chest. She leaned forward and rested her forehead on the table.

The meeting room was small and tight, and the smell of coffee lingered in the air.

"So it's not over yet," Alicia whispered. "They still have to choose whether they believe the witnesses?"

Hennessy nodded. "That means the closing statement has to be focused on the fact that you acted in self-defense and that the threat of serious bodily injury had not ceased when your stepfather turned around. That's been our tactic this entire case, and if we can convince the jury of it, you can walk out of those doors without a conviction." Hennessy nodded and looked at his watch. "It's time to finish this."

As he walked out of the courthouse meeting room, he wished Garrett had been waiting for him, ready to withdraw the case. But there was no one waiting. After Alicia rejected the offer early in the day, Garrett decided he would see the case through to the end, no matter the result.

After the brief recess, the public gallery had filled with spectators.

When the court was settled, Judge West spoke to the jury about their duty and how they needed to use legal definitions to guide their decision-making. She then called for Garrett to make his closing statement.

Garrett walked to the lectern, looking like a petulant child who hadn't got what he wanted.

*****

"Ladies and Gentlemen of the jury, you have a case where the facts are clear.

Alicia Fenton struck Dennis Fenton on the back

of the head with a baseball bat. That's indisputable. That's a fact. It was a blow to the back of the head. Dennis Fenton was facing away from his stepdaughter when he was struck.

You have to decide whether you believe she was acting in self-defense or not. To determine if she legally acted in self-defense, she must have met these criteria.

One—the defendant was without fault in bringing on the difficulty. She must not have provoked the attack. Two—the defendant believed she was in imminent danger of being killed or seriously injured. Imminent danger means the danger that's immediately present and real. Three—a reasonable person would've had the same belief about the imminent danger. And four—there was no probable means of avoiding the danger.

You've heard from expert witnesses, including body position experts, crime scene experts, and forensic experts. You've heard from police officers at the scene of the crime. They have all said the same thing—Dennis Fenton was struck in the back of the head.

All the evidence is clear. Alicia Fenton swung the baseball bat when Mr. Fenton was walking away. Can you still be a threat when walking away? That's a decision you will have to make.

A person is criminally responsible for their conduct. While you deliberate, I need you to remember that fact—a person is criminally responsible for their conduct.

The cold, hard truth is that Alicia Fenton swung a baseball bat and hit Mr. Fenton.

Mr. Fenton died as a result of that blow.

The application of the law in this case is simple, and there's no hard evidence that Alicia Fenton was acting in self-defense.

The decision is yours to make. Thank you for your service to this court."

*****

Garrett walked back to his seat after his short closing statement. He slumped in his chair and wrote a note on his pad. He turned and tossed his pen back down on the table.

Hennessy made several notes across his closing statement, and when invited by Judge West, he stood and moved behind the lectern to begin.

Garrett's case rested on one fact—Alicia Fenton had hit him from behind.

Hennessy's case rested on establishing Dennis Fenton's intention and state of mind before he arrived at the Logan Street address. He had to present the idea that the threat was not over to Alicia, even though Dennis was walking away, and he had to convince twelve regular people Alicia had acted in defense of herself.

*****

"Dennis Fenton's intent was clear.

We have established that throughout the case. That night, after five weeks in prison, Dennis Fenton went to the property to rape his stepdaughter, Alicia Fenton.

Miss Fenton is allowed to defend herself in her own home. She saw an opportunity to defend herself, and she took it. That's all there is to this case. Nothing more.

She acted in self-defense.

As the prosecution has stated, the following elements are required to establish self-defense.

First, she must be without fault. Legal provocation is any act in violation of law that would be reasonably expected to produce the fight. The prosecution has produced no evidence that Alicia provoked her stepfather. In fact, Dennis Fenton's arrival surprised his stepdaughter. She was the owner of the property, and as the experts have explained, Dennis Fenton was not a current resident. He was supposed to be residing in the Lieber Correctional Institution for another fourteen months. You have heard the experts explain that Dennis Fenton entered the apartment and physically cornered Alicia. Then, he assaulted her. He made his intent to rape her clear. Alicia Fenton was acting in self-defense.

Second, she had to be in imminent danger. Imminent danger means the danger that's immediately present and real. We've established that Dennis Fenton physically assaulted his stepdaughter, with the intention to rape her. That's classed as imminent danger. Dennis Fenton attacked her, evidenced by the cut above her eye and the fact that her blood was on the kitchen wall. With this evidence, it's clear that Alicia Fenton was acting in self-defense.

Thirdly, given Alicia's situation, you must consider whether a reasonable person would have felt the same threat. You should consider all the facts and circumstances of the crime, including the physical condition and characteristics of the defendant and the victim. For example, you can consider Dennis Fenton's size and age. We've established that Dennis Fenton was a larger than average man and an intimidating figure to his stepdaughter.

You may also consider the victim's violent reputation. We've heard from Dennis Fenton's sister that he had a history of violence, and she witnessed her brother hit Alicia in the past.

And you may also consider the victim's intoxication level. We've heard from the Deputy Coroner that Mr. Fenton had high levels of alcohol and morphine in his system when he died. You've heard from character witnesses who testified that Dennis Fenton had a problem with alcohol for many, many years. We've heard from witnesses who have stated that Mr. Fenton became violent when drinking alcohol. With this knowledge, it's clear that Alicia Fenton was acting in self-defense.

The last element of self-defense is that the defendant had no other probable way to avoid the danger of death or serious bodily injury than to act as the defendant did in this particular instance. She had no other choice than to defend herself. Alicia Fenton was acting in self-defense.

You have heard a witness state that they heard Miss Fenton yell, 'Not again.'

'Not again,' she yelled before anyone else was in the room.

Let me repeat that for you so it's clear—Alicia Fenton acted in self-defense. If she had not acted, she would've suffered great bodily injury or perhaps even death. And because of that, you must find Alicia Fenton not guilty.

What are the facts of this case? The fact is Dennis Fenton talked to his fellow prisoners about raping his stepdaughter after he was released from prison. The fact is Dennis Fenton talked about raping his stepdaughter on the drive to her address. The fact is he physically struck his stepdaughter in the face after he arrived.

In this case, you have heard from Mrs. Edith Chapman, who detailed the abuse she saw Alicia Fenton receive as she was being raised. You've heard from the school nurse, who documented that she believed Alicia Fenton was being beaten at home, and there was the possibility of sexual abuse. And you've heard from blood spatter experts who have detailed that the blood in the kitchen was from when Dennis Fenton struck his stepdaughter only moments before she defended herself.

You've heard from the paramedic who attended to Alicia's wound at the scene of the crime, who stated that Alicia was scared and had a cut above her eye. You've heard from domestic violence expert Dr. Julia Owen, who explained the pattern of behavior that abusers use and how, given all the evidence available, it was likely that Alicia had suffered regularly at the hands of her stepfather.

You've heard from witnesses who have clearly stated that it was Mr. Fenton's intention to arrive at the address and rape his stepdaughter.

Listen to the facts, listen to what the evidence is saying because it all points to the fact that Alicia Fenton was acting in self-defense.

If you believe Alicia Fenton was defending herself

against the threat of rape and serious physical violence, you must find the defendant not guilty.

Thank you for your service to the justice system."

*****

After the closing statements, Judge West turned to the jury and explained the legal requirements that must be met before they could deliver their decision.

"The defendant has raised the defense of self-defense. Self-defense is a complete defense, and if it's established, you must find the defendant not guilty. The state has had the burden of disproving self-defense by proof beyond a reasonable doubt. If you have a reasonable doubt about the defendant's guilt after considering all the evidence, including the evidence of self-defense, then you must find the defendant not guilty. On the other hand, if you have no reasonable doubt of the defendant's guilt after considering all the evidence, including the evidence of self-defense, then you must find the defendant guilty. I wish you well. Thank you for your service to the court."

CHAPTER 46

HENNESSY LOOKED at his watch. It had only been an hour.

He hated the waiting game.

Alicia was taken back to the holding cells, and Hennessy walked back to his office with Jacinta. It could take hours, days, or weeks for the jury to reach a decision, Hennessy told Alicia. All they needed was one person to disagree in the jury deliberation room, and they would be in for the long haul. Alicia looked like she was about to vomit as the guards took her away.

Hennessy understood the nerves. The first hours after the closing statements were the worst. That was when the doubt set in. Had he done enough? Had he convinced the twelve regular people she was acting in self-defense?

Both he and Jacinta spent time either slowly pacing around the room or taking up one of two more popular positions; one next to the main window looking out at the street, the other leaning against the far end of the table. They didn't pace together.

While one was leaning, the other slowly worked their way around the outer edge of the room itself, usually looking down at the floor. After several minutes, the pair would swap, one taking up whatever leaning position was open.

Hennessy stopped at the window to his office and watched a helicopter skim across the rooftops a few miles in the distance. The helicopter didn't appear to be any news chopper but a private one with no corporate markings. He watched the helicopter fly off until it disappeared over the horizon.

"You couldn't have done anything more," Jacinta said. "You presented the perfect case. Whatever the jury decides, you did the best you could."

Hennessy didn't respond. He looked at his watch again. It had been an hour and fifty-five minutes. His office phone rang. Jacinta leaped to her feet and answered it. She spoke for a moment and then turned back to Hennessy. "The jury has a decision. Judge West wants us back within the hour."

Hennessy swallowed hard. The decision had been reached in under two hours. He didn't know if that was good or bad. He drew a deep breath and looked at the liquor cabinet. He decided not to have a drink, even though the nerves were filling his stomach. He hated this part. Why couldn't they just tell him the decision already?

Within twenty-five minutes, he was back in front of the Charleston Judicial Center. Word had gotten out to the media that the jury would soon deliver their decision. The courtyard in front of the courthouse was humming with the noise of media. One reporter spotted Hennessy approaching, and he soon had five microphones in his face. He declined to answer their questions. He was too nervous.

After he stepped through the security line, he stood in the foyer and looked around. When Jacinta joined him, she patted him on the back. He walked into the courtroom and sat behind the defense table.

His knees felt weak, his fingers numb, and parts of him reacted to the nerves in a way he didn't think possible. He'd always believed himself stronger than most, and here he was close to panic as he waited in the courtroom.

Aaron Garrett and his team arrived next, and the public gallery filled with onlookers, bringing nervous tension with them. The media stood at the side of the room, pens ready. The five older cops shuffled into the back of the room last.

Alicia was brought in via the side door. She looked nervous, more nervous than he'd ever seen her.

"Ready?" Hennessy asked.

Alicia nodded. "Let's get this over with."

Hennessy looked around the crowd. He couldn't see Sean Carver.

There was no hiding from the pressure. The silence was intense. It was the last play after months of stress. The last chance Hennessy had to learn the truth about his son.

At five minutes past 5pm, the bailiff stood and brought the murmurs to a close. The combined shuffle of feet sounded almost regimental. All eyes watched the judge return to her bench, the silence louder than ever. Once everybody had retaken their seats, Judge West called for the jury to be brought back in.

Hennessy looked for any sign from them as they walked to their seats. He saw no clue from them, with not a single member of the jury looking up as they walked from the door to their seat.

"Has the jury reached their verdict?" Judge West's voice broke through the silence.

"It has, Your Honor," the foreman said. The

bailiff approached him, took the slip the man held out, and then walked it back to the bench. Judge West accepted it. Time stood still as the court watched the judge's eyes stare at the slip of paper.

Finally, she looked at the foreman and asked him to reveal the verdict. The man did so without hesitation.

"In the charge of murder in the first degree, we, the jury, find the defendant not guilty."

CHAPTER 47

IT TOOK five hours for Alicia Fenton to be officially released.

After the decision, Hennessy drove her to the Sheriff Al Cannon Detention Center, where she was processed. It was past ten o'clock at night by the time she was a free woman again. Instead of celebrating, all Alicia wanted was to go home to her own bed. Hennessy drove her from the detention center to her apartment. He led her inside, checked the apartment for anybody lurking around corners, and then wished her good night.

She grabbed an arm and thanked him. "Without you, I would've taken the deal for ten years. You don't know how much it means to me."

Hennessy nodded. "Just make sure you pursue that nursing career and make someone out there happy."

"I will." She reached up and wrapped her arms around him. "Thank you. You've changed my life."

Hennessy gave her another nod, and tiredness took over as he stepped out to his car. He drove back to his apartment. Although physically exhausted, he was too mentally wound up for sleep. He poured a glass of whiskey and returned to the small porch at the front of his house. He sat there, listening to the loud bugs, looking out to the park opposite. He watched the Spanish moss gently sway under the oak trees, highlighted by the bright moon.

There was simply nothing as peaceful as sitting on a South Carolina front porch on a summer evening.

He took another sip of his whiskey and thought about Sean Carver. Carver's GPS data had shown him driving from the Rebel Sons clubhouse directly before he picked up Dennis Fenton. If exposed, that evidence was sure to see him fired from his job. Internal Affairs had his name, and he was already skating on thin ice. He'd already been warned not to contact any of the Rebel Sons. A trip to their clubhouse was a major mistake.

After he picked up Fenton, they drove to the Whiskey and Vine Liquor Store off Market Street. Carver's GPS data showed he was parked directly out the front of the store at the moment the silent alarms went off and drove away one minute and fifty-five seconds later.

Did Dennis Fenton actually say those words to Carver in the car? Hennessy wasn't sure. He knew Carver didn't want the information about his whereabouts presented in court, so Carver would say whatever he needed to stop Hennessy.

As he took another sip of whiskey, he thought about the Brandon McDermott case and how the evidence exonerated him from the Grand Larceny charge. It had been Dennis Fenton who broke into the liquor store that night, desperate to snatch an expensive bottle of whiskey and celebrate his release. McDermott could still face charges for vandalism, but Hennessy suspected that the Circuit Solicitor's Office would drop all charges in an attempt to wash their hands clean of the mess.

But Brandon McDermott's case would have to

wait.

His first appointment would have to be with John Cleveland in the morning.

The cell next to Hennessy buzzed. He looked at the number. It was Alicia.

Her voice sounded petrified as her words registered barely above a whisper. At first, Hennessy could scarcely hear, and when he asked her to speak up, she didn't.

"I don't know what to do," she said. "Someone's been banging on my door repeatedly, and my phone has been ringing nonstop." She spoke so fast. Her words tripped over each other, and Hennessy could barely distinguish one from another. "Someone's out there."

"Alicia, Alicia… slow down." He could hear her breathing erratically, and it took her a moment to calm down enough to listen to him. "Alicia, take a breath."

He heard her take a long breath.

"Ok, now tell me, who's been calling?"

"I don't know. There's just silence when I answer." She almost took off again but calmed herself. "Mr. Hennessy… I'm scared. I didn't know who else to call."

He could hear the struggle, her voice breaking with fear, and he hoped she could hold it together long enough for him to get there. "I'll call the police and—"

"No," she pleaded. "No, please. Don't call the police. It's them I'm scared of. I think it might be—"

She didn't finish the sentence. Hennessy heard some muffled sounds before she came back.

"Alicia, you need to hide."

"I already am hiding," she whispered. "I'm in my wardrobe, but…" Another pause, more shuffling before she came back. "I think someone just broke into my—" but her words were cut off, and just before she disappeared, he heard the beginnings of a scream.

The line went dead, leaving Hennessy to listen to nothing but silence.

CHAPTER 48

HENNESSY GRABBED his keys and raced to his truck.

He hit the accelerator hard, giving the engine all the fuel it wanted. It roared to life, the tires kicking up enough smoke as they slid around in a wide arc before sending two tons of steel hurtling back toward the main road.

Hennessy hung on for life as he drove the truck along at a breakneck speed and hoped no random pedestrian chose that moment to step out into traffic.

Once on the main road, he initiated the recall button to try to get Alicia back on the line again, but he stopped himself just before he pressed the call button. What if she was still hiding, and phoning her would only alert whoever had broken into her apartment to where she was?

Hennessy tossed the cell phone aside in frustration and gripped the steering wheel tighter. The next corner was tight, and the squeal of the tires losing purchase as he rounded it gave him a fresh dose of adrenalin. He felt the rear end threaten to slide out completely, but the tires found purchase at the last second and kept him on the road. Once he was pointing the right way again, his right foot worked the gas pedal with hostility.

The drive from his place to Alicia's apartment

would've normally taken at least twenty minutes, but Hennessy pulled up out the front in just ten. He'd run red lights and slalomed his way through the worst parts of traffic and was sure a few cameras would have picked him up, but none of that mattered.

He grabbed his gun from the glove box and leaped onto the sidewalk. Almost immediately, he sensed something was wrong.

A faint whimper floated through the night. Hennessy held his breath and turned his head a little to focus a single ear in the direction of the sound. A woman's crying. It was Alicia.

Hennessy paused a couple of yards from the open door, tightened his handgun grip, and took a deep breath. He was close enough for the subdued whimpering to turn into faint sobbing, but he needed to know whether she was alone. Nothing else showed an intruder other than the open door and the phone call.

A noise broke above the sobs, a kind of shuffling, annunciated by a brief grunt. The voice behind it didn't sound feminine, confirming that someone else was waiting for him. After another deep breath, Hennessy locked his elbow, pointed the pistol at the door, and pivoted into the doorway.

The confrontation was instant. A man was holding Alicia. He had an arm wrapped around her neck and a pistol aimed at her head.

Sean Carver's eyes were far from the man he'd last seen in the courtroom.

The detective looked almost unhinged as he eyed the man he considered responsible for his downfall. Between them, a young girl stood terrified, a bruise already coloring one cheek with a deep shade of blue.

"Couldn't keep your nose out of it, could you?" Carver sneered as he tightened his arm around Alicia. He hid most of his face behind her head, using her as a shield. Hennessy kept his sights trained on the part of the man he could see.

"Let her go, Carver."

"Don't think I will. Think I'll just end her here and now. Just like she ended Dennis' life."

"Why would you hurt her?" Hennessy asked as the distinctive scent of whiskey filled his nostrils. With bloodshot eyes and sluggish movements, it was obvious Carver had been drinking.

"She should've let him do what he wanted like so many times before. It would have been the last time, anyway. Brock Roberts was here to do the job."

"What are you talking about?"

"You think we would've just let Fenton snitch on us like that? No way. We were going to clean up the mess, but Alicia did it for us. And the number of times I had to listen to Fenton talk about how much he liked his stepdaughter, I thought I'd come and taste her for myself."

Carver licked his tongue over Alicia's neck. She closed her eyes and grimaced through the tears.

"Do you have any idea what this has done to me?" Spit flew from his lips as he snarled his words at Hennessy. The lawyer refused to move, standing perfectly still as he kept his gun pointed at the detective. "Because of your games, I'm now suspended and under investigation. They know about the GPS data, and Internal Affairs will pull me over the coals once they find out. Know where that leaves me?"

"Hung out to dry," Hennessy said.

Alicia met Hennessy's gaze, her eyes willing him to save her, but it was impossible with Carver's hold on her.

Carver kept stepping from one foot to the other, shifting his and Alicia's weight just enough that Hennessy's sights kept aiming from the detective's face to his hostage.

"Just put the gun down, Carver," Hennessy tried again. "We can talk about this. Nobody needs to get hurt."

"Hurt?" Carver's voice sounded slurred, but Hennessy knew the man still had enough control to operate the trigger. "If only you had kept your dog on a leash instead of getting him to sniff around my business."

Without warning, Carver aimed the gun at Hennessy and grinned. His other arm tightened around Alicia's neck, and Hennessy saw her face grimace in pain.

"Want to know hurt, Counsellor? Real hurt?"

Hennessy stared down the barrel of the pistol, his heart ready to explode out of his chest as the beating erupted in his temples. He could feel the pulsing in his hands, his finger held firmly on his trigger.

Carver's shoulders slumped as he relaxed the hold on Alicia. His lips pursed just enough to give the man a sense of indecision.

Carver pulled the gun back, aimed the barrel at his own temple, and pulled the trigger.

His head kicked to one side as a flood of blood and brains blew onto the wall.

Alicia screamed. She fell away from the detective's body.

Hennessy rushed forward, and checked on Alicia.

She was crying but unhurt.

Hennessy told her to remain still until she got herself back under control, then went to where Carver lay. He kicked the gun away and looked at the man's self-inflicted injuries.

He didn't check for a pulse.

CHAPTER 49

THERE WAS another prison riot at the Lee Correctional Institution.

Five people were beaten badly, one clinging to life. The Royal Nation was heavily involved. The prison would enter a seven-day lockdown while an investigation took place. Hennessy tried to pull enough strings to bypass the lockdown and meet with John Cleveland, but it was no use. The prison guards wouldn't budge. There would be no meetings until the lockdown ended. Hennessy's information would have to wait.

Five days after the shooting at Alicia's house, Hennessy sat in his office, unable to control the growing nerves. He constantly tapped his index finger against the edge of his desk, unable to focus on anything. He'd done the work, he'd done the hard yards, and he wanted the information. He needed to know what happened to his son.

At five minutes past 2pm, Brandon McDermott walked in. He looked as nervous as the lawyer. He sat in the chair opposite Hennessy's desk, sitting on the edge.

"You said it's good news?"

Hennessy nodded and snapped himself out of his slump. He removed a file from the side of the desk. "It is."

McDermott exhaled loudly and leaned back in his chair. "What have you found?"

"While looking at the GPS data of Mercedes in Charleston, we found one new Mercedes which belonged to a police officer parked directly outside the Whiskey and Vine Liquor Store precisely one minute before the robbery, and then left the location exactly one minute and fifty-five seconds after the alarms went off."

"A police officer? Who was it?"

"An officer named Detective Sean Carver. That detective is now deceased in a different incident."

"I'm sorry to hear that."

Hennessy nodded. "They've also matched one of the bottles stolen to another crime scene. A rare bottle of Orphan Barrel was found in the hands of a man named Dennis Fenton. After I alerted the police department to that fact, they've been able to match that particular bottle to the one stolen on the night of April 15th."

"Are you saying the detective drove this other man there, and they broke into the liquor store?"

"That's right," Hennessy agreed. "The police have since requested the detailed GPS data for that Mercedes, and it came back this morning. I received a call from the prosecutor on your case, and they're dropping all charges against you, but they've asked that you pay for the damage to the security camera outside the store." Hennessy removed a piece of paper from the file and placed it in front of McDermott. "This is the invoice to fix the cameras. Fifteen hundred dollars. If you pay that to the store, the police will drop all charges against you."

"That's it?" He pulled his cell out of his pocket

and opened his banking app. "If I pay this, it's all over?"

"That's right."

"Consider it done."

"Send the receipt for the invoice to Jacinta, and she'll forward it to the officers and the liquor store. After that, we'll get an official statement from the police saying that all charges are withdrawn. Then you're free to go."

McDermott didn't answer. He typed the details into his cell and then looked up at Hennessy. "It's done. All paid for. I've sent the receipt to Jacinta."

"Then we're finished. Jacinta will send you our invoices, and I'll call you once we receive that official statement from the police to say the charges have been withdrawn."

McDermott started laughing and threw his hands up like he had just won a marathon. "Yes. Yes. I can't believe it. My wife's going to be happy. Thank you, Mr. Hennessy." McDermott stood and offered his hand. "Thank you."

The two men shook solidly for a long moment. McDermott gripped the lawyer's hand hard.

"Thank you," he repeated.

"Just stay out of trouble," Hennessy grinned. "I don't want to do this again."

"You bet."

Brandon McDermott walked out of the office with his arms raised again. For him, it was all over.

Hennessy smiled at the success and then checked the time. He had agreed to meet Alicia at 3pm, at her local café. He left his office a few moments later, taking an extended stroll through the historic streets of Charleston. When he arrived at the café, Alicia was waiting for him.

She greeted him with a hug and sat back down. She looked different, relieved of a great stress. Her skin looked softer, and her eyes looked brighter. Her hair was combed, and her smile was broad.

"You look well," Hennessy said after he ordered a coffee and sat down. "Being free looks great on you."

"Thanks," she smiled. "I can't believe it. After all these weeks, I can't believe it."

"And you weren't injured in the incident with Sean Carver?"

"I was a little shaken up, sure, but no physical injuries." She paused for a moment and then looked at Hennessy. "I know I said it before, but thank you. Every man in my life has abandoned me, and you were the first one to see it through, so thank you. You've restored my faith in men."

"Just doing my job."

"I don't believe that."

"Well, even bad men have good moments. I've heard that while Dennis left his estate to you, Sean Carver had written in his will that he wanted half of his estate donated to the study of PTSD. He didn't want other people to suffer the pain he went through and wanted more research done to help those struggling with the condition. You should remember that bad men can do great things, and good men can do very bad things. Nobody is perfect."

"My birth father wasn't a good man," she said bluntly. "Has he told you what you needed?"

"Not yet. There's been a lockdown in the prison for the past week, and it's not due to lift for another couple of days. I'll see your birth father as soon as the lockdown is lifted."

She noticed the apprehension on his face. "But?"

Hennessy drew a breath. "But I'm not sure he'll tell me the truth. He's a lifer, and he's got nothing to lose. If he doesn't tell me the truth about what he knows, there's not a lot I can do."

Alicia sat back. She didn't know how to help. She didn't know the man.

"So, tell me," Hennessy continued. "What's the plan now that you're free?"

"With the money from Dennis' estate, I'm going to study nursing at the University of South Carolina. I just want to help people like me."

Hennessy smiled. He didn't have the information he wanted, but he had helped save a good person from a terrible fate.

CHAPTER 50

WHEN THE Lee Correctional Institution reopened seven days after their lockdown, Barry Lockett insisted on driving Hennessy to the meeting. Hennessy thanked his investigator, and they drove the two hours mostly in silence. They arrived at the prison, and Lockett said he would wait in the truck. Hennessy thanked his investigator again and walked through the security alone.

While waiting in the prison meeting room, Hennessy was flooded with anxiety. He felt his pulse, the beating in his chest quite intense, but nothing prepared him for the dump of adrenalin when the door finally opened behind him. He watched Cleveland walk in, and the two men exchanged a brief look before the inmate sat down.

"Alicia called me this morning, right after the lockdown had finished," Cleveland said and blinked back a tear. "She called me and said thanks for hiring you. She said she would still be in prison if it weren't for you. And then…" He scoffed and shook his head, blinking back another tear. "And then she called me Dad. I don't know why that tears me up. I've only met the girl twice. But there's something about it, ya know? Something about being called 'Dad.'"

Hennessy didn't respond, keeping his glare on Cleveland.

"Before that phone call, I wasn't going to tell you the truth. I was going to let you walk in here, and then I'd tell you I knew nothing, just to watch you spin out. I would've enjoyed that. I would've laughed so hard at you." Cleveland chuckled. "But after being called 'Dad,' I changed my mind. That call meant somethin' big. Hit me right in the heart. It's all I can think about. I'm excited because some girl I haven't seen in a decade said, 'Thanks, Dad.' Can you believe that? She said thanks for getting you as a lawyer, and thanks for getting Dan Coleman to testify. She even said she'd like to see me. I was shocked, you know? I've never been so happy."

Again, Hennessy didn't respond.

"And knowing what that feels like, I've decided I'm going to tell you the truth."

A silence fell over the men. For one, the confession would open up things he'd carried for too many years; and for the other, it would lift a veil of pain and suffering he'd thought he'd keep for eternity. Both needed it, yet only one had the power to help them.

"So, I guess it's time for me to pay up." Cleveland scratched his face. "What do you want to know?

"I need to know everything. Tell me straight."

"I will. But before I do, I need you to know that I'm not the same person I was back then. People change, and I've had a long time to understand that the man I was back then was a prick. I was just a stupid guy. Just a dumb idiot looking for work. It was before Alicia was born, and I was just looking for money."

"What happened?"

"Twenty years ago, I was approached by an

acquaintance of mine, Justin Fields, who asked me to drive a van. No reason, just here are the keys and drive. Being young and naïve, I did. I didn't ask questions, and he didn't tell me. He said he'd pay a few hundred just to drive the van. I thought it was the best deal ever. He directed me to a football field, and we hung out there for a while until Justin spotted this kid and told me to get closer, so I did. Before I knew what was going on, Justin opened the van's back door and grabbed the kid. He was kicking and screaming, but Justin dragged him into the back and slammed the door shut."

Cleveland paused to take a breath. Hennessy could see he was struggling but didn't care. He needed answers.

"If only the kid had listened and shut up." He looked over at Hennessy. "I didn't know it was supposed to be a kidnapping; Justin didn't say so until afterward. I mean, to be honest, I doubt it would have mattered much to me at the time, you know? I was already knee-deep in stuff, and this was just something else for me to get involved in. He said we were supposed to hold the kid for a couple of days while a ransom demand was made." Another break, another breath. Cleveland let out a sigh, long and slow, as he looked down again. "If only he had shut up," he repeated. "The kid just wouldn't be quiet, and he fought back, not just a little, either. He was a fighter. Justin tied him up and put a mask over his head, but this kid head-butted Justin and then kicked him. He gave Justin a couple of decent kicks before…"

Hennessy watched the man stare at his fingers, curl them up and tap the table.

"I don't know why, but Justin flipped out and began hitting the kid repeatedly, over and over, until he finally quit yelling. By the time I pulled over and checked on him, he was dead. There was nothing we could do… not that we really tried. We panicked and drove around for like an hour, trying to figure out what we could do. In the end, I drove to the bridge, and we dumped his body."

Hennessy sat in silence, the shock of hearing about the final moments of his child's life ripping his heart apart. He felt tears well up but blinked them into submission. One tear broke loose and rolled down his face, but the destroyed father flicked it away with a finger.

"Who paid you to kidnap my child?" Hennessy asked, his voice barely registering.

Cleveland didn't look up. "Justin told me he got paid by some prosecutor. He wasn't anybody back then, but I was told they had a problem with you. They kidnapped your kid to break you into submission."

"Who?"

Cleveland stared at Hennessy. "He's a Senator."

"Richard Longhouse."

Cleveland nodded.

Hennessy could barely sit still as the name tore through him, his fingers shaking uncontrollably as he fought to keep his anger in check.

Finding himself unable to keep calm, he stood and walked to face the nearest wall. Closing his eyes, he felt the tears return, his lip quivering with the rawness of grief.

"I'll testify if you need me to," Cleveland said from behind him. "After what you did for my daughter, and that moment when she called me 'Dad,' I owe you. I've already written a letter saying everything I know. I wrote it last night. And I'll get up on the stand and say everything I know."

Hennessy didn't answer for fear of his internal screams breaking out. All he wanted was to avenge his son, to bring those who had taken him from his family to justice. He opened his eyes but remained staring at the wall.

"I know you want to avenge your boy, but unfortunately, Justin died five years ago. He was in and out of places like this his whole life and got killed in a bar fight in Florida."

Hennessy closed his eyes again and swallowed hard. This wasn't the time or place to lose control. There would be plenty of time for grief, but it had to wait.

"We're done here," Hennessy whispered and, without another word, walked to the door and banged on it.

A guard came and let him out, and he walked out before Cleveland could say anything else.

By the time he exited the prison's front door, Hennessy had suppressed most of his emotion deep into his soul.

"You ok?" Lockett was cautious.

Hennessy glared at Lockett and then walked to the passenger seat of the truck. "I need you to drive me to Senator Longhouse's office."

CHAPTER 51

"HELLO, SIR. It's Sunday afternoon, and the Senator isn't taking any appointments today. Can I help you with something else?"

Hennessy didn't answer the secretary. He stormed past her desk and pushed hard into the door that led to the office of Senator Richard Longhouse.

Behind the large and imposing dark mahogany desk, Richard Longhouse sat with his reading glasses on, scanning over a paper file. To the side of the desk sat a glass of whiskey. Longhouse squinted and then placed his pen down. Calmly, he took off his glasses.

Hennessy stormed around the desk and grabbed Longhouse by the collar of his shirt. All the calmness went from Longhouse's face. Hennessy pushed the chair back and dragged Longhouse into the open space in front of his desk. He threw him to the floor.

"Joe?" Longhouse held his hands up in surrender. "What's going on?"

Lockett stood by the door. The secretary tried to come in, but Lockett held his hand up as a stop sign. She left to get help.

"Joe?" Longhouse repeated.

Hennessy stood over Longhouse, his towering figure silhouetted by the light coming in the window behind him. His fists were clenched.

"You ordered my son dead."

"I did no such thing!" Longhouse scuffled back. He looked at Lockett, but Lockett didn't offer any sympathy. Longhouse looked back up to Hennessy with pleading eyes. "I don't know what you're talking about."

"You paid someone to kidnap him."

"No, no, no." Longhouse shook his head. "I didn't do that."

Longhouse went to get up, but Hennessy placed his hand on the Senator's shoulder and pushed him back to the ground.

"Don't lie to me. I know you paid Justin Fields to kidnap my son."

"Justin is long dead, Joe." Longhouse shuffled back further, still with one hand raised, until he was at the bookshelf at the side of the room. "I don't know where you're getting your information from."

Hennessy reached down, full of rage, and gripped Longhouse's collar again. He dragged him up and slammed him against the bookshelf.

"Why?" Hennessy hissed through clenched teeth.

"Why what?" Longhouse whispered.

The fear in his eyes was clear. His hands went to Hennessy's forearm, trying to push him back, but Hennessy was too strong and too full of fury. Longhouse tried to keep his chin down, trying to stop Hennessy's hand from pressing into his throat, but it was no use.

"Why did you kill my son?"

"Whatever Justin Fields did had nothing to do with me."

Longhouse tried to push Hennessy off him, but Hennessy slammed him back into the bookshelf. It was hard enough for several books to fall around them.

"Joe," Longhouse pleaded. "Joe."

Building security arrived at the door, followed by a desperate secretary. She told security that the Senator was inside. The two security guards pushed through the door. Lockett stepped back.

The two security guards had their hands on their weapons, but their guns remained holstered. "What's going on?" the first guard asked.

Lockett walked forward and patted Hennessy on the shoulder. "It's time to go."

Hennessy grunted as he brought his nose within inches of Longhouse's face. He released his grip around his throat, and in one swift movement, he landed a clean right hook into Longhouse's stomach, sending the man crippling to the floor.

Hennessy leaned over the fallen man and whispered, "I'm coming for you."

CHAPTER 52

HENNESSY SPENT the next two days in a daze, confused about his next steps.

He needed to get a statement signed by Cleveland and hand it to the police. Would they touch it? He didn't know, but it was his best option, besides putting a bullet in Longhouse's skull. He wanted to shoot Longhouse, but logic took over his emotions. He had checked the Glock 19 that he kept in his apartment, cleaned it, and ensured he had enough ammunition. He thought about pulling that trigger over and over and over until that was all he could think about. But every time he went to leave his apartment, his logical brain kicked in.

If he shot Longhouse, he would lose everything, including Luca's Vineyard. He couldn't do that. His wife still needed a husband, and his daughters still needed a father. He couldn't let Wendy down, and he couldn't let his daughters down.

He hadn't told Wendy the whole truth yet. She called him that morning, and he said he would tell her everything when he drove up to the vineyard on the weekend. It pained him deeply that Longhouse was still walking the streets, free from the justice he deserved. Hennessy's hands shook every time he thought about Longhouse and all their interactions in the past. Longhouse knew, he always knew the truth, and yet, he pretended like nothing had happened.

Hennessy sat in his office alone as the Tuesday afternoon drew to a close, looking out the window with a glass of Jack Daniels bourbon in one hand. He had sent Jacinta home, telling her he needed to be alone. She saw the look on his face and didn't argue.

He sat and stared at the wall, quiet and distant.

He took a sip of whiskey and looked into the glass as he held the liquid in his mouth.

Without thinking, he grabbed the bottle from the desk, and took it to the office kitchen. He poured the contents down the sink. He didn't want to find solace in the bottom of a bottle. He watched the amber fluid partially fill the sink before whirlpooling out of his life for good. He dropped the bottle into the trash and went back to his office.

Instead of sitting, he leaned against the edge of the window and looked out at the world, knowing that somewhere out there, another man went about his day without a clue that his days were numbered. Hennessy imagined Longhouse sitting in his car, driving to an unknown destination, assuming he was in the clear for Luca's death.

"I'm coming for you," Hennessy whispered.

"Talking to yourself is the first sign of insanity," a voice said from behind him, and he turned to see Lockett standing in the doorway.

"I'm on the edge of insanity," he said. It was the truth. The past twenty-four hours had almost driven him into madness.

Lockett didn't smile. Hennessy could see immediately that his investigator had something on his mind.

"What is it?" Hennessy asked.

Lockett avoided eye contact. "I'm sorry to be the one to break it to you, but there's been another riot at the Lee Correctional Institution this morning. The reports say that two men died during the worst of it. Members of the Supreme Brotherhood attacked members of the Royal Nation. Two members of the Royal Nation were beaten and stabbed." He paused, processing what he'd said and what he still had. "Joe, one of the men killed was John Cleveland."

Hennessy's mouth dropped open as he tried to process the flood of emotions that overwhelmed him. Had Cleveland told him everything he knew, or was there more? Did he hold anything back? He'd already used him once to get his daughter out of prison. What if he had plans for more services that would lead to more revelations?

"Joe?"

Hennessy looked at Lockett, but words still failed him. He snapped his mouth shut but remained standing, his brain trying to process everything.

He looked at his investigator again and mentally reached for words that would make him sound in control. None came. Fearing how he looked, Hennessy went back to his seat and fell into it. The chair creaked in protest, loud enough to sound as if it was ready to give up and fall apart, but it held.

He sat like that for fifteen minutes, unable to move or find the words to express his thoughts.

His case against Richard Longhouse was finished before it even started.

CHAPTER 53

JOHN CLEVELAND had written a statement before the riot.

Among his final belongings was a letter addressed to Hennessy, which included everything he had told Hennessy earlier, and even added more details. The letter named Richard Longhouse as the man who commissioned Luca's kidnapping. The prison guards gave the letter to Hennessy, and he went straight to the police, who assured him they would look into it.

A day later, the police called to say they couldn't touch it.

They said there was not enough evidence to reopen the cold case. There was nothing concrete and nothing to investigate. All they had was a letter from a deceased prisoner that named the killer as another deceased felon. They couldn't question Cleveland about it, and they couldn't question Justin Fields about his actions either. The police couldn't find a reason to reopen the file.

Joe pleaded with the police to interview Longhouse, but they refused. Interviewing a sitting South Carolinian Senator was fraught with issues. Joe told them that politics shouldn't matter, and they assured him it wasn't because of politics, but he knew the spin. He'd heard it a hundred times before.

Joe returned to the vineyard after the police said

they weren't reopening the case. On the first afternoon of Joe's return, Wendy found Joe loading two shotguns into his pickup truck. He said if the cops couldn't deliver justice, he would have to do it himself. Wendy tried to stop him, but he brushed her aside. She continued to plead with him not to shoot Longhouse. She didn't want to lose him as well. He ignored her and got in the truck. He roared the engine and spun the vehicle around in their gravel driveway, kicking up dust.

With tears streaming down her face, Wendy stood in the middle of the driveway. He tried to go around her, but she refused to step out of the way. When he moved, she moved. She stood in front of his truck and told him she would need to run her over to get past.

After a minute-long standoff, Joe broke down, sitting in the driver's seat.

Once the tears started pouring out, they didn't stop. Sitting behind the steering wheel of his beaten-up old truck, he cried heavily.

He had failed.

He had failed Luca, he had failed justice, and he had failed his family. He had failed as a man.

He sat in the truck, bawling his eyes out as Wendy opened the door and rubbed his shoulders. After ten minutes, she convinced him to turn the engine off and return inside. She packed his guns back into the cabinet and locked it.

For the next week, Joe stayed at the vineyard.

He spent days wandering aimlessly, walking between the vines, surrounded by so much greenery. He knew every inch of the land he wandered, but he was lost. He didn't speak to anyone. Lockett called, as did Jacinta, but he didn't return their messages. Wendy talked to them and asked them to give him time.

Joe wasn't sure if time could heal his wounds. He wasn't sure if anything could. Wendy gently suggested that he could try the church in Greenville, perhaps a priest, but Joe refused. He hadn't stepped inside a church in twenty years, and it seemed disingenuous to step inside one now.

He spent the long, hot days outside, inspecting the crop, checking the fences, and ensuring the vineyard was running smoothly. The yield was looking good. They had the right amount of rain, the right amount of sun, and the right amount of humidity. If the weather stayed consistent, it would be a bumper year, perhaps even their best.

His moods had lurched about wildly. The grief was corrosive, and he spent much of the time rocking between anger and disbelief. At times, he felt numb, like it was a dream, and at others, he felt pure rage bubbling deep inside, desperate to get out.

Somehow, he had managed to get through the last twenty years. Putting one foot in front of the other, completing one task after the next. Emotions were like that. Easy to forget about when life was busy. But in the quiet moments, it was always in the quiet moments, those repressed emotions found their way back to the surface.

One night, after a long day on the land, he fell asleep under a tree at the west end of the property. Wendy had found him around midnight. She said she was worried about him, but she understood.

Under the bright light of a full moon, she lay next to him, and they cried together. They stayed there until the early hours of the morning.

Joe struggled to sleep, only managing small naps at inconvenient times. Every time he closed his eyes, thoughts of Luca came back into focus. His great laugh, his energetic bounce, his innocent smile. Wendy found Joe in the armchair in the living room several times at night, his head tilted forward and his eyes closed. Each time, she wrapped him up and gave him a pillow.

After the second week on the property, Jacinta called Wendy, concerned if Joe would ever return to Charleston. Wendy assured Jacinta that he would. He just needed time to process what he was going through. Jacinta said she would push all the meetings back another week, but they were cutting the timeframes close on several issues.

Lockett arrived on the tenth day, and the two men shared a bottle of Merlot. They didn't say much, but they didn't have to. They sat outside, watching the sunset, and bonded in silence.

On the twelfth day of Joe's self-imposed exile, Wendy found him at the top of the vineyard, sitting on the grass next to his tractor, staring out at the view as the afternoon shadows grew long. The lands were green, stretching on beyond the rows of vines that snaked down the side of the hill and into the valley. Dark clouds had gathered on the far horizon. Storm clouds. So big and so aggressive, so powerful and so dominant, rolling toward them with an ominous threat.

Hand in hand, they sat on the grass and watched as the storm clouds drowned out the sun. As the rain fell, gently at first, she felt a change in him. As if giving him her blessing for taking the next step,

Wendy kissed his hand, then held it a little tighter.

"I'm ready," Joe whispered to her.

After all the years, after the decades of pain and grief and anguish, Joe finally knew what had happened to his son.

And now, armed with the truth, it was time for justice.

<u>THE END</u>

ALSO BY PETER O'MAHONEY

In the Joe Hennessy Legal Thriller series:

THE SOUTHERN LAWYER
THE SOUTHERN CRIMINAL

In the Tex Hunter Legal Thriller series:

POWER AND JUSTICE
FAITH AND JUSTICE
CORRUPT JUSTICE
DEADLY JUSTICE
SAVING JUSTICE
NATURAL JUSTICE
FREEDOM AND JUSTICE
LOSING JUSTICE
FINAL JUSTICE

*****

In the Jack Valentine Series:

GATES OF POWER
THE HOSTAGE
THE SHOOTER
THE THIEF
THE WITNESS

Made in United States
Troutdale, OR
01/17/2025

28039252R00183